ETERNAL INFINITY

A THRILLING ROMANTIC ADVENTURE

ROBERT MIRANDA

Eternal Infinity
Copyright © 2020 Robert Miranda
All rights reserved.

ISBN: 978-1-7356567-0-0 (paperback)
         978-1-7356567-2-4 (hardcover)
         978-1-7356567-1-7 (epub)

Editor: Caitlin Berve
Publishing and Design Services: MelindaMartin.me

This book is dedicated to my late mother, Esther Miranda. Her unwavering love and encouragement were the primary motivators for the imagination and hard work that went into this project.

ACKNOWLEDGMENTS

I would like to thank Anna Laurel.

Without her help and dedication,
this project could never have been completed.

CHAPTER 1

It was the middle of the night in this European capital. In the wee hours of the morning, the streets of most neighborhoods are usually so quiet, one can hear a pin drop. This early morning would be different.

A small dark sedan was traveling along the side streets faster than the speed limit. It became obvious the driver was in a hurry as the wheels screeched around the corners and headed for the highway.

The lone occupant was a middle-aged man wearing a tie with a sports jacket. The man was called Sten. He received this nickname due to his proficiency with an old-style machine gun. Although he was well-dressed, his tie was crooked and his shirt was partially hanging out of his pants. This disheveled appearance indicated he got dressed with urgency.

The passenger seat next to him had a cell phone facing up. There was a typed message. The wording was curious as it was typed in English even though that was not the official language in that country. The message read, "Come quickly, we have a big problem." English was only used in case of an emergency.

Once on the highway, Sten's speed increased to an unsafe level. He only began to slow down when he saw the sky light up with flashes from police cruisers as well as the faint sound of sirens.

He exited the highway and got closer to the action. He could see two uniformed police officers several blocks away. As he approached, he noticed the police had cordoned off the area.

Sten pulled up and stopped by the officers. He spoke to one of them and showed his identification he had taken from his breast pocket. One of them called on his two-way radio. Sten was quickly directed through the blockade. The officer saluted him as he left.

Sten drove a couple of blocks and noticed an officer motioning for him to approach. He made hand signals directing him where to park. The space was right in front of the building, which was his destination.

The building was towering over him in all its grandeur. He walked over to a massive set of steps. The public entrance was at the top where there were two huge doors.

Before ascending, Sten looked around. His panoramic view showed twenty police vehicles, many officers, and neighborhood residents. They were dressed in their nightclothes and were curious as to the disturbance.

Sten looked to the sky and gritted his teeth. He made a fist and pounded his thigh a few times. This was not the picture of a happy man.

This was one of the most famous museums in the world. It contained the largest collection of priceless works of art.

Sten started walking up the stairs and passed a large sign. It read CLOSED. He reached the top and was greeted by two officers. They held the doors open and saluted him.

The lobby was large enough to hold dozens of people. While there were many uniforms present, Sten immediately noticed two men conversing: One was the chief investigator in charge and the other was the curator, a very old man named Endo.

Endo saw Sten and excused himself. When Endo was near, Sten said, "English only." Endo told Sten he told the chief the same thing. Evidently, the lead investigator was the only other person that spoke English in this group. He acceded to Endo's wishes.

"I told the chief you needed to speak to me privately first on government business."

"He agreed?"

Endo was told it would be fine, but the next request was not received well. Endo had asked to please cease his investigation temporarily. He said Sten would explain.

Sten walked over to the chief. After introducing himself, Sten explained everything would be clear after he spoke to Endo privately for a short time.

"Is this really necessary?"

"Do you think the ministry would send me here if it wasn't?"

"I don't understand. Oh, go ahead. Please make it brief."

Endo and Sten entered Endo's office which was near the lobby. Endo was extremely nervous. Sten walked to the small bar by the wall and poured Endo a stiff drink. He then sat

Endo down behind his desk and seated himself facing Endo.

"Now, what happened?"

"There was a burglary."

"When we put you in this position, you were told that there would be no alarms. You promised all would be disabled."

"The insurance inspector called. He came when I wasn't here and cited the violations. I tried to speak about the lack of necessity and he threatened that any robbery would result in my prosecution."

"That's just a blind threat. He's doing his job—"

"I tell you most sincerely, I'm an old man and I don't want to spend the rest of my life in prison."

"Calm down."

Sten asked Endo what he saw. He said he looked around as quickly as he could before the police arrived.

"I only saw one piece missing."

When he told Sten which painting, Sten's eyebrows raised because it was arguably the most valuable painting in the world. It was a household name.

"I asked the investigator to cease after he noticed it was gone. I don't think he saw anything else."

"It shouldn't matter. We can put another copy there. If they decide to send an expert, we'll temporarily hang the original."

"That's the problem. This was the original."

"What? Are you mad.? We've been through this one hundred times."

"You don't understand. We had an advanced warning a

famous art expert was coming. He would have seen through the copy."

"You fell for that? It was a ruse. You were set up. I don't understand the alarm angle, but that's for another time."

"I don't know what to think except my life may be over."

"Relax."

"Did you tell anyone else about the special room?"

"Just my assistant, Vera."

"How could you? You know this is top secret."

"She accidentally saw it. Please don't suspect her. She's been with me since she was a child. She would never do anything like this."

"We have to forget about her for now. The chief will have to know what's been going on."

"Sten, please don't. The scandal would put us and many others away."

Sten assured Endo that things would work out. He instructed Endo to open a door behind a bookshelf. With a flip of a switch, the bookshelf moved aside exposing a heavy metal door. It was similar to the vault doors used in banks.

"I'm worried this will blow up in our faces."

"Just be calm and let me do the talking when the chief comes."

The vault opened revealing a small room. The floor was lined with many paintings leaning against the walls. There were also statues as well as what appeared to be ancient artifacts.

They both walked to a stack of paintings, one behind the other. The covering was removed showing each was an exact duplicate of the one that was stolen. They flipped through them and took the one that was the best copy. Only the very top authenticators would even suspect it was a phony.

"Remember, don't say a word. I've already made a call. Exposing ourselves will only demonstrate the need for secrecy. I hope he buys it."

"What will you say?"

"I'm just going to try to stall him. I hope he gets a call before he sends me packing. He needs to understand his actions could send people at the highest levels of government to prison."

It was time to sit with the chief. Endo gulped down a large whiskey in an attempt to calm his nerves. It would be a tense discussion. If the chief balked, everyone would be in the soup.

Endo opened his office door and invited the chief in. Putting the investigation on hold like this was making the chief agitated. He was already irritated that he was awakened at this late hour.

The chief was invited to sit facing Sten with Endo in the background. Endo kept his hands under the desk because they were shaking so much. The chief noticed it but didn't bring it up. Sten would need to keep things calm.

"Would you like a drink?"

"No, thank you. I'm on duty."

Sten showed his confidence by walking to the bar and pouring the chief a drink. He said, "Just in case you change your mind. I suspect you'll need one."

The trained detective was looking around the room

for clues. He saw nothing out of place. His attention then turned to the other occupants.

"This is highly irregular. Have both of you been discussing this case?"

"No, we've been discussing the tennis matches. Of course, that's what we've been doing."

"Please don't try my patience. After losing sleep, I lose courtesy also."

"Touché."

They began to speak about the result of the present investigation, so far. The chief confirmed he would continue to examine the entire museum after this talk. Sten's fingers began tapping on the arm of the chair. He had to think quickly. He morphed the conversation into family and children, but that didn't go far.

"I'm not sure what game you're trying to play, but say what you have to say and let me get on with my work."

Sten knew it was time to lay it all on the line. He figured the best approach would be a direct frontal attack.

"What are you going to write in your report?"

"I'll put the most valuable piece of art in the world was just stolen and all borders must be sealed."

"No, that's incorrect. Your report will read there was a burglary attempt, the alarm scared the perpetrator, he ran, and all inventory has been accounted for."

"I think you're looking for a one-way ticket to an insane asylum. If I wrote that, I'd be dismissed and maybe put behind bars."

"You know who I am?"

"All I know is you're an important person in the ministry. I still don't understand what the ministry has to do with this."

Sten instructed Endo to move the bookcase and open the vault. Endo asked one last time if it was really necessary.

"Just do it."

The chief saw the secret vault, got up from his seat, and just stared at the contents behind the door. In his mind, he knew there was something nefarious going on.

"What's this all about?"

"Just come with me."

As they walked into the vault, the chief looked around in awe. He first thought it was just a storage room for valuable pieces. That idea was quashed when he saw the duplicates of several masterpieces including the stolen painting.

"You can't tell the difference, can you?"

"This is the first time in my career I don't know whether to arrest you or how to proceed."

"The first thing to know is things are working here that are much bigger than both of us."

"I have to go by my oath—"

"Don't take this as a threat, but you can endanger yourself along with your family."

The chief became angry and pointed to his gun. He made it clear that any danger to his family would be met with shooting. Sten put up his palm.

"Just wait and use your head. Let's sit and discuss this further."

"You were right about one thing, I need that drink you

offered."

They sat back down. Endo closed everything up. Everyone kept silent as the chief was drinking vigorously. After every sip, he would put his head back and look at the ceiling. It became quite apparent he didn't know how to handle the situation.

There was a knock at the door. An officer opened the door and stuck his head in.

"You're wanted on the phone."

This was the opportunity Sten was waiting for. His biggest concern was whether the chief would be told to back off.

Endo was finally smiling and said, "You handled yourself well. I just pray we can bury this."

Several minutes later, the chief returned. He had a relieved look written all over his face. It was almost as if the weight of the world was lifted off of his shoulders.

"You really do have a lot of juice."

"What were you told?"

"I was told to give you my full cooperation and do exactly as you told me. I suppose one way or another my career will be coming to an end."

Sten put his arm around the chief and they sat down once again. The chief didn't argue as Sten refilled his glass. It was needed for Sten to reassure the chief so he didn't have second thoughts.

"Don't worry, this will work out."

"How can you be so sure?"

"Anyone who isn't living under a rock recognizes this painting. Isn't that right?"

"I guess so."

"Sooner rather than later, this thing is going to surface. It's way too famous. The thief's, or buyer's, ego is going to make a slip. The minute someone else sees it, they'll squeal and we'll get it back with no harm done. We can't publicize it, but the best thing is there's no reward necessary."

They had to work together with time being of the essence. They made calls to get any exit using the seaports, airports, train stations, and border roads temporarily closed. They would re-open when special inspectors were in place.

Once again, there was a knock at the door and one of the police stuck his head inside.

"The reporters are waiting."

"Tell them to be patient. I will address them shortly."

The chief told Endo and Sten to stay in the room until the reporters had left. He had experience giving reporters the runaround.

The chief left the room and nodded to the officer at the door. The door swung open and a group of reporters rushed into the lobby. He figured they were sharks anyway and wanted to have some fun with them.

"You folks have your scanners on this time of night? Don't you ever sleep?"

One of the reporters yelled, "Why are you speaking English?"

"Because I feel like it."

They all knew this chief had little sense of humor and no tolerance for yellow journalism. He held up his hand and they quieted down and became more civil.

"I'm going to make a statement. There will be no questions tonight. Please hold them until tomorrow."

There were soft murmurs as the reporters were looking at each other. Then the chief began to speak.

"A short time ago, there was an attempted burglary here. The perpetrator was an obvious amateur. His clumsy ways set off the alarm. There is no evidence he ever entered the building. A preliminary check found nothing of value missing. The investigation is ongoing. That is all."

Some of the reporters couldn't help themselves. They shouted meaningless questions except one yelled something about a cover-up.

The chief stopped and said, "Detain that man." He was in no mood for these antics. He also knew this was an unfounded attempt to merely push an official's buttons.

The chief then waived everyone off as the police gently pushed them out of the building and proceeded to the room where Sten and Endo were sitting.

By this time Endo was almost drunk, but Sten and the chief were staring at each other. Each took a turn asking the same question.

"What do you think?"

Each had the same answer as if they were programmed. They both shrugged their shoulders and said, "I don't know."

There was one unspoken thought they both felt in their hearts. That was the silent belief this painting will never be recovered.

CHAPTER 2

This northern area of the Midwest USA is extremely mountainous. The vista has a wonderful view of nature. There's green everywhere along with lakes and waterfalls. An abundance of wildlife is all around.

The area is also quite remote with the closest town being more than 100 miles away. The only tangible item that suggests modernization, is a two-lane state road. It's been recently paved and winds through the mountains.

Facing north and south, the road has high posted speed limits with some reductions for sharp bends. There are very few motor vehicles except for a few state trooper cars, due to the local barracks being less than 20 miles away.

Today, a white van was cruising leisurely down this road. The driver was admiring the beauty around him.

The van itself had an unusual look. The only windows were the windshield along with those on the driver and passenger sides. Its sides and rear were completely blocked, similar to a commercial van.

The unusual nature was evidenced by the various projections emanating from the roof. Some looked like different sized antennae commonly used for many purposes.

Others looked like old-fashioned horns with the bells facing sideways. The horn-shaped objects could pivot facing any direction. The oddest looking thing was a dome-shaped object with arc-shaped projections around its perimeter.

The driver was casually dressed. There was a protective suit on the passenger seat. It resembled a beekeeper's suit, only much thicker and heavier. It was more like a hazmat suit except it even had a lot more shielding. He was constantly touching his chest.

The other strange look of the interior had a grouping of meters attached to the dashboard. Some had dials and some had digits. The one thing they had in common was the second by second changes to the readings. They were wired to a box sitting on the passenger side floor. The box had the look of the black box used in commercial aircraft.

There was a constant level of noise coming from the back of the van. It consisted of clicking, clacking, buzzing, and bells. This was all consistent with machinery that was used to process some sort of collected information.

There was a sudden surge in the readings. The meters started going crazy and the noise got louder.

The driver split his attention. He was concerned as to what was going on. He pulled over to the side and started checking the calibrations. Everything was correctly set, yet the strange reactions continued.

His instruments could vaguely pinpoint the position of the causation. He decided to follow the signals.

Once again, he was on the road. The signals became more intense and he became more distracted. He took one look too many at the meters.

The road curved and the van began to swerve. As luck would have it, he nearly hit an oncoming car being driven by a state trooper. He knew this would be bad news after looking in his mirror and seeing the cruiser make an abrupt u-turn.

The trooper was gaining speed and closing the distance. He activated his emergency flashers. With little choice, the driver pulled over on the shoulder.

The trooper exited his car and approached the van as he would with any normal traffic stop.

"Have you been drinking?"

"No, sir."

"Taking any prescription drugs or hallucinogens?"

Each time the answer was no. There was one obvious factor missing. There was no odor of alcohol or marijuana.

"License and registration, please."

"I can't give you that."

"I'll ask you one more time—"

"The answer will be the same."

"Please turn the van off and exit the vehicle."

The driver complied and the trooper escorted him to the back of the van. While walking the driver clutched his chest again.

"Are you ok?"

"Yes, I think so."

"I'm going to give you some field sobriety tests. Are you familiar with nystagmus, finger-to-nose, Romberg, one-legged stand, and toe-to-heel?"

"I was a grand juror once, so I know all of them. I can't do the stand because my balance has been bad since I was a kid."

"Do you have any physical limitations that would prevent you from doing the others?"

"No and honestly, I was distracted and not drunk."

"We'll see."

The trooper gave all the tests and all were passed. He next wanted to figure out why he wasn't given the license. It seemed unnecessary to arrest the man.

"What's all that noise coming from the inside?"

"Nothing I can talk about."

"Alright, open up the back door."

"I can't, it's welded shut. The handle is just for appearances."

"Then open the door next to the driver's seat."

"Can't do that either. It's locked and I don't have a key."

The trooper was quickly losing his self-restraint. He didn't understand the lack of cooperation. He was also wondering why this man kept grabbing at his chest. All he knew was he had enough of the nonsense.

"Do you realize you're a few seconds away from getting arrested? We'll impound your van and take it apart bolt by bolt."

The driver had been trying to avoid something that was only to be used in dire circumstances. He pulled what looked like a business card from his breast pocket. He gave it to the trooper.

"What's this?"

"Just read it, please."

The card read as follows: THE BEARER OF THIS CARD IS NOT SUBJECT TO ANY STATE OR LOCAL LAWS. HE SHOULD NOT BE DETAINED NOR SHOULD HIS PROGRESS BE IMPEDED IN ANY MANNER. IF HE IS KILLED, DO NOT REMOVE THIS CARD FROM HIS BODY. IF STATE AND/OR LOCAL AUTHORITIES HAVE ANY QUESTIONS, PLEASE CALL THE NUMBER ON THE REVERSE SIDE.

"Is this a hoax?"

"I'm afraid it's as real as you and me."

"Come with me."

The trooper escorted the driver to his cruiser. He opened the back door and locked him in the back seat. He sat in the front and immediately got on the radio.

When he called his headquarters, he asked for the captain. He was the highest-ranking person in these barracks. The trooper glanced in his mirror and noticed the van driver taking deep breaths and rubbing his chest.

"Are you sure you're ok?"

"I think it's just a little indigestion."

Finally, the captain came on the line. He was inquisitive because an on-duty call to him was most irregular.

The trooper explained the situation and read the card.

"You can't be serious. This guy is pulling your leg."

"I'm not sure. The van has these weird instruments and sounds. Everything seems so official. Do you want me to arrest him?"

"I suppose I can give a quick call to that number. I wouldn't be surprised if a bartender or pimp answers."

The van driver leaned over to the plexiglass separating

him and the trooper. He told the trooper the call would take a long while.

"There's a lot of protocol, you know."

The driver was right. They first kept the captain on hold for ten minutes and transferred him to different departments. He finally was allowed to identify himself. He was switched once again. Although he was exasperated, he knew by now this was no joke. He finally told a person not to transfer him and he said the magic words … those being on the card the van driver gave him.

He was told to hold again but was also promised to be connected to the right person. The man who picked up sure sounded official. They started discussing the situation and the captain became convinced this man was the real deal.

Meanwhile, the trooper and the van driver were engaging in a light conversation with the trooper speaking about the trooper's wife and kids. He just bought his first house and the family enjoyed the swimming pool in the back.

He was proud of his children doing well in school. He was also saying that his wife was a teacher. They just couldn't afford to lose him in his dangerous job.

"You don't want to tell me about your family, do you?"

"I can't. I don't have one."

"How long have you had that indigestion?"

"I'd say about a week."

"If I release you, I'd advise you to get to a doctor right away. I don't like the looks of this."

The captain broke into the conversation and told the trooper about his call. He said it was the strangest call of his career.

"You can release this man along with his vehicle."

"But—"

"Don't ask any questions."

The trooper was more concerned about the driver's health than making an arrest anyway. He pulled out a card with the barrack's phone number. He insisted on a call if his indigestion gets worse and an ambulance would be summoned expeditiously.

The trooper watched carefully as the physical discomfort grew. The driver was slow getting back in the van. He felt a little winded, dizzy, and nauseous. He also felt he was able to continue.

When he pulled away, the trooper stayed and watched until the van was out of sight. He went on with his patrol.

The instruments in the van were still acting wacky. The driver felt it was time to put on his protective suit. He pulled over to a rest area. Since he felt a little better, he put the suit on except for his head protection. That would have been too hot and made breathing difficult.

He decided to put his head back and close his eyes for a few minutes. He slept for a couple of hours.

When he awakened, he felt pretty good. As long as the instruments were showing such a volatile reaction, he decided to follow the trail.

There was a forest on both sides of the road, leading to mountains. There was also an occasional clearing with overgrown weeds.

He thought it strange when he saw one of these clearings

with two narrow swaths that had been flattened by a heavy weight. They almost looked like the trail a car would leave.

Rather than stopping, he followed the signal which appeared to get stronger a short distance ahead. He then saw flattened weeds, only much larger.

This time, he stopped. There were unmistakable tire tracks, likely made by a tractor-trailer. It appeared that the terrain was drivable, so he got back into his van and slowly went past the clearing and into the forest.

As he followed the trail, its winding nature made the sight of the road disappear after only a short distance.

The forest ended along with the tracks at the foot of a mountain. By now the instruments were at their limit and he knew he was close to the source.

After attaching the head protection, it was time to take a walk. As he put the gear on, he noticed a faint rumbling sound like machinery or an engine of some sort.

Theoretically, those instrument reactions should have already been debilitating with the previous exposure. He thought maybe that was causing his discomfort. Whatever it was, he should have already received a lethal dose.

The terrain was rocky and nothing seemed to be out of place. Even with the head protection, he could hear a grinding or sliding sound as if something was opening. He still saw nothing.

It was hard to believe this was happening in an area of such wilderness. The only thing he was convinced of, was that all of the sounds were not made by nature.

He stopped and heard what sounded like the cadence

of feet moving through the brush. His peripheral vision was hampered by the head protection and he couldn't see behind himself.

The sounds stopped. He took off the headgear. Before he could turn around, he heard the bolts of two automatic carbines being pulled.

He looked towards the top of the mountain and just started to raise his hands. He didn't get very far as he got an excruciating pain in his chest. His eyes rolled into his head and he collapsed on the spot.

CHAPTER 3

There was a small airport in the southern part of the Midwest, in the USA. This one was built for specific needs. The short runway and lakes at both ends made landing difficult. It was only suitable for small aircraft and skilled pilots.

The owner had substantial landing fees which kept student pilots and weekend sky jockeys away. It was as private as it gets.

With all the "stay away" features, the ground was still a picture of beauty. The grass areas were kept mowed like a golf course. Bushes were neatly trimmed and there were a few picnic tables behind the tower.

As a small private jet got closer, it was shortly after dawn and the pilot radioed the tower. This was a Unicom airport, so there was nobody to control air traffic. Only occasionally was a person in the tower and that was for giving wind speed and direction to assist the pilot in landing.

Today, there was someone in the tower. He had a foreign accent and spoke in a friendly manner. The short conversation was less official and more like a friendly exchange.

"I'll be landing in a few minutes."

"It's a beautiful day. Let's meet outside. I made a fresh pot of coffee. Do you want me to bring you a cup?"

The pilot accepted since he had been traveling a good portion of the night. He made a smooth landing and taxied to the tie-down area. He noticed only a couple of planes which was normal because of the remote location.

The pilot left his jet and walked behind the building the tower was in. He was tall, handsome, and about forty. He saw another man waiting by a picnic table. This was the same person that was on the radio. He was older, approaching the normal retirement age.

After a distant wave, they came together. There were a handshake and a hug. They sat down because they had some business to discuss.

"Your trip went well?"

"It's good. The painting will be in the usual place. It'll be ready for your pick up in a week."

"There's a snag here. My client isn't convinced it's real."

"Why?"

"The media reports that the museum and the police both state that nothing was stolen. When you're spending a billion on something, you have every right to be suspicious."

"You know I wouldn't fool around with a fake."

"I know, but he needs more. I've never asked you to divulge your secrets, but I'm afraid we've got a lot of convincing to do."

"I'll try my best."

Many years ago, a very young man was visiting the museum neighborhood. He had little money, so he worked a few odd jobs and stayed at a cheap flophouse.

He had a habit of having his lunch in a park across from the museum. It was usually just a sandwich and a container of milk.

One day, he saw a relatively young woman sitting at a nearby bench. She was accompanied by a young child of about eight. The child was her daughter. It was strange. Their clothes looked ragged but clean. They just didn't have the look of homeless people.

He noticed the child kept looking at his sandwich and milk. He got up and walked over to the couple. He looked at the child.

"Would you like some?"

"Leave the man alone."

He was a bit surprised at their perfect English. The traveler later found out they spoke several languages. He didn't want to go against the mother's words, so he shrugged his shoulders and walked away.

"Mister? I'm very hungry."

That's all he had to hear. His heart broke in half as did his sandwich. He walked back and forced them to share his meal. The mother thanked him profusely.

He sat with them and spoke a bit. The child's name was Vera. It turned out their husband and father left them. The mother couldn't work because she was very sick and required an operation.

The couple found a kind janitor in an apartment building. He allowed them to live in a small room next to the furnace in the basement.

As the days passed, he would give them whatever food and money he could spare. He spent his spare time minding Vera as her mother recovered. She spent time in the museum almost every day. She loved it so. The curator developed such a liking for her, he made sure she could come whenever she wanted, free of charge.

There came the day when it was time for the traveler to move on. Vera sobbed when the news was broken. As he said goodbye and walked away, Vera looked at her mom who gave a quick nod.

"Mister? Someday, when I grow up, I'm going to do something special for you and I always keep my promises. It'll be something you'll never forget."

He came back, hugged and kissed her, and also fought back the tears. He sent them money from time to time.

Many years later, he returned to the area and looked Vera up. She was now happily married with a child. It shouldn't have been a surprise that she worked her way through college and was now the assistant to the curator who was so kind to her.

She needed to speak to someone she could trust. She told him she walked into the curator's office and accidentally saw him with a secret door open and several forged art pieces. Being caught, he sat her down and explained the whole mess with the ministry.

"You remember your promise?"

"I'll never forget it."

He took the bold step by asking her to help him with the theft. The only way she would help was by refusing any compensation.

Vera helped him with setting up the situation so the original painting was on display. She had the insurance people informed about the alarm and made up the story of the art expert coming. His plan worked out and it was over in a matter of minutes.

The older man asked, "I don't understand why you had her make sure the insurance company threatened the curator and the alarm go off."

"It was a simple matter to disable that antiquated alarm, get the painting to a safe place, and reactivate it. With her internal info, I knew how the interested parties would react."

"You purposely turned it back on?"

"By doing that, the insurance company was satisfied. The police had to play along and the ministry avoided a scandal. It was a win all around."

"Your plan was absolutely brilliant."

"It worked out pretty well."

"I just don't understand why she would hurt the old man who was so kind to her."

"I asked the same question."

When queried, Vera never blinked. She said this terrible situation with the ministry was eating Endo up inside. All he wanted to do was get a small place near the sea and have relative peace for the few years he had left. They couldn't do anything to him because he hid many incriminating papers.

"This way I could fix it so my dear Endo could live out his life in happiness and I could also fulfill my childhood promise to you. To me, that's a lot more important than an old piece of art."

"My client will love the story, especially the heart angle. He might buy into it. I just wish we had something else to put it over the top."

"I was saving the best for last."

When Endo was a young man, he was part of a group exploring what was left of the reputed homes of the old masters from centuries ago.

One of the places was of particular interest to Endo. Rumor had it that one of the greats lived there. It was never really substantiated. He had a keen interest in this artist and inventor.

While they were rummaging through the place, the chilly weather that day turned windy and rainy. The others in the group didn't want to walk home in the inclement weather, so they decided to leave and come back on a nicer day.

Endo wanted to see what artifacts he could find without group differences of opinion regarding the disposition. The government had strict limitations on what items could be moved or areas disturbed. He wanted no interference from the government or his group.

He was curious about what could be behind the walls of every place he explored. Previous locations turned up nothing. All the walls here were either cracked, rotted, or had holes. It was still forbidden to break a wall to look behind it. He knew, if he was caught, he would either be permanently banned from the site or possibly arrested.

Endo put on his protective gloves and mask. It was quite dusty with a lot of broken ruins with sharp edges. He had to be careful reaching inside a wall because of rats.

Wall after wall yielded little. There was an occasional broken cup or pieces of unknown wooden things. He would just leave them there so they could be dated at a later time.

What seemed like a bedroom was his last stop. As with the other rooms, Endo looked out the window for anyone who shouldn't be there. He pulled large chunks out of the walls to make it easier to inspect.

His flashlight revealed what looked like a piece of paper. He reached and gently pulled out what looked like an envelope. Endo gingerly moved the flap and saw there was paper inside. This was not the place for an examination. Without proper care, the paper would have crumbled.

Endo knew he had something good, so he cautiously slipped it into a plastic bag. He had a special oversized pocket inside his jacket for just such an object.

As soon as he hurried out, Endo appeared to have taken nothing and he felt safe. He passed several people who didn't even look at him.

When he got home, the fine delicate instruments were unpacked. Endo began the process of delicately removing the paper. After an hour's work, he was finally able to remove the paper and safely unfold it.

Endo was surprised to see it was a letter written by the great artist. His fluency allowed him to translate it since it was a similar romantic language. It was evidently written to a student.

The artist wrote about his sorrow that people, including his students, were trying to copy his work. He devised a plan to have a way to identify his work unknown to forgers of his time.

The artist had made trips to the Middle East and copied hieroglyphics of a language that was unknown at his time. He was and still is recognized as a genius. He was able to decipher the characters.

Then, just as now, the public never saw the back of his work where he would make a small inscription. It was in the ancient language and would identify something in the painting. Should someone copy it, they wouldn't know what it was and would be exposed as a fraud.

The weirdest part of this episode was that language was never officially deciphered until the 20th century. He worked this out all by himself: a superior intelligence.

"This painting has one of those marks?"

"Yes. He refers to it in the letter. It translates to a woman's head."

"How do you know the letter is authentic?"

"Endo had it analyzed. The paper and ink are from that period. Most importantly, the handwriting was absolutely his."

"Where is the letter now?"

"You'll get it along with the painting. Vera gave it to me."

"It sure seems like we'll get our money now."

The older man seemed relieved as they sipped their coffee. He noticed a pained look on the other's face. He started tapping the table with his fingers. Their business was concluded, but there was something else.

The older man waited patiently for the other to say

something. He didn't want to talk in circles, so he became direct.

The older man said, "We have known each other for a long time. You saved my life once. I can read mental anguish on my friend's face. Perhaps it's time for you to tell your confidant what's on your mind."

"I should know better than to fool my closest friend. I'm afraid I will have to retire from all this."

"I've never asked anything about your operation. You don't have to tell me now. Can I help?"

"There's no hope of help. What I've been doing has been exposed. I hope my associates will be ok."

The older man said, "My sources tell me there's some trouble up north involving the government. You wouldn't know anything about that?"

With a smile and a wink, the response was, "Never heard of it."

"Ok, I've set up the coded accounts for quite a few people. They should have enough money for years. I assume we're talking about the same people."

"They're the same."

"What about you? You've given me pennies for your account."

The pilot said, "I don't need much money."

"As usual, you're always thinking of someone else and never yourself. Remember, if you ever need money, come to me."

"You're the first person I'll call."

"My crystal ball tells me there's something else on your

mind."

"It's not that important. It's just that I never stole any-thing before. It cost me some sleep. All those millions we made, it was just legitimate."

"You'll get over it. You come from nowhere and you go nowhere. Now hop in your jet and get out of here."

CHAPTER 4

In the same mountainous area where the white van disappeared, a very plain sedan sped north on the same road. The driver was a middle-aged man who was neatly and casually dressed. He seemed to be in a hurry but there wasn't a trooper in sight.

He came upon the only building for several miles. It was the state trooper barracks. After he parked the car, he walked at a rapid pace into the building. There was a table straight ahead and it was manned by a desk sergeant.

He asked for the commander who was actually the rank of captain.

"He's very busy. Can I help you?"

"I really need him."

"Do you have an appointment?"

"Just remind him that he spoke to me over the phone regarding a traffic stop of a van with an unusual situation."

The sergeant made a call and explained what was said.

"Is your name Jim?"

"That's correct."

"He'll see you now."

The sergeant pointed to a door down the hallway. When

he reached it, he knocked and was asked to enter. The captain offered him a seat.

"Do you remember the situation with the van?"

"I remember speaking with you. That was the craziest traffic stop I've ever heard of."

"Has the trooper done any follow-up?"

"The driver was just released as per the instructions. Oh, wait, the trooper did say something about the guy seemed to be in discomfort— his heart or something."

"Well, that's a new wrinkle. I need the cooperation of you and your trooper. I'm going to stop you right there until I know exactly who you guys are, who you represent, and what this is all about."

Jim deduced the only way he was going to get any help was by being forthright. He reached into his breast pocket and pulled out his credentials. There was no badge but a government eagle was emblazoned on the ID along with four large letters, SMVA.

The captain looked and returned the wallet. He leaned back in his chair and took a deep breath.

"Ok, I'll bite. What the heck is SMVA?"

"It stands for Strategic Materials Verification Agency."

"Never heard of it."

It was Jim's turn to take a deep breath. He wanted to limit the information he gave, but he knew he would have to give some details to break the stalemate.

"Our agency is not a household name. We are associated with the other intelligence agencies, but we have our own budget and report directly to the president."

He went on to explain their purpose, at least for public consumption, was to monitor radiation leaks from nuclear reactors.

"What's so secret about that?"

He continued that the reactor business was only a minor part of their mission. They were mainly concerned with foreign agents either stealing strategic materials or planting them as a sort of attack.

"The monitoring devices in that van are top secret."

"That's a wild story, maybe too wild."

"Would you like me to call the White House? You'll get a good tongue lashing."

"I suppose it's not necessary. What's going on? What do you want from me?"

"That van, the driver named Billy, and all the equipment has gone missing."

"Do you want to file a missing person—"

"I want this quiet. Is the trooper on duty?"

"He's on patrol."

Jim requested the trooper be called in and take him to the exact location of the traffic stop. That was all that was needed.

"You and the trooper also have to forget I was ever here."

"I hate this cloak and dagger business, but I'll comply with your wishes."

The captain personally got on the radio and recalled the trooper who was a little puzzled.

"Is there anything wrong?"

"Just return to the barracks immediately. That's an

order."

It only took ten minutes. When the trooper left his car, he was greeted in the parking lot by Jim and the captain.

"Follow this man's instructions. I'm going back to my office."

The trooper was asked to lead Jim to the point of the incident. The two cars left. After a distance, the cruiser pulled onto the shoulder with the sedan behind him.

They met after leaving their cars. The trooper pointed to skid marks in the road where Billy had swerved. They walked a ways ahead and the trooper showed where he stopped the van.

"I was worried. Billy was in obvious pain but I couldn't legally help him. He left heading north."

"Right now, he's missing. I want you to forget you saw either of us."

"Maybe I can help you find him."

"Thanks, but no thanks. Just go about your patrol. I'll take it from here."

After the trooper departed, Jim followed the direction. For miles, he saw nothing suspicious. Then he spotted the first turn off that Billy had noticed. The high brush and weeds were flattened by what could have been car tires.

Jim didn't have Billy's instruments, so he didn't see an immediate reason to drive further. He wasn't sure his car could take the drive in that forest area. He decided to park on the shoulder and take a walk in the direction of those flattened weeds.

The path wound so many times that Jim quickly lost

sight of the road the same as Billy did at the other location. After walking about a quarter of a mile, he came to the foot of the mountain just like Billy did. It was a small clearing with the heavier forest on either side.

Jim looked around and right before the forest was a metal box. It was welded to the top of a metal pole. The pole itself was cemented to the ground. The box looked similar to a mailbox except it was much larger and shaped like a cube with a door on the side. There was also a strange light sitting on top of the box. It looked like the dome lights they used to use on police cars.

Suddenly the light started flashing like a beacon. It was an eerie blue color. It sure looked like an invitation if Jim ever saw one so he decided to open the little door.

Inside was a small device that looked similar to a cell phone except it had only two buttons. It seemed like some sort of communicator. He decided to press one and a voice came on.

"You're trespassing. Please leave immediately."

"I'm looking for someone."

"You're trespassing. You were told to leave immediately."

Jim was growing impatient. He thought it best to start flexing his muscles. He also needed to be more specific as to who and what he was looking for.

"I'm with the government and—"

"If your superiors know you're here, you will be in big trouble. This land is off-limits."

"I'm looking for a white van and the driver. I'm not leaving until I get some answers."

"I see. Wait."

Jim heard a door opening and closing. There was silence for a few minutes. He heard the same door open and close, only this time with the sound of wheels rolling.

"Your man had a heart attack. He almost died. We had to throw a few stents in him."

"You speak about it in a cavalier manner."

"What's the difference? His life was saved."

"You will give him to me now?"

"No, it's not that simple."

Jim started thinking. Either Billy needed more time to rest or it was a hostage situation. He had to know what was required to secure Billy's release.

"You want money?"

"That's an insult after we just saved his life."

"Just tell me what you're driving at."

It became very clear. There was concern in the words of the voice at the other end. If Billy were released, there would be an investigation of what was happening in this area. Assuming there was a lack of cooperation, the government was sure to use the military to force their way into a solution for their curiosity. It seemed Jim needed to stall for time as much as the others did.

"What exactly do you want for his release?"

"A substitute."

"You mean a substitute hostage."

"Your man needs more after-care than we have the personnel or time for. It will take time to resolve this situation. Do you understand?"

"I'm not sure I can—"

"You have plenty of agents in your department. Get one of them before your man gets sick again."

"How about me?"

"No. From now on, you will be the only person we will have outside contact with. Get someone else."

"Can I speak with Billy?"

"He's sitting next to me in a wheelchair. Go ahead."

"Jim?"

"Is that you, Billy? How do you feel?"

"I feel great. It's the best I've felt in weeks. They tell me I died for twenty seconds."

Jim didn't know if his man was speaking under duress. He had no choice but to try to see any kind of hint in his voice.

"Are they taking care of you well?"

"They treat me like a king. They're always stuffing me with food and vitamins. It's the best treatment I've had since the way my mom took care of me as a kid."

Jim felt a bit easier because the word mom was code for everything being good. The voice broke back in.

"Are you convinced now?"

"You know my name. What's yours?"

"That's unimportant. Call me the voice or whatever."

As Billy was being wheeled away, he shouted out, "Don't rush Jim, I'm having a ball."

They began to go over the parameters of the timing and the exchange of personnel. The voice was very clear as to exactly how it would take place.

"Just make sure there are only two of you. If you bring anyone else, with or without weapons, you won't be seeing Billy for a long time, if at all. Also, I would prefer someone with a technical background. like chemistry or physics."

Jim tried one last time to figure out what their goal was with this whole exercise. He kept getting evasive answers. There was a denial of any religious, nationalistic, political, or any other kind of fervor. The voice kept repeating they wanted to be left alone. He knew the voice was right when it was implied the government would never let that happen.

Jim would have to work in a hurry. He needed approval from someone in another department in his agency. He would then have to find the closest agent who was in-between assignments.

Jim's biggest fear was the general who was in charge of the military unit assigned to his agency. The rules clearly stated for any situation like this he was required to inform the highest officer attached to his unit.

If the general ordered any kind of maneuver in the area, it would endanger Billy's life. The bigger question was what these people were capable of. Jim suspected they were heavily armed.

CHAPTER 5

Jim was waiting at a crossroad about thirty miles from his destination. He was accompanied by the replacement agent. He was instructed to wait for some military to guard him along with getting Billy safely released. Jim assumed there would be possibly two military police. How wrong he was.

He was horrified when he saw three vehicles resembling large pickup trucks approaching. They were loaded with soldiers. He flagged down the lead vehicle and spoke to the lieutenant in charge of the operation.

"What's going on here? You brought an entire platoon."

"Those are my orders, sir."

"Bringing half the army is going to endanger my man. It's bad enough I gave my word that there would only be two of us. This is crazy."

Jim understood he didn't have the authority to stop this parade. He just hoped the voice wouldn't notice the platoon.

When they reached their destination, everyone parked their vehicles on the road. Jim shook his head as the soldiers started deploying carrying their rifles.

"Lieutenant, stay behind me and try to remain out of

sight."

"I'll do my best."

Several soldiers climbed trees and took up a sniper position. The rest fanned out behind trees in the forest. As Jim and the agent walked, the soldiers crept closer.

When Jim reached the box, the blue beacon was already flashing. If an inanimate object could project a restless mood, this was it. He retrieved the communicator. He didn't even get a chance to say hello to the voice.

"The deal is off."

"Why are you—"

"You heard me. The deal is off."

"Please tell me why."

"You think we're fools. Instead of the two of you, you brought a military attack force. We have sensors and cameras everywhere. The trees are booby-trapped. You've put these soldiers' lives in danger, let alone your man. Do you think you're a Trojan horse?"

"This wasn't my doing. I was overruled."

"I believe you but you don't understand the seriousness of where you are and what you're doing. You're making a mess for your own government. We'll try to keep your man alive and healthy as long as we can."

"I don't understand what you mean by a mess."

"You'll find out soon enough. Do you have anything else to say before we end this communication?"

"Wait, please. If I can get rid of them, can we continue our business?"

There was a short silence. Jim could hear the voice taking a deep breath with a sigh.

"Go ahead. Last chance."

Jim left the agent and walked towards the troops and the road. He was frantically trying to make a phone call. Before his call was even connected, he saw the troops moving past him. The snipers had all climbed down the trees and joined the other troops marching to the road and eventually the trucks.

He asked one of the soldiers for the lieutenant. The private pointed toward the last group remaining. Jim called out.

"Excuse me. Where are you going?"

"I've been ordered to bring my men back to the base. Good luck, sir."

Jim couldn't understand how this occurred but he wasn't looking a gift horse in the mouth. He scurried back to the box and got on the communicator.

"Now, can we continue?"

"You're a heck of a field commander."

Jim knew the voice was just playing with him. He wasn't happy, but he wanted to get this over with.

"It's been a long day for me. It's nearly dusk, I don't want to get lost in this wilderness. Can we please conclude this quickly and make our next appointment?"

The voice began to give Jim and the agent instructions on how they would proceed. There was a package in the box. Jim had seen it but left it undisturbed. He was told to take out the contents, which were a pair of handcuffs. He was instructed to cuff the agent to the pole which the box was sitting on.

"The cuffs are on and the agent is attached."

"I already know that. The sensors picked that up."

"If you see that large rock to the right of the box, the key to the van is underneath."

"Got it."

"Now, turn around and follow that path behind you into the forest. You'll see your man inside the van in about half a mile. Hurry, it's getting dark."

Jim waved to the agent and trotted into the forest. He could retrieve his own car tomorrow.

Jim was apprehensive as he lost sight of the clearing behind him and saw nothing ahead. He knew it was going to be a very dark night and wanted to be out of there soon.

The van was finally seen in the distance. He rushed over and saw Billy in the passenger seat. Billy looked at Jim and smiled.

"Long time, no see."

"Are you ok?"

"I was telling you the truth. I haven't felt this good in quite a while."

"Just enjoy the ride."

The van was started and they retraced the flattened grass to leave. Jim was surprised Billy looked so good. He also noticed a box between the seats with three packages in it along with a folder and papers.

"What's this?"

"They said to read it as soon as possible and handle with extreme care. They contain very dangerous materials."

"I'll check it out as soon as I drop you off. You'll be

airlifted to a military hospital to be checked."

As they would be driving for some time, Jim figured he would do some debriefing. He asked how the events happened.

"I'm not sure. I was unconscious and I woke up on what I think was an operating table. There were three men in scrubs hovering over me. I'm pretty sure they were doctors."

"What did they look like?"

"I couldn't tell because they wore masks. They all had foreign accents."

"What did they do?"

"One said he was going to make it stop hurting. Each time he inserted a stent, he asked if it still hurt. Twice I said it felt a little better, but I still had pain. Whatever he did the third time was wonderful. I couldn't believe it. The pain was completely gone."

Billy didn't see much as he was restricted to a few rooms. They wouldn't let him out of a wheelchair for his own safety.

"They checked on me 100 times a day. They couldn't do enough. The food was really good. The veggies were fresh, the meat was tender. My mom would be jealous."

"Did they talk much?"

Billy described the conversations as resembling idle chatter and the reason he was there never came up.

"One doctor always wanted to play chess."

"You're the agency champion. It doesn't sound like a fair match."

"It was frustrating. We couldn't get far into a game. He kept correcting my moves."

Finally, Billy convinced the doctor to play a real game. By the middle of the game, Billy resigned.

"I don't even know how I lost. He was that good."

It turned out the doctor was a grandmaster. He didn't play internationally because he hated beating people.

"Only once he took pleasure in defeating a very bad man."

The doctor played anonymously as a participant against another grandmaster playing a simultaneous exhibition against ten other players. He described the man as arrogant and poked fun at inferior players, even children. He sneered at opponents taking the fun out of the game.

The doctor destroyed him and he got so mad, he threw the pieces and stormed out of the room leaving all the games unfinished. The doctor said he wanted to teach him a dose of humility.

"Everybody in this place was the same way. They all seemed like decent, caring people. I'm pretty good at judging character."

"Did you see anyone on a phone type device?"

"No, but I saw at least twenty people walking around the halls. I even saw a couple of children."

Now Jim knew the military option would not be one of his preferred methods for resolution.

"What places did you see?"

He described the operation room and his bedroom. The only other place he saw was what looked like a kitchen with tables.

"It was a really comfy bed. I don't think the females that

attended me were nurses. They spoke more like doctors."

"Did you see them without a mask?"

"They were mostly middle-aged but very sexy."

"You're speaking like the single man you are. Down there, tiger. You're a sick man."

"I tried to talk them into giving me a massage, but they just laughed. They didn't take the bait."

"Anything unusual they did?"

"The only thing was they gave me no prescription drugs. They came in several times a day with natural things. They called them vitamins, herbals, homeopathics, and unclassed supplements. They made a big deal saying these were powerful, yet harmless for my condition."

"Anything else?"

"I did see someone trotting through the hall wearing a hazmat suit. Maybe this has something to do with my instruments and the things next to our seats. There is one last important occurrence that confused me. What my instruments registered … we all should have received a lethal dose and be dead by now."

Nobody was even sick. That was something that couldn't be explained right now. Jim knew it wouldn't be easy getting info out of the voice. He was hoping the agent would do a good job spying and bringing back something meaty for intelligence to examine.

They finally reached the closest airfield and Billy departed for a thorough examination and convalescence.

For now, he would have to be satisfied with the contents of the box next to him.

CHAPTER 6

Back at the exchange point, it was completely dark with a fog rolling in. The agent was still cuffed to the pole under the box and getting a bit tired.

The agent decided to sit with the pole supporting the back. As the eyes began to close, the chin sank and a nap was commenced.

The agent was aroused when the sound of footsteps was heard squashing leaves and breaking twigs. Nothing was observable for the moment. Then a green light was seen through the fog coming closer from the forest.

The agent rose and was able to distinguish a tall, muscular man. He was wearing the green light over his eyes which helped for night vision and the fog.

When he came within a few feet, he stopped. His head reared back in a position of surprise. The night glasses only gave a general outline of the agent without much detail of the face. However, the body shape was unmistakable.

"You're a woman!"

"That's what my gynecologist says."

"You know I have to search you."

"Go for it. I'm a big girl."

He first pressed a remote button in his pocket. There was a click and the cuffs were unlocked.

"You can leave them there. Someone will pick them up later tonight."

He began to pat her down. The man was obviously uncomfortable as he took great pains to be gentle. He barely came in contact with any of her private areas. He finally reached her ankles.

"I could hit you over the head right now and run away."

"You won't do that."

"You're pretty cocky about it."

"Not really. You've been told to cooperate and find out what's going on. I have to blindfold you now."

He tied the blindfold around her head. He took the time to spread the top and bottom so there was no chance of seeing. The man then turned her around to disorient her a bit. He then held her arm and led her into the forest with a slightly different route than the one he approached from.

"You better hold on to me. The ground is pretty uneven."

"No thanks. I'm capable of walking on my own."

They walked about ten steps into the forest before she tripped, fell forward on her knees, and then face down.

"Are you ok?"

"Wounded in pride only. Let's go, wise guy."

She got up, grabbed his arm, and walked with higher steps to avoid a repeat. After a couple of hundred yards, they stopped. He pressed another button and she heard a sliding sound. There was a camouflaged door on the ground.

When the opening was completely exposed, he helped

her take a seat. This was just an ordinary stair lift that was mostly used in the homes of handicapped people.

He put one foot next to hers and held on to the back of her seat. He activated it and they began to descend. She could feel it was way more than a flight of stairs.

"How far down are we going?"

"The equivalent of a few flights."

They finally reached the bottom and he helped her up. They went through a metal door into a small room. He turned on the light.

"You can take the blindfold off now."

She took it off and shook her head to fluff her long, blonde locks. She was stunning. She was in her thirties but looked much younger. She was tall with a magazine cover face. She looked more like a runway model than a trained operative.

He took a look at her and started laughing.

"What's so funny?"

"So they sent me a temptress."

"Listen buster, you asked for someone who knows chemistry or physics? Well, I have more degrees than a thermometer. By the way, I'm sure you figured I'm trained in counterintelligence."

"Ok, I'm convinced. I think."

She was doing a slow burn. She finally decided to put her abilities on display to garner more respect.

"You think?"

With a martial arts move, she kicked out his legs. He went down while she barred an arm and had a dangerous grip on his throat. Used correctly, it could be fatal.

When he went down, he said nothing except for a slight grunt.

"So you're going to kill me now?"

"I wanted you to be convinced without the words."

"What's your name? I'm Bret."

"I'm Ani."

"Is that a nickname for Anne?"

"No, that's my name and it's pronounced ah'nee."

She helped him off the floor and actually started brushing his clothes. She gave him a strange look.

"Let me ask you something."

"Go ahead."

"When I took you down, you hardly said anything. Those big muscles were relaxed. Your breathing and heart rate were normal. Could you have broken that hold?"

"I sure could have, but it would've meant injuring you and I hate hurting people."

Ani immediately started gaining some respect for Bret. She finally noticed he was quite handsome.

Bret led her through another door into a hallway. They continued walking before reaching an elevator.

"You're taking me to your jail?"

"You watch too many movies. I'm taking you to your quarters. You'll have to learn to trust me."

"I should trust anyone? Every time my husband says he loves me, I want a notary there."

Bret laughed at her clever remark but seemed disappointed.

"You're married?"

"Nope, it's just my expression."

"I have to confess I like your style for an enemy."

"Ditto."

They took the elevator up several flights. They exited and walked down the hall.

"We have to make one stop first."

"Your torture chamber?"

"You know, I haven't figured out yet when you're kidding."

Ani said, "It's not important for you to know. It's only important for me to know."

"I won't even try to win this argument."

They passed several doors. They stopped at an ordinary looking door like the rest. He opened it and led Ani in.

The room looked like a doctor's examination room. It had a reclining table, lots of instruments, and several pieces of machinery. There was a door in the back.

"That door is the operating room, where we saved Billy's life."

A woman was standing in the room wearing a white lab coat. She was about Bret's age and also attractive. Her name was Lana. She kept giving Ani an icy stare.

"I'll wait outside while the two of you do your thing."

Bret stepped out and left the women to stare at each other. Lana grabbed a gown and threw it at Ani.

"Take your clothes off and put this on." Lana had an eastern European accent.

Ani saluted her, but that wasn't taken kindly.

"Don't get smart with me. Just put the gown on and get behind the x-ray machine."

Lana proceeded to give Ani a thorough examination. She even examined her teeth and private areas.

"What are you looking for?"

"Where I come from, women have hidden everything there, weapons, drugs, contraband."

She finally took a blood sample and began examining it.

"Get dressed and sit down."

"Yes, ma'am."

Lana completed her work and opened the door. She invited Bret back in.

"She's healthy as a horse. Her organs are perfect for transplants. Maybe we can use them."

Bret was startled. He didn't understand Lana was just giving Ani the business because of Ani's attitude. They left and got back in the elevator.

"Did she eat a worm for breakfast?"

"Don't mind Lana. She's a brilliant doctor, but wary of strangers. She's actually very nice when you know her."

"For a minute, I thought she was going to drink my blood."

"Now, now … behave."

They were already getting familiar with each other. They used expressions like people who have known one another for years.

The elevator reminded Ani of a department store or office building.

"Can we stop for lingerie and shoes at this floor? I need

a few things."

"How about diamond rings?"

They exited the elevator to yet another hallway. She looked around at the fresh paint and rows of doors.

"Just how big is this place?"

"It's a labyrinth of caves and tunnels. I'll explain later."

They stopped in front of another plain door. This would be her room. It wasn't too big, but it reminded her of a typical nice hotel room. There was a bed, TV, bath, computer, bookshelf, internal phone, and dresser.

"Is there room service?"

"If you want."

"All kidding aside, this is really nice."

"There's some movies and books over there to help you sleep."

Ani bounced up and down on the bed. Even the mattress was soft with fluffy pillows.

"Are you hungry? There's a kitchen nearby."

"I'm fine. Why are you being so nice?"

"Since your people want you here, you're more of a guest than an adversary or a hostage. It's late. Why don't you get some sleep?"

"I don't see a lock on the door."

"There's no need. Besides, if a burglar or rapist walks in, I suspect you're more than capable of making him sorry. If you need anything, just dial zero."

"If I want something, can I get it myself?"

"Not tonight. you'd be wasting your time walking around. Tomorrow, I'll give you a complete tour of the place and answer all your questions. Deal?"

"You got it. Nighty night."

As he left, Ani was thinking and talking to herself.

"Ok, Ani, don't forget your assignment. So what if he's good-looking, sweet, kind, considerate, and caring. He's still the enemy. Maybe."

CHAPTER 7

Ani woke the next morning thinking about what the weather was like outside since there were no windows. She wondered if and when she would see the sun again. She had no cell phone because she knew it wouldn't be allowed. She also knew the computer would have no internet. More than likely, it was just loaded with games. Ani just grabbed a book from the shelf and thumbed through it.

There was a knock at the door and Bret walked in. Ani was famished, so she was hoping the first order of business would be to grab a bite. They would be taking the elevator several times today.

"Are you ready for the grand tour?"

"Of course, but how many days will I be fasting?"

"Our version of a restaurant will be the first stop. Actually, it's just a kitchen with a few tables and chairs. Do you have a food preference?"

"I'll eat anything that won't eat me first."

They only had to walk a short distance. They skipped the examination room since she'd already been there. She wouldn't see the operating room behind it.

"There's nothing special about the operating room and

I hope you never need to use it."

They arrived and sat down in the eating area. It was all open with no doors. Ani noticed a large open kitchen with all the standard appliances. She saw two doors on either wall in the back. There was a man who was limping sweeping the floor.

"That's Henry. He's a little slow upstairs but he would give you the shirt off his back—a real angel. He does a little of everything like cooking and cleaning."

Bret motioned for Henry to bring some food. Henry was happy to do it. Ani would notice, as time progressed, just how attached Bret and Henry were.

"You can gorge yourself because this tour will take most of the day."

"What are those two doors in the back?"

"I'll show you when we're finished here."

After eating, Bret brought Ani to the back. He opened one of the doors. It was a fairly large room with shelves against every wall. The shelves were stacked with cans which were freeze-dried food.

"There's enough here to feed everyone for a year."

"I'm surprised because the food tasted so fresh."

"I'll show you why."

They went to the other door. Ani was shocked because it looked like a large greenhouse without the sun. Still, it was quite bright. The fruit and vegetables were abundant and looked delicious. Ani walked around and examined everything.

Bret pointed to a large hole in the ceiling.

"This room location isn't an accident. That hole leads to the outside and is in direct sunlight. We've taken that sunlight and projected it. All the bulb lighting is full spectrum. If you add that to pure mountain soil and water, you see the results. A little added plant food doesn't hurt either."

"What about fresh meat?"

"We buy it from the locals. We pay them more than the market rate, so they're happy. You can't tell from the road, but there are villages not far from here."

Needless to say, Ani was impressed. They went to the next stop. It seemed every working area they would view had a large window next to the door. The room was lined with shelves consisting of small glass bottles, plastic jars, vials.

There was a woman about Ani's age, sitting at a desk and working on her computer. She looked up, smiled, and waved. Ani's training had her look closely. Ani noticed this woman was outwardly something special. From the neck up, her hair, makeup, lipstick, and everything else seemed perfect. Ani was hoping she could speak to her later on.

"This is the dispensary."

"Those are all drugs?"

"If you mean prescription types, those are only on one group of shelves. The rest are nutritionals and various unclassed supplements."

Ani looked more closely. Although many were standard vitamins and such, most of the labels contained names she couldn't recognize, let alone pronounce.

"This is Dina."

"She's a pharmacist?"

"Yes, she's a Pharm D and more. The doctors all have their specialty, but she researches all holistic fields and pulls together all the doctor's info. She recommends which modality she believes works best for a given situation. I would stack her knowledge of body chemistry against anyone."

Next door to the dispensary was a room filled with books, tapes, CDs, DVDs, and flash drives. There were a couple of tables with computers on them. There was also a door on the back wall.

"This is a sort of library and entertainment room. If you want to read, listen to music, or watch a movie, feel free to take what you want back to your room."

They suddenly heard a muffled sound of a full orchestra playing behind the door. Bret led the way and opened the back door. It was similar to a large home theater. There was a projector, a huge screen, and an obvious audiophile array of speakers. There were three rows of seats. The lone occupant stopped the music and turned to Bret and Ani.

"Was it too loud?"

Bret shook his head. He explained to Ani she could come here if she wanted a bigger theater experience or concert hall sound.

"Are you sure you're not running a resort here?"

"We just want it to be as homey as possible for everyone."

They left the area and proceeded, taking the elevator for the third time.

When they left the elevator and started walking, there was the sound of several children behind them. They were running, giggling, and participating in horseplay. Before she could turn around to look, one of the larger kids wasn't watching and bumped Ani pretty hard.

She was knocked off balance and Bret grabbed her waist as she grabbed his arms. Their eye contact was that of two people who had emotions brewing. They both thought that two days were way too early for any attachment and they released.

Bret then gave a stern look at the guilty child.

"Sorry, ma'am."

Ani smiled and said it was ok.

Bret wasn't as forgiving.

"You all know recess is over so it's back to the class unless someone wants to miss that new science fiction movie."

Seeing a movie in that theater was a big deal, so they all flew to the classroom.

"You have children hostages? That's horrible."

"Don't be ridiculous. They live here with their parents. They get plenty of sun outside and take regular vacations. That is until you barged in."

"I'd like to see their so-called school."

"Next stop, coming up."

The children had their backs to the door. The teacher wore a lab coat and smiled at Bret and Ani. It looked like some sort of science class.

Ani noticed a variety of ages. She wondered if they could learn being taught on the same level.

"They're all close in age except for the two belonging to Alex and Lana. They're a bit younger. They're so bright, they have no trouble keeping up."

"This is the same Lana—"

"Yes, and Alex is her husband."

"They seem pretty obedient and well adjusted."

"They are, except maybe one. That one over there."

Bret continued explaining the one child he was speaking about had his own ideas about everything.

"He's bright … maybe too bright. His knowledge has been increasing faster than his wisdom."

Bret explained the boy would go around espousing collectivist theories going against what his parents had experienced.

"One thing we frown upon here is discussing politics because it's so polarizing. It hurts his parents so much because of their relatives that were tortured in their country in the name of a revolution. He's really a good teenager. Maybe he'll someday realize he can't be both a revolutionary and an elitist living off his mommy."

They kept walking and stopped in front of an oversized room with a large window in front. There was a large table with people meeting there. Some waved to Bret. This was obviously a conference room.

They were all doctors and in charge of their areas. Charts and papers were being passed around. This was serious stuff and a large board displayed both chemical and mathematical equations.

"You can see Lana there."

"Yes, the ice queen."

"Be nice. There's her husband, Alex, along with Pramesh, Wang, Nkuma, Carlos, Red Hawk, and Hans."

"A liberal would call this a proper diverse group and a conservative would call this a quota."

Bret said, "Neither is correct. They serve important functions. They're doctors with expertise in homeopathy, Ayurveda, traditional Chinese medicine, African herbs, American herbs, and South American herbs as well as allopathy. They also provide contact with others like us in their former countries."

"That's a mouthful. Anything else?"

"They're all engineers."

"What's the significance?"

"How do you think this place got built?"

Ani said, "Ah, touché. So what do they really do?"

Bret and the others discovered what they believed to be a better way to treat people medically. Pharmaceutical companies have to spend over a billion dollars to bring something to market.

This group, being holistic, knew you can't patent natural substances. At the same time, big pharma pays their people to invent a new molecule first and see if it's effective second.

Here, they already have effective treatments that can't be patented. All they need to do is invent a harmless molecule that can be added to the natural substance. It will not affect the resulting compound.

They can then sell it to the pharmas for much less than the billion-dollar cost it normally takes. Big pharma can then patent it.

"This is a large part of our income. Many of the products you've heard of are really ours. Now you know why I wanted someone with a technical background to replace your Billy."

"How do they communicate with the outside?"

"That's where we're going next. Patience my dear."

They came to a place that would answer her question. The window exposed four men sitting at tables with short walls separating them. This was the communications center.

"They send signals to our satellite."

"Where'd you get one of those?"

"Thousands are orbiting the earth. Many are for sale. All we had to pay for was the code for the operation. We communicate with others through our own codes."

"The government can easily break any code."

"Yes, but they have to want to do that. Our codes are embedded in the commercials we write. They're broadcast on the internet, cable TV, and the like."

"But how do you—"

"Different ways. Part of our agreements with pharmaceutical companies allows us to advertise a product we sold them as we feel necessary. Of course, we get compensated."

Bret began to list the products and the advertisements. Ani was amazed as she recognized several of them along with the particular commercial.

"You need four guys for that?"

"They actually do something else."

The leader, named Stan, was actually a computer nerd. He actually developed the program for the satellite communication using commercials. He also developed the programs for coordinating their utilities.

"The plumbing part was easy. There are fresh mountain

lakes all over the place. They act as a reservoir. The sewage was easy also."

"I noticed the temperature is comfortable."

"The temperature inside this mountain is constant. All we need is a group of fans to funnel fresh air at a good temperature."

"That and the lighting takes electricity. You obviously have it."

"We figured we'd need various sources. Some are for immediate needs and some to keep the emergency generators going."

"I didn't notice anything outside."

"You wouldn't. We have wind turbines at the top of the mountain disguised as trees. The wind blows there 24/7."

"You mean the trees actually turn?"

"Yes, but to an aircraft or satellite, they look like plain, old trees."

"I'm guessing that's not enough."

"There are loads of high, powerful waterfalls around here. The turbines produce a lot of hydroelectric power."

"That sounds like everything."

"No, you've seen how the ugly solar panels stand out. We developed a way to camouflage them to look like the exposed ground in a forest. They also generate a lot of power. The only thing left was to figure a way to bring them together. He developed several complicated programs that work off each other and take over control the machinery in case of any kind of failure."

"I can't begin to say how impressed I am with all of this."

"We've worked very hard. Now it seems it's just a matter of time."

"Is this the end?"

"No, there's one more very important place I have to show you."

Bret took Ani to a remote part of the operation. They stopped in front of a heavy metal door. The door had a skull and crossbones with words above and below it.

Above it were the words DANGER: LETHAL SUBSTANCES.

Below it was the words NO ADMITTANCE WITHOUT PROPER PROTECTION.

"This is the one area I'll ask you never to enter. There are radioactive isotopes as well as both chemical and biological items. Any contact with any of these will mean death in a very brief time."

"Is this what Billy's instruments picked up? If so, why aren't we dead already?"

"We had no idea he was in the area. We were testing a harmless gas we invented. It can mimic a deadly dose of gamma radiation. That simple gaff has destroyed our whole operation. On a positive note, that mistake saved Billy's life."

Now, Ani was wondering what a peaceful group was doing with deadly materials. She knew her situation here was an attempt to buy time.

"If the government decides they want to sacrifice me, why would they believe you have such materials to stop an attack?"

"I gave Billy samples of everything to take with him. It's all safely encased. Any failure to follow the provided directions will be catastrophic."

"Can you give me details of what you gave him?"

"First, there's a small working nuclear bomb."

"How can you get your hands on one of those?"

"One? We have more than that. Don't be naïve. After the breakup of the major power, the newly created countries were starving. Getting this and many other destructive weapons were easy for the right price."

"What else?"

"The biological weapon is something I really don't understand. The germ has something to do with a deadly bacteria. An even deadlier virus was planted inside the bacteria. If the bacteria doesn't kill the host, it will release the virus which will finish the job because there is no immune system left. There's no prevention and no cure. I've been told it wouldn't take long to wipe out an entire city."

Ani was starting to lose respect for Bret. He sounded so much like a man of peace, and now he sounded more like a potential mass murderer.

"What's the last one?"

"The chemical is like simple nerve gas. It's really not a gas at all. It's a liquid not unlike gasoline's consistency. We don't know its lifespan. We do know exposure in a room would mean death in seconds."

"How could you be involved in such a thing? I was having such good thoughts—"

"Let me say something. When we got all of this, we thought of an old expression. It was peace through superior firepower. Now we learned we could serve mankind better by working on health issues that the money and power brokers don't want to touch."

"You're ashamed?"

"Of course I am. I have thought long and hard on how to legally dispose of this material without compromising my people. You know what the government would do to us. There is just no way without destroying my friends. I would gladly sacrifice my life if it meant their survival."

Ani began to gain back her respect for Bret. She already knew how he abhorred taking a human life. This sequence just reinforced it.

"What happens if the government buys your story of having more weapons?"

"Then, there's a chance. I have a few tricks up my sleeve if they'll play ball. I'll need your cooperation."

"I don't know. Let's see."

"It's funny. The peaceful solution is using the most destructive weapons anyone can imagine might mean our salvation."

They started heading back to Ani's room. They didn't say much. Then Ani grabbed Bret's arm.

"Wait. I've been thinking. Putting emotions aside, there's a dollars and cents issue here."

"I'm a little confused. You're a scientist, not an accountant."

"I did some very unscientific calculations in my head and the numbers don't add up. The money you generate from drugs and advertising, just won't pay for running this operation and especially those weapons."

"I wish we didn't get into that."

"Hey, you holding out on me? You promised to answer any and all questions. Now you're backing off?"

"It's just that—"

"It's just that I'm beginning to think of myself as a fool."

"Don't hurt me like that. It's only a couple of days and you know we have something special going."

"Then fork it over."

"When you're right, you're right. I'll show you the last piece of the puzzle. Please don't hate me."

Ani's emotions were in a spin. By rights, she should remember her mission and do whatever it took to destroy this group. What about those life-saving events? What about the children? What about Bret? Every time she thought about him, she got a pain in her stomach.

They finally reached the point of the puzzle. It was another one of those unassuming doors. Bret opened the door to a very small empty room. He then walked to the door in the back. He opened it and switched on the light.

The room was empty except for four things. There were three tables with objects on top and covered by sheets. The fourth looked like an easel holding a piece of art that was also covered by a sheet.

Bret uncovered the painting first.

"So it's a nice copy of the most famous painting in history."

"Right, except it's not a copy. Remember where it was hanging?"

"Oh, ok, I read that they were burglarized, but nothing

was stolen."

"That was to prevent a scandal. I have indisputable evidence that it's the original."

"Even if I believed you, what's the point? Nobody could ever show it without being arrested."

"You have to understand billionaires. Sometimes they get something because they just have to have it. This one will probably be put it in a vault and looked at from time to time. You were asking about money. What do you think it's worth?"

"I've read it's priceless. Perhaps up to ten figures?"

"Bingo, you nailed it."

"Someone's giving you a billion dollars for that?"

"That's about the size of it."

"So you're nothing but a common thief."

"It's the only thing I've ever stolen in my life. I won't personally profit from this. Does the end justify the means? I don't know. I guess I'll find out on judgment day when I meet my maker."

"You say I'm clever with words. Compared to you, I'm an amateur. Alright, what else you got?"

They walked over to the first table. Bret removed the sheet, exposing a chest measuring about a foot all around. It didn't take guessing to know there was something valuable in there.

"It looks like a fancy jewelry box."

"You're very perceptive. Look at this."

He opened the box and inside was a huge egg-shaped rock. He gently pulled it out. It filled both hands.

"It looks like a big piece of quartz, but I bet it's not."

"It's the largest diamond in the world. It's more than double the size of the previous record holder and that one had a big black spot."

"It's so clear. It looks like glass."

"It's D color and flawless. There's no diamond like that in the world, even one-tenth of its size."

"Let me guess, ten figures?"

"You're two for two and that price is a bargain."

"You stole this also?"

"I told you no before. This was a gift from a tribe that lived near the mine. They worked in it. I saved a bunch of people who were very ill. They gave it to me. If I refused, that would have been the end of me."

As long as the going got weird, they continued to something even stranger. Bret took the sheet off the next, much larger box. After opening it, they saw it contained what looked like random bones from a fossil.

"I know fossils can have pretty good value but usually nothing extraordinary. I suppose this is different?"

"It sure is. It looks mundane but the DNA sure isn't."

"What is it?"

"I'm not sure what it was."

Bret alluded to man's unsuccessful search for the missing link. He said it would neither confirm nor deny any of the theories such as creationism or evolution.

"The DNA in this is partially human, bird, ape, and reptile. It's about 500,000,000 years old. There's not enough of a fossil to reconstruct what it looked like, but I don't think it was bred for beauty."

Ani laughed. Bret was getting more clever in matching her sarcasm.

"I won't even guess the price but I assume it's at least what the others are."

"Let's just say, the bidding starts there."

Bret covered it up and started escorting Ani out of the room. She stopped and pointed to the fourth piece.

"What about that?"

"Oh, that's not for sale."

"I still want to know what it is. Don't tell me you're holding out again."

"Alright, alright."

The sheet covered a chest similar in size to the last. When Bret opened it, Ani took a look and started scratching her head.

"This looks like something made in a pottery class. Ok, give me a hint."

"You can see it's all the colors of the rainbow. It's actually another fossil."

"Let me take a closer look."

Bret carefully lifted out the tray the parts were laying on.

"I'm guessing it's some kind of mutation."

"It's not from this earth. It's an alien. Look at the round mouth and the eyes below the nose. The skull has a bigger braincase than a human."

"You'll need a better story than that to convince me."

"Ok, try this. You have a chemistry background. What's the basic element for all life on earth?"

"Carbon of course."

"No exceptions?"

"None that I know of."

"This thing is based on nitrogen."

"That's impossible."

"Our experiments are absolute. From samples, the best we can determine is it had some kind of grayish liquid flowing through its body that it called blood."

"This is so crazy."

"It's my prized possession and no, I didn't steal it."

That officially ended the tour. As they walked towards Ani's room, Bret said he would be unavailable for a few days and both Lana and Alex would see to her needs.

"What am I supposed to do with my time?"

"How about volunteering to teach the kids some science classes. You can choose the subject. I think you'll do great. You can also go into any of the labs and watch the experiments. Feel free to examine our research papers. They're all available. Don't forget the media room for fun."

Both of their emotions were in a whirlwind. Neither could believe they were getting attached that quickly. Only time would tell where it goes.

CHAPTER 8

Jim was sitting in a small motel room. He had poured through the information that was provided with the packages for several days. He first verified the information on the flash drive, disc, and hard copy all matched.

Although his technical knowledge was limited, Jim had a basic understanding of the three alleged powerful weapons he sent to the laboratories for analysis.

He kept making sounds of surprise, despair, and sorrow.

"This can't be … Oh, no … I can't believe it."

The explanations of the use and care of the objects were quite convincing. He was even given the chemical and mathematical equations.

His phone began to ring. It was the cardiologist in charge of caring for Billy at the military hospital. His first concern was to ask how Billy was doing.

"Billy was doing so well, we discharged him today.. No infection, no rejection. He told me quite a story."

"The stents were done properly, then?"

"All I can say is the person who did this was a well-trained interventional cardiologist."

Jim didn't have a lot of time since he was expecting calls

from the laboratories. He kept pestering them for updates and wanted to make this brief.

"What were his chances of survival if this procedure wasn't performed?"

"It's hard to say. The most accurate assessment I can make is he wouldn't have lasted the night. I absolutely believe this procedure saved his life."

Jim had to consider this when he made recommendations for handling this situation. On one hand, he was facing an unpredictably dangerous group of people, capable of destroying entire cities. On the other hand, these were humane types that were exhaustive in their approach to save and release Billy. He thanked the doctor and ended the conversation.

If he got bad news about those packages, he would have to go to the highest levels and take some browbeating because of the delay.

Once again, his phone rang. It was the chief scientist examining the nuclear device. It was a secure cell, so he could talk freely.

"I have an update for you."

"I'm afraid to ask."

"The tests are entirely conclusive. This is a working nuclear bomb."

"Is it armed?"

"Not in its present state. If we activate it, there would be severe damage within miles from the point of detonation."

Now Jim felt a little nauseous. He knew what was ahead of him. He began rehearsing in his mind exactly what he would say to the next level which went to the top.

"Please let me know if there's any change. I know you will give it top priority and care, but make sure to limit those who know about this."

"That will be easy. I don't even know where you got it from."

Jim was still thinking before his ultimate phone call. His phone rang again. It was the biological weapons lab and the lead scientist.

"I would love to know where this came from."

"I can't tell you that."

"Eventually you'll have to. This could give us a real edge over our enemies."

"I've read it's a virus implanted into a bacterium."

"It's so much more than that. It reproduces so fast, from a little in a reservoir, an entire city could be depopulated. Death is within minutes. We can't find anything to destroy it."

"Nobody outside of your team is to know about this. Foreign agents are all over the place. It'll be like a shooting gallery."

"At this point, I'll recommend locking it away in a safe place. We don't have enough material or equipment to go any further safely."

Jim was in full agreement. As he disconnected, he thought he'd try one last time to get the third and final report.

After his call was answered by an administrative assistant, he spoke nervously. Instead of going through channels, he asked for an emergency talk with the lead scientist.

"This is Josef, may I help you?"

Josef was the highest-ranking civilian at the base. He had a heavy accent but was cleared and trusted. Coincidentally, he was the managing scientist for this sample. He had to ensure the sample was properly secured so no unauthorized personnel could get near it.

"I need your expertise on that sample you've been working with."

"There's nothing much I can tell you."

"Please, Josef. Take your best guess."

"It could be anything from a mild nerve agent to something much deadlier than VX. It's my guess it's the latter."

"How long will it take for a definite analysis?"

"It won't be soon. We don't have the proper way to seal it in a workable area. If my suspicions are correct, any leakage could be fatal for half of the base. I recommend removal to another lab."

"Do you have a date?"

"You know the red tape involved. I think it will take several weeks."

"Ugh. Thanks for your time."

Jim had to take a step that he wanted to avoid. With the information he had, the next call would determine the entire direction of a major episode in history.

Jim gathered all the papers along with his notes. He left his laptop on with the most pertinent sections. He dialed and an operator put him on hold. He nervously paced back and forth in his room.

"He is busy at the moment but he wants to speak with you."

Being put on hold for the second time just made Jim edgier. He finally heard what he was waiting for.

"The president will speak with you now."

"I was wondering when you'd get around to calling me. You've given me a bit of a headache with your little adventure out west."

"I try not to bother you even though we report directly to you. I didn't realize until now the importance of it."

Jim didn't know that the president would be speaking about something different than the reason for his call.

"Using the military isn't important? Do you know where this is?"

"I just know it's a remote area."

"Don't go simple on me. Answer the question."

"I think you're going to tell me something I should know."

"You brought the military on to a reservation. That's patently illegal. I have the Indian Agency on my back from a complaint. The residents called and complained the moment it happened. They're threatening to picket the White House. How do you think those soldiers got recalled so quickly?"

"It wasn't my idea. The general—"

"He's been relieved. It seems I have to remind everyone I'm still commander in chief."

"I'll remember."

"The road is the border. I don't want anyone going past there wearing a uniform with any kind of exposed weapons without my explicit orders."

Jim now understood the president had no idea as to the real reason for his call. He first wanted to clear up the circumstances that led him to the reservation in the first place.

"So this man you're telling me about, what's his condition?"

Jim not only explained the lifesaving event that took place, but also the fact that he had to replace Billy or they wouldn't let him go.

"Extortionists? I won't give them a dime."

"They haven't asked for any money."

"Terrorists?"

"I don't think so, yet. To my knowledge, they have no religious, nationalistic, or political ax to grind."

"Define yet."

"That is the reason for my call. The reservation situation just makes this more complex."

Jim explained the three packages as well as the analysis. As the details became more explicit, the president's voice grew angrier and louder.

"Why am I always the last person to know? Do they actually have more of this stuff?"

"They say they do, but there's no way of knowing."

"Anything else you can tell me? We may have to inform the leaders of the reservation that an armed attack is a possibility. I don't have the luxury of pondering the legal implications."

"They did save Billy's life."

"That's a consideration."

"Billy said they have children there."

Jim knew that would hurt the president since he had children of his own.

"Oh, no. What a mess. Hostages?"

"Billy thinks they just live there voluntarily."

"I can't … this needs some thought."

"Based on Billy's observations and my conversations with this mysterious voice, I think they would probably be remiss to use any of these weapons. I can't be sure."

"Then why do they have them?"

"I don't have an answer for that. You certainly have quite a few decisions to make."

"Not the least of which is the international implications. That's why the president has close advisors. This is way beyond some crazy people living inside a cave or mountain or whatever. Keep me posted."

Jim had done his duty. He retired to a local bar to get himself a good, stiff drink. His itinerary for the near future would include almost daily conversations with the voice and the president.

The president, on the other hand, had bigger problems. He already had a domestic crisis. This could easily morph into an international crisis. He had a nation to think about. There were also human lives at stake. He couldn't get the idea of child casualties out of his head.

The only thing that could be certain was the resolution of this situation was not going to happen in days. It would likely take weeks or months for this mess to be cleared up.

Although most presidents had a large number of advisors, this one kept a small group for these situations. It was a group that didn't blindly agree. They had strong feelings and varying opinions. Their voices would play the central role in the president's decision to resolve this matter. Others who had a title of advisor were kept on the periphery.

The president only wanted the new general who was attached to Jim's agency to be involved. He was to secretly develop an attack plan if needed.

CHAPTER 9

Jim would spend the near future speaking with the president and Bret (who he called the voice). He continued hounding the last lab on the list for some kind of result.

While Josef always accepted his calls, he always had little update to give. There was no approval to transfer the sample to a lab that was better equipped.

He used a double chamber to be sure there would not be any leakage from a sealed area. A tiny sample was released in a sealed room and it proved deadly to insects, birds, and mice almost instantaneously.

The problem arose when the same fate befell living things in an adjoining room, albeit not at an instant. Josef didn't dare take more chances, so he was trying to rely on instruments from machinery rather than live examples.

This day, Josef didn't answer. The operator said it was a workday for him. Since he was prone to meetings, Jim assumed this was a long meeting day. The circumstances were quite different.

During the morning, Josef removed the secure case from a locked cabinet, as he did every day. He would read through research papers that gave the info regarding similar weapons.

Josef would pause and just look at the container as if he might somehow get instantaneous knowledge. He'd also glance at the marker board hanging on the wall. It contained equations and other technical data with plenty of erasures.

Josef was sitting with his back to the door when he heard it open and shut. He got up and turned around.

"Kannat, what are you doing here?"

Kannat had a heavy accent. Josef and he had a relatively good relationship. The only thing that Josef wondered about is Kannat's accent did not match the derivation of his name. He never bothered to ask or question it since Kannat had received security clearance.

"I wanted to see if I could help."

"You are not assigned to this project."

"I've been told about it. I worked on similar objects in my old country."

Josef immediately smiled. After all, he needed help. He had no idea Kannat was bluffing. He was too naïve to suspect anything at the moment. Kannat just kept staring at the container.

Josef started showing Kannat his papers. He then walked over to the marker board and asked Kannat what was wrong with his equations. Kannat walked over, erased some of Josef's work, and wrote his own equations, which made no sense in this application.

"No, no, no."

Josef erased Kannat's work and wrote some other calculations. Once again, he wrote something on the board. He went back to the table with the research papers.

Once again, Josef erased Kannat's work and said this is a different substance altogether. He then noticed something strange. He watched as Kannat was silently mouthing everything written on the board. It was obvious he was trying to memorize Josef's work.

It was as if a light went on in Josef's head. His head swiveled back and forth between looking at the board and Kannat's mouth. His voice became a crescendo of sound from slightly above a whisper to a loud vocalization.

"You told me nothing. You know nothing. I forbid you to leave this room!"

Josef walked quickly to the door to lock it with the key he was simultaneously pulling from his pocket. His mistake was turning his back on Kannat.

Kannat pulled a heavy, blunt object from beneath his lab coat. It resembled a crowbar. He struck Josef's head with thunderous, brute force. Josef crumbled to the floor.

Although Josef was unconscious, he was still alive. Kannat put a gag in Josef's mouth and bound his feet and arms with some heavy cord.

Kannat sat there for a moment with the package cradled under his arm inside his lab coat. He spoke to Josef as if he could answer, but it was a one-way conversation.

"Josef, my friend, I will not kill you. They will find you soon enough. I pray you recover and don't hate me. I guess that's what friendship does. I have my duty; you have yours. I will be long gone by the time they discover you."

Kannat walked out with the small case in his lab coat, supporting it with his hands in his pockets. It was quite inconspicuous. He moved quickly to his car in the parking lot. He went back to his office and a working area next to gather anything of value and personal articles.

Kannat walked through the base with a casual gait. There were a few hellos and nothing was out of the ordinary. He knew enough to stay calm and go slowly until his car left the gate.

The military guards were unaware and passed his vehicle as people with security clearance came and went all day long. He drove rapidly for several miles and stopped at a familiar shopping mall. Parking in the back, there was a place he knew would be out of sight from the general public. Kannat changed the license plates and headed out.

He knew his carefully planned escape route because he'd practiced it several times. There would be several highways and side streets. It would be next to impossible to follow him.

Traveling more than 200 miles, Kannat finally turned off onto a dirt road leading to an abandoned farm. He couldn't help but wonder whether Josef was discovered yet. His violent episode bothered him because he was, after all, still a scientist.

Kannat finally arrived at a barn that was in very poor condition. The door was large enough to drive through. He did that and abandoned the car, walking a short distance to a large shed.

Although weather-beaten, the shed was clean inside. There were a few pieces of laboratory equipment such as a microscope. He sat there and waited.

At that time, Josef didn't show at a scheduled meeting. Some thought he wasn't feeling well. Others thought he was bogged down with his work. Being occasionally absent-minded, it wasn't unusual for this to happen.

When he didn't answer calls to his lab or office, a procedure called for the base security to be summoned. They first went to his office and found nothing suspicious.

When the MPs went to the lab, they knocked. Getting no answer, they opened the door. It would only open a few inches because of some kind of blockage.

They started pushing harder, moving the impediment slightly. They heard a muffled moan and broke in with full force. This rolled Josef over.

They immediately called for medical help and removed both the string and gag. They asked what happened.

Josef mumbled almost incoherently. He kept repeating the same words. Most were unintelligible, but some were clear.

"Kannat, Kannat, Kannat … Sample gone, sample gone."

One of the MPs was told to bring Kannat. He first checked his office and then his lab. It was crystal clear. Anything that was the least bit significant was gone as was Kannat.

Security was alerted as well as the general alarm. The search unit was informed to approach the subject with extreme caution. He might be carrying a deadly substance.

Kannat was still waiting impatiently when the sound of a car became audible. It pulled up next to the shed. Out walked a tall burly man. Entering the shed, he greeted

Kannat. They both had to speak English because they had different native tongues.

"Do you have the item?"

"It's sitting on the table in front of me."

"You summoned me for something of grave importance. What is it?"

"I don't exactly know."

"You got me here for a top emergency regarding secret material and you don't know what it is?"

"I tried to get the lead scientist to talk but it was for naught. What I do know is they brought it through the gates as a top-secret item. Security was heavy and nobody was allowed near it."

"It sounds like something we can use."

"Enough talking. They're looking for me by now. We have to leave."

"Just wait. This was so sudden, it will take time for you to be evacuated home."

"How long?"

"I'll take you there in about an hour."

"In the meantime, I'll get hung for espionage."

"Take it easy. You weren't followed?"

"I'm almost positive of that."

"Your car is in the shed?"

"That was the arrangement."

"Let them look. The best they can do is send helicopters and they'll see nothing. There's a disguise in the drawer."

Kannat felt a little better and they both sat, looking at the package. The burly agent shook it gently. He shrugged his shoulders and smirked.

"It sounds like a liquid but I bet it's not a new kind of vodka."

"Theoretically, it should be some kind of poison—probably fatal if ingested. It could also be a germ."

"We have some time. We have rubber gloves. Let's look under the microscope."

Kannat was a little uneasy but he assumed if it didn't kill Josef, he could safely handle it with care. They took out a syringe and slide for the scope. They proceeded to open the case.

That was the last thing either one of them would do in their lifetime.

As the search continued, the base called Jim. They let him know what happened.

"You're supposed to be one of the most secure places."

"Never mind that. You have to find out something from the perpetrators."

"Go on."

"We need to know how long this stuff lasts. Days, weeks, months? How long before it dissipates?"

"I need an aspirin. How the heck am I going to do that?"

"You have to figure out a way unless you want a tragedy."

Jim disconnected the call. The last such call gave him a bout of nausea. This time, he hit the daily double with nausea and a headache.

Jim knew the voice would be displeased. He also didn't like the precarious position this would likely put Ani. He had to give it some thought whether to beat around the bush, just lie, or tell the truth.

His first move was to call the president. The news was not received warmly. The president was furious.

"This is now officially a crisis. Where is the poison?"

"We haven't found the spy who took it yet. We're pulling out all stops to get him. My best assumption is he's hiding while on the run and he hasn't handed it off to anyone yet."

"If this stuff escapes and it kills any of the public, these people just wrote their own epitaph."

"I'd get more info, but I'm not scheduled to talk to the voice for a few days."

"Isn't there anyone else in that place you can speak with?"

"Nobody will speak to me. I'm always told I have to wait for the voice."

"Let's still keep a lid on this. If it can be found and disposed of safely, I don't care if the thief escapes."

"I'm not sure we have a choice."

"What are you going to do next?"

"What can I do? We have to wait until it's located and the time I'm allowed to speak with the voice."

This time Jim gathered up all the technical info he had and started reading it again. He didn't know where to start. He felt like a carpenter without a hammer.

As this situation was becoming more dangerous and complex, Jim was now carrying a bottle with him. His last thought of the day was that he wouldn't become an alcoholic.

CHAPTER 10

Bret disappeared several times. None were for more than a day or two. Each time he returned, Bret would ask Ani what she had been doing. This was out of interest, not suspicion.

Ani spent a lot more time with research rather than entertainment. The one task she hadn't devoted time to was teaching. This last time, she made it her business to help out with classes.

"How did it go?"

"The children were quite nice. I was surprised at their eagerness to learn. Their heads are like sponges."

"Were there any problems?"

"Just the one you told me about. He's a wise guy that needs to grow up. He's still one of the spoiled kids that thinks he's a revolutionary but still needs mommy's care. He'll be ok."

"What did he do?"

"It's very minor. I took care of it."

When Ani turned her back, he hit her with a spitball. The culprit led the class with laughter. She turned and smiled but didn't say anything. Her silence quieted the class. It was fear of the unknown.

Still smiling, she asked who the offender was. There was still silence.

"Oh, cowards huh? It's ok. I don't like squealers anyway. I would like the guilty one to voluntarily stay after recess and apologize."

Nobody stayed after recess. When it was time to be dismissed for the day, Ani kept the class for a few moments. She looked around the room without making eye contact with anyone.

"I know who did it. The next time any disruption happens, I'm not going to yell, I'm going to get some fun out of the deal."

The next day, little changed. Children don't understand their whispers can often be heard. Ani overheard him whispering what a jerk she was and he would fix her. Ani ignored him.

Ani caught him in the hallway during recess and politely asked to speak to him. She led him to a storeroom with no window. He hesitated.

"You scared?"

"I'm not afraid of you."

They went in and being a young teen, he was already bigger than her. She said she knew it was him with the spitball. He just smirked.

"I guess we have to do this the hard way. How would you like to slug me?"

"I'm not allowed to hit a woman."

"Go ahead as hard as you can."

"I'll get in trouble."

"Why? You're not going to hurt me. I'm going to hurt you."

"I don't trust you."

"You little baby. You're frightened of the teacher."

"You promise not to tell anyone?"

Ani returned the same smirk he originally gave her. He quickly made a fist and swung as hard as he could. She intercepted the swing by grabbing his wrist. She simultaneously punched him in the stomach and bent his arm around his back. She wrapped her arm around his neck. He had tears in his eyes.

"You're hurting me. Please stop."

"Listen, you little creep. If you ever give me a hard time again, I'll beat the tar out of you. Now apologize."

"Ok, I'm sorry. Let me go."

"Only if it's a sincere apology."

"I mean it. It's just the world is tough for me to understand."

Ani released him. She started rubbing his arm for circulation.

"You know what I was like at your age?"

"You were probably a good girl."

"Wrong, I thought I was a tough guy like you. Then I learned what life was all about. You're a good boy … a bright boy. If you learn to channel your emotions, there's no limit what you can accomplish."

"I want to change so badly."

"I'll make you a deal."

"Like what?"

"Let's go back to class and you'll see."

They were sitting in the classroom and Ani made an announcement.

"You know, I could use some help, a sort of deputy. This person would have to help me grade tests, review everyone's homework, things like that. Any volunteers?"

The class was so surprised, they sat there stunned. Ani looked around and then looked squarely in the eyes of her former nemesis.

"How about you?"

"That would be so great. I want it."

The class looked at him. They were shocked. It took Ani a very short time to turn this kid from a beast to a productive student. Everyone noticed. His mother even queried Ani and thanked her.

"How did you do it?"

"We just had a little talk."

Bret was impressed with the story. It seemed everything Ani did, thrilled him. The infatuation was becoming mutual.

It's usually hard for people who become smitten and are adversaries to hide their emotions. They didn't do a good job keeping people from seeing their feelings.

Bret and Ani started going to the public areas and would have some limited contact. There were whispers as they often walked holding hands or arm in arm.

It seemed Bret was more confident as he kept his demeanor at a steady level. It was more difficult for Ani. Her heart would race and start pounding when he so much as touched her.

They both knew it would be wise if that was the limit of their contact, so they tried their best to keep it that way. They would go to sleep at night thinking of each other, even though they hadn't so much as kissed.

It was right after the school story that Bret found a message in his room. It read that Jim needed to talk to him as soon as possible. The time he would call was within an hour.

Bret wondered if it had to do with their recent conversation. Jim wanted to know the dissipation times for all the samples. Bret told him the time was the standard half-life for radioactive isotopes. The biological substance would survive an unknown period but likely would die without a host or water within days. He was pretty sure the chemical (if escaped) would dissipate in twenty-four hours, but forty-eight would be a safer time frame.

Bret fetched Ani and waited for the call.

CHAPTER 11

Jim wanted to wait on the call to the voice with the bad news until Kannat and the sample were located. It took more days than anticipated. The government secured the area with the maximum distance they thought chemical could travel.

It was discovered through a lot of dead animals in the area. The shed was the center of where all this happened. The search team released some birds, insects, and mammals in the area and funneled them towards the shed.

Jim would now need to confirm the safety factors with Bret. Nobody was even sure a hazmat suit would provide sufficient protection.

The latest info was the apparent survival of every living thing for several hours. When that information reached Jim, he knew it was time to get hold of the voice and spill the beans.

"Your note my guy received read there's something important to talk about."

"All the samples were verified and we are in full agreement regarding their authenticity."

Bret noticed Jim's voice cracking. He sounded shaky.

Bret looked at Ani with her palms in the air. She was also confused.

"You still haven't told me about the emergency."

"Ok, here it is. The chemical was stolen. We think the thief and his co-conspirator might be dead."

"What? Are you nuts? I gave you explicit instructions. You're supposed to have the tightest security. You—"

"Shut up and listen. How sure are you about the forty-eight-hour safety period? Lives of the search team are at stake."

"No guarantee, but it should be a harmless liquid. Send some animals—"

"We did that. The originals died, but the recent ones are alive."

"Then it's all clear."

"I have to end the call—"

"Now it's your turn to listen. You tell the president to not have any knee-jerk reaction. You talked about the lives of the search team. If he starts acting like a cowboy, he'll be endangering more innocent lives than he could ever imagine."

"I'll relay the message."

With the communication ended, Bret put his elbow on the table and his forehead against his open hand. He started nervously running his fingers through his hair. Ani could see him clenching his fist.

"This is all my fault. I never killed anyone before. I can't even stand when someone's in pain."

This was all Ani could take. She jumped out of her chair and went behind where Bret was seated. She hugged him from behind.

"I'm so sorry, baby. It's not your fault. I want to make you feel better."

Ani kissed the back of Bret's head, along with his cheek and forehead. He turned his head towards her and kissed her on the lips.

He stood up and hugged her tightly while he was still sniffling. Bret appreciated her caring and thanked her. Their lips met for a longer period of time. Their passion was burning.

They left the room holding hands and immediately went to Bret's room. They knew nothing could stop them now. The door to his room closed and the lights went out.

Later in the evening, they cuddled together. It was time for pillow talk. Ani heaved a sigh.

"I'm worried."

"About the situation with Jim?"

"No. About the fact that I've known you such a short time and now I've fallen in love."

"I thought about it a lot. The way I look at it, we're not kids. Sometimes in life, even after a brief time, you just know this is the one. Give me your hand."

Bret reached over to a drawer in his night table. He pulled out a ring and put it on her finger. It fit pretty well. The ring wasn't expensive. It was made of very lightweight gold. There were no stones. All it had was an infinity symbol. Ani looked at it and kissed Bret on the cheek.

"It's so pretty. Why infinity?"

"It was to be saved for that special person. I was told

true love lasts into infinity. Once you're trapped in there, it's impossible to escape."

"I know so little about you except you're the most caring person I've ever met. Tell me about yourself."

"I was a normal kid, I guess. I played sports and all that. Maybe I used to think too much."

"Think in what way?"

"I was a dreamer. Some would say an idealist, but I didn't think the word was a good fit."

Bret thought there were different forms of idealists. Some just sat around, dreamed, and accomplished nothing.

Some were overly emotional. They spent more time demonstrating and rioting. They also accomplished nothing.

Some took on the powers more quietly. If it came to a struggle, they were brave and stood up alone if necessary. Most of them ended up in labor camps or worse. Bret wanted to be different.

"How so?"

"I was a young man and I decided to travel the world. I wanted to talk to people and see if anyone had similar thoughts and ways to fulfill their dreams."

"Did you find many?"

"I was shocked at the number of people who thought exactly like me."

That's when Bret started devising a plan to start having a better world without wars, where people had more respect for others like many years ago.

"You thought these weapons could work?"

"Yes, but I saw it was useless without teaching the proper rearing of children. Too many entitled parents are fixated with self-esteem."

"Isn't self-esteem a good thing?"

"It's very good, but not when you're taught to disrespect others in the process. Politeness, courtesy, and consideration are a lost art."

"You've seen a lot of this."

"When the handicapped elderly are pushed out of the way so a child can enter a door first, it's not right. I've always taught kids to respect anyone in authority."

"I guess I saw it from the other end."

"It's your turn. Tell me about it."

"I was brought up in an orphanage. I don't even know how I got my name."

"It was rough, huh?"

"Double that. The people that ran the place were evil. I could handle myself, but other kids were tortured."

Ani spoke about her best friend, Lisa. She was a bit younger.

"She was beautiful, much prettier than me. She was just sickly—bad immune resistance, I think. One day a cold, the next a fever..."

"They were tough on her?"

"Those sadists were mean to her every chance they got."

Ani spoke about the time in the lunchroom when Lisa was feeling pretty bad. She was too sick to eat.

One of the matrons would walk around carrying an oversized ladle. It was quite heavy and she used it for discipline.

"She was the usual stereotype—overweight, hair in a bun, her facial expression looked like she ate a worm for breakfast."

"Scary, huh?"

"She walked behind Lisa, saw she wasn't eating, and crowned her pretty hard. Lisa started sobbing."

"That's disgusting."

"I scooped up some mashed potatoes in my hand, stood, and threw it in her face."

"What did she do?"

"Before she could do anything, I got into a boxer's stance and asked her if she wanted to try the ladle on me. Of course, she ran away."

Ani got a reputation as a protector. Even the boys looked to Ani as the one who would defend them.

"This quieted down at the home?"

"Just with me. They continued their inhuman ways with the kids. Any outside complaints were out of the question because of the fear of retribution."

The final straw came when Ani walked into the kitchen one day. There were always whispers the director was a pedophile. When Ani walked in, she saw the director with his hands all over Lisa. She was crying. The director was startled and jumped back. Ani lost her cool, grabbed a large carving knife and pointed at him.

"If I ever see you touch that girl again, I'll cut off your penis and wrap it around your neck!"

"Wow, what did he do?"

"The coward ran out the side door."

It was then the director and the people who worked for him decided they had to get rid of Ani. Foul play was out of the question. One of them came up with an idea.

Ani was turning sixteen. She was so smart, she already graduated from the equivalent of high school. They made her an offer to pay for an apartment off-site as long as she would keep a job and go to college.

"I couldn't say no to getting away from that awful place."

"Have you kept in touch with Lisa?"

"No, I couldn't."

Shortly after Ani left, the same nonsense started again. Lisa was easy to pick on because she was so meek. She really did nothing bad, but they built an infraction against her.

There were temporary army barracks used during the war to house soldiers over the summer. They had been empty for many years. As punishment, they made her sleep there a couple of nights. This was in the middle of the winter.

"Can you imagine a sickly girl being made to sleep in a place where the walls were just thin wood and full of holes? Sub-freezing temperatures didn't help. There wasn't even a stove for heat."

"This is so criminal."

"It didn't take but a day for Lisa to get really sick. The poor thing didn't last a week."

"Sounds like murder. Did you go after them?"

"Sadly, I couldn't. There was an immediate investigation and the whole crew was arrested, tried, and convicted. Everyone was put away for a long time. That's when I promised Lisa I would try to succeed for both of us. That's why

I had three degrees by age twenty-two."

"What did you do next?"

"With the flow of rent money now gone, I couldn't earn enough with a girly type job like waitressing. I tried working for a contractor doing roofing and siding. He paid pretty well."

"But?"

"He sent me to pick up some siding. The place was filled with contractors. The manager was taking care of everyone except me, even guys who walked in after I did."

Ani had to get back to work. and, after waiting an hour, her patience was wearing thin.

"I got so mad, I asked him if he was doing this because I was a woman. The contractors just looked and the manager snickered. He thought he was making a fool out of me."

Ani said, "You know that famous women's organization? They have an office on the next block. Maybe you'd like to deal with them?' "

The manager said, "Those dishrags? Well we're pretty tough."

Ani said, "Oh, yeah? If I call them, those dishrags will come down here and pick at your bones like vultures until there's nothing left."

The contractors all got hysterical and the manager turned red. He knew they were laughing at him. He just got mad and brought out the siding for Ani.

Bret said, "You kept that job?"

"Not for long … the winter came and I got laid off."

Bret started stroking her hair and cheek.

"I feel so bad, you had it so tough. What was next?"

"I thought it over. I hadn't finished my first degree yet. I was too young to get any kind of decent job. The only way was to prove myself was with a commission job."

"That's an idea. What kind?"

"I started with real estate. They're so unscrupulous, my broker would let me sell without a license. It didn't last long though."

"You couldn't sell anything?"

"I could. You know their reputation."

The broker wanted Ani to sell land that couldn't pass a percolation test and couldn't be built on. She told Ani to say the land is pristine and the potential is limitless.

"I told her the only thing I would tell anyone is the land is a swamp and the potential is malaria. That was the end of my real estate career."

As usual, Bret roared at Ani's quips. She apologized and said she hoped he understood why she was a little rough around the edges.

"Are you kidding? I love the way you speak. Anything else?"

Ani was going to try one last time working a commission job. She landed something where she sold vending machines for a manufacturer. The showroom looked more like a warehouse.

Ani wasn't doing very well. The crude types that walked in just weren't a good match for her manner.

Ani was ready to give up. This would be her last day without a sale. The company also noticed so it would be a mutual separation.

In walked six rugged-looking guys. Ani was the only one in sales available.

"I was scared."

"You don't scare easily."

"You have to realize these guys were marked up. You knew they made their bones. They all had the same uniform—short, stocky, muscular, heavy eyebrows, hair combed back, known by nicknames."

The men walked around looking at machines. Ani followed them, but they purposely ignored her. There was one that was a higher ranking. Ani overheard him say, "I wanna see this hot chick sell me a machine."

Ani finally realized her only chance was to come down to their level of speech. She would learn the leader was called Bags, which was short for money bags. He got that name for his frugality by always reaching in his pocket and never coming out with anything. He was joined by Tunnel.

"Why Tunnel?"

"You'd know if you saw the space between his front teeth."

The others were Dinny, called that way because it was short for Anthony and his grandmother called him Andinny; Fantastic, because he'd say that no matter how he felt; DS, which stood for department of sanitation, because he owned private pickup routes; and Mr. Low, because he always blew transmissions and rode around town in low gear.

Ani gave it a try. "Excuse me." There was no answer. She tried again. "Excuse me!" Once again, no answer.

Exasperated, she finally said, "Hey, sport!"

That finally got their attention.

"You guys want a machine?"

Bags was doing the talking.

"What kind you got?"

"Come over here."

Ani walked next to a machine, cupped her hand, and slammed the side of the machine causing a bunch of rattles.

"You hear that? It's a piece of crap. You don't want it."

The boys nodded and started speaking in low voices. She led them over to another machine which was a lot more money. Once again, she slammed the new one. It made a rock-solid thud.

"This is what you want. It's a real whore. It'll vend anything—candy, condoms, put your old lady in there, it'll vend her too."

After the cackling stopped, Ani had made her first sale. One strange thing was a well-dressed woman watching and quietly laughing. She wore clothes that Ani couldn't pay for with a month's salary.

Bret said, "At least you made a little to get you started."

"Not quite. They owned most of the buildings by the airport. It was a protected area."

This was a sideline for their building investments. They owned catering halls, garbage routes, funeral homes. Like Ani said, they had the whole uniform.

"Credit card?"

Bags opened his eyes wide.

"Cash, only cash. Don't bother with a receipt."

This time, Bags actually took a wad of bills out of his pocket.

"Bags ordered so many machines, I set a one-day record for company sales."

"You were a real hero."

"It didn't end. About twenty associates came in. They ordered so many machines, the company couldn't manufacture them quick enough."

Bags was so enthused, he invited Ani to his home to meet his wife. He was having a gathering for several associates and wives. She saw the house was very ethnic. There was a lot of masonry in front, including stone lions and religious statues.

At dinner, the wives were very interested in Ani's life. She told them of the orphanage and her trying to pay for college. They all knew about the scandal because it was in the same city. The media spoke about the trials and convictions without much detail.

Ani saw no problem relating to some of the events. The stories were continuously met with gasps. Then something weird happened when she got to the circumstances of both the kitchen incident and Lisa's death.

Everyone became quiet. The men just started staring at one another. They said nothing and remained expressionless.

"It was as if they were speaking with their minds to each other."

Three days later the media reported a fight in the prison. The former director was killed.

"Do you think that they—"

"You never ask questions from these kinds of people. At least Lisa got justice. I hope she's looking down and smiling."

Shortly thereafter, Bags returned to the showroom. Ani was mortified. She was certain something was wrong. Any cancellation would ruin her.

Bags walked up to Ani and pulled a white envelope from his pocket. It was bulging.

"Me and the boys took up a little collection to help you with college."

"You accepted the money?"

"You don't decline a gift from someone like Bags. Besides, the commissions didn't come through yet and the rent was due. I figured a few hundred dollars would come in handy."

Ani told Bags she would leave it in her desk drawer. The desk was next to her.

"Stop! There's fifty big ones in that envelope. Keep it in your pocket."

Ani couldn't believe anyone would give her fifty thousand dollars. Between that and the commissions, she could pay for college and buy a car.

Bret said, "That's another great story."

"It doesn't end there."

A manager approached Ani and said the president of the company flew in and wanted to see her. After escorting her up, he let her in an office where the president was standing. He was an elderly gentleman, but well-groomed and wearing a silk suit.

"Since I started this company thirty years ago, I've never

seen a sales performance like this."

He walked around her, looking Ani up and down.

"You're a lot younger than I thought you'd be, but this may even work better. I'd like you to transfer to the headquarters and become my marketing director."

Ani was stunned. "You said something about being better?"

"I have a lot of deadwood there. There are some vice presidents. I don't even know what they do except play golf. Someone like you might scare the bejeebers out of them."

"I'm very flattered."

"Don't give me an answer now. Think about it a few days."

Ani left the office on cloud nine.

"Did you accept the position?"

"I ended up turning him down."

"What a great opportunity. Do you regret it?"

"Not at all. They went bankrupt a few years later."

Bret was mystified at how anyone could refuse something like that. He wanted to hear more.

Ani was walking from the president's office when another manager approached. He said his sister wanted to speak with her. She met the sister who turned out to be the same well-dressed woman who was watching Ani.

"My name is Myra. I'd like you to have lunch with me."

"They only give me a half-hour so—"

"I've arranged for you to have the afternoon off."

"Free lunch and a half-day off? That works for me."

Myra had a taxi waiting. She took Ani to a very expensive French restaurant. They spent some time with idle chatter. Then Myra got down to business.

"Have you ever considered a job in the service?"

"I don't know anything about the army or navy."

"Not that, silly. I meant the service with a semi-secret government agency."

The more Myra said, the more Ani ate it up. It was all domestic but would be in the intelligence area. Ani decided that same day, this was the life she wanted.

"So here I am, in my baby's arms."

CHAPTER 12

Bret was relaxing with Ani the next morning. He had some major decisions to make before his talk with Jim later that evening. Every option on the table was predicated on Bret getting approval from his inner circle of managers. Ani noticed he was more relaxed.

"Do you feel any better than last night?"

"You know I do. My head's a lot clearer. How about you?"

"For anyone who says I'll hate myself in the morning, I have a very forgiving nature. How are you going to handle things?"

Bret said, "I have an idea about the only course of action. It'll involve sitting down and getting an agreement with the same people you saw in the meeting on the first day."

"It sounds pretty drastic."

"I'm afraid so. That recent event changed things. To be sure, those samples I gave Jim have outlived their usefulness for buying time."

"Your next step will have to be more serious. I mean, have more consequences."

"I'm already up to my neck. Now, it's a matter of survival for my friends. The powers that be have to think they'll pay too high a price for any attack."

"Be careful. I don't want to lose you. I just can't."

"When I speak to them, it would be best if you weren't present. I think they would be more comfortable and give me honest feedback. I'll tell you everything later."

"I understand."

Bret set out to gather the people who would help him make a decision. Those not included, such as Dina and Stan, had agreed to abide by any determination and put their full faith in anything Bret would tell them.

One by one, they trickled into the conference room. Red Hawk asked to speak to Bret ahead of time. Bret excused himself from the group to speak to his friend.

Red Hawk said, "The time has come for a decision on the future of my people."

"You're very perceptive. You probably know what I'm going to tell everyone."

"I think something is coming on my end. I've been requested to attend a meeting of the member nations in the near future. I suspect it has something to do with the things that are happening here."

"You think your nations may affect the decision-making process on a national level?"

"I'm certain of it. I have no idea what they'll say or do."

Bret said, "Whatever we decide now, you know it can endanger your people. We have to do whatever we can to buy more time."

"And you think—"

"I think it's the only way. I trust your judgment. I think

we all do. If anyone disagrees in this meeting, I'll try to support your opinion."

They made their way back to the conference room. Everyone was chatting. Bret came right to the point.

"Everyone knows why we're here. The situation is becoming more dire. We need to agree on our next course of action."

The first topic was whether surrender is an option. The questions about that were directed at Bret.

"I'm against it. I have no doubt you would all be imprisoned. With the weapons we possess, the term would probably be for the rest of your life. Those of you with children would be unlikely to ever see them again."

It only took a few minutes to garner unanimous agreement that surrender served no purpose. It was asked what could be negotiated.

"The incident with the chemical has boxed them into a corner. They have to act soon unless we can stall them long enough until an understanding is reached that any aggressive action would meet with catastrophic consequences."

There was a concern for friends and relatives in other countries. Bret was understanding, but firm.

"I don't want to sound cruel, but they will have to fend for themselves. You're all here because of the problems you had with your governments. Once again, you will have to concern yourselves with the survival of you and your families."

Bret decided to cut to the chase. He saw the exchanges were too concerned with too many peripheral issues. The order of the day would be to decide if there would be an international demonstration. He became very blunt.

"Folks, we really need to pare things down to whether we're going to send out a signal to our friends to do something that will get the government's attention. It could blow up in our faces or be the beginning of a way out for us. If we agree now, I'll have Stan send out the word. We should get a response very soon."

The main questions focused on his belief in a lack of casualties. Bret wasn't a fortune-teller. Some weren't convinced this action would save their own lives.

"There are no guarantees. We've taken great precautions to have human life spared."

At that point, Alex broke in.

"I find it hard to believe that people here are actually wondering about Bret's judgement. Most of you would have been in a labor camp or worse if it weren't for Bret."

Then it was Red Hawk's turn.

"The people I represent have the most to lose if things don't work out. With things unknown, I still have decided to agree with Bret."

Bret reminded the group that only a unanimous vote would make this dangerous action proceed. The first roll call gave it wings. It was a go.

After everyone left, Bret summoned Stan. He would be sending the message. Stan arrived in a few minutes.

"It's time for the major pharma commercial."

"That's a desperate measure."

"You weren't asked to vote, but I'd like your opinion."

Stan thought about the circumstances of how he came to the group. He wasn't only a computer nerd. He developed some very dangerous programs.

Stan wasn't a bad person. Computers were his love and he got bored easily. He fooled around with developing video games and other more useful business applications.

An acquaintance of his wasn't so nice. He would go to Stan and discuss mild topics like simple programs. The subject always turned to dangerous hacking.

The pseudo-friend wasn't as good with programs. He always asked Stan for tips. On more than one occasion, Stan questioned his motives. The answer was the same each time. It was just a hobby.

Stan became more involved with this hobby. He always tried to maximize the effectiveness of his programs. He ended up creating something so fierce it could destabilize the military of countries that were on the brink of war. He thought his acquaintance was using it for a sophisticated computer game.

It was used for the real thing. The erstwhile friend was caught and arrested. He denied being behind the fiendish plot. He was given immunity and pointed the finger at Stan.

Stan spent time in prison and finally was paroled for good conduct. His life was a disaster. He could never work in the computer field with his background.

Bret found him working at a fast-food restaurant for minimum wage and gave him a way to use the skills he loved while being provided a place to live. Stan was always appreciative of what Bret did for him. He told Bret in the past he would never doubt him.

"Bret, I don't care what the situation is. When opinions differ, I'll always be on your side."

"Do you think this massive action is warranted?"

"I don't know. I can't see an alternative."

"It makes me feel better that you weighed in."

"Even if things don't work out, I'll always appreciate the time you allowed me to pursue the one thing I enjoy most."

"If you broadcast this commercial now, when can you expect a detailed answer?"

"They usually get back to me within a few hours."

Stan left and broadcast a commercial for a drug that was making the company billions. They never questioned the content and the rights were in their contract anyway.

Bret had time to speak with Ani about the plan. He hoped he would have an answer before he spoke to Jim.

"You think I'm a madman?"

"Actually, I agree with you. The situation is out of hand already. This may be the only way to get out of this."

In a couple of hours, Stan showed up. He was wearing a big grin, waving a piece of paper, and nodding.

"I have your confirmation."

Bret took the paper from Stan and thanked him for the speedy work. As Stan was leaving, he looked back. "Good luck, my friend."

Bret examined the info on the page. It listed a date and local time. It also had two locations along with their latitude and longitude. Bret was now ready to speak with Jim.

Bret and Ani waited for Jim's call. When they finally

spoke, Jim didn't waste any time. The bodies of the chemical thief and his cohort had been recovered along with the sample which had dissipated.

Jim said, "Are you ready to surrender? I've been assured they'll go easy on everyone. I think it's your only way out."

"What does go easy mean?"

"I can't commit, but I think prison time would be limited if you cooperate."

"I have a better idea. Why don't you surrender?"

"Sure, the world will get down on their knees to accommodate a group of outlaws. Surely you jest."

"Do you really believe I'm an outlaw? You disappoint me."

"I suppose you're not. Do you have any terms for me to forward? Maybe they'll listen."

"Our surrender is out of the question. It seems your superiors don't take us seriously."

"I think they do. They probably question your additional weapons, if you have any."

"I have an idea. Let's put that question to rest."

"What do you have in mind?"

Bret told Jim the major news. There would be two nuclear explosions in unpopulated areas. Jim would be provided one hour's notice to evacuate any military in the area. At that time, he would be given the latitude and longitude of the detonations.

"Are you insane? You can't do that."

"Watch me."

"What about fallout?"

"It's set up so it won't reach any populated areas."

"What are you going to accomplish with this?"

"Jim, I'm going to be frank with you. We have a lot more than that at our disposal. I've said that all along. I have to buy enough time to get a satisfactory way of ending this mess."

Jim said, "The president's running scared. You may be forcing his hand."

Bret said, "I'm betting he doesn't want another holocaust. You really think he's going to attack a reservation for the first time since the 1880s?"

"Ani, are you there?"

"I'm listening."

Jim said, "Can't you talk them out of this mistake?"

"That's impossible. You have desperate people here. They're not going to listen to me."

"You have to do something. I can't present this to the president."

"Exactly what do you want me to do? I'm lucky they haven't chained me in a dungeon."

All the while Ani was smiling and winking at Bret. She put on a good act and it was obvious Jim believed her.

Jim was now carrying a flask. He took a drink and said to give him the info. Just when he thought this crisis couldn't get any worse, it was now progressing from a national to an international crisis.

Bret gave Jim the date and time of their communication. The actual time of day and location would be given to Jim with one hour's notice.

Now Jim had to make the difficult call and likely get dressed down the same way he had been before. He was still waiting to wake up from this nightmare.

CHAPTER 13

Jim was put in the familiar position of being put on hold for a long time. He finally got through to the president. He had previously informed the president that the two perpetrators of the strategic theft had expired.

The news for the media coverage didn't have many legs as the search teams and vehicles involved were explained away by releasing a statement of an escaped convict. A false name was used and the sharks in the media didn't see it as a rating booster. This emboldened the president.

"Have they offered to surrender yet?"

"No, they've upped the ante on this crazy situation. It's becoming a travesty."

"Alright, tell me the bad news."

Jim's synopsis was met with silence. It seemed the president was pondering a response.

"If you think I'm going to fly into a rage, well, I'm not. My advisors agree that we have to proceed with caution. They just may have these weapons."

"What should I tell the voice?"

"Nothing, he wants to stall us, so let's do the same. Let him start thinking."

Both of them rolled around the possibilities. The president wouldn't normally share this info with someone outside his inner circle.

Jim had more understanding of the voice and his people than anyone else. That's why he was becoming more and more privy to the possible actions.

"This is going to happen soon. Are you getting the word out to the international community?"

"I can't make that many phone calls. My staff will make the calls. Better yet, just my close advisors will do it. I will handle the other major superpower personally."

Now it was a waiting game for Jim. The president and his staff would have to deal with a lot of different opinions and deflect accusations. These would assuredly come.

The inner-circle started pouring through the list of countries to contact. Most would only require a foreign minister level. They could speak to their leader and respond with questions.

There would be no answers until the event did or did not take place. The diplomatic problems were going to evolve. Some smaller countries were going to point fingers at their main rivals.

The countries selected were the major nuclear powers as well as the strategic allies. They anticipated a much calmer reaction from some of the nations that were considered enemies of the USA on the world stage.

This proved to be true. The larger and more powerful the nation, the more they agreed to a wait and see a progression. The main question was what were their chances of being affected by the explosions.

The brains were working and deduced that the most un-inhabited areas would be islands, the poles, and the deserts. That mostly eliminated any fallout effect as long as it didn't get high in the atmosphere.

The president wanted to hear the results of several of the phone calls before he made his own. He felt the additional input might avoid surprises and help him in his tête-à-tête.

He looked out the windows and saw flowers, trees, and heard birds singing. He thought what a beautiful world this could be if this scourge was stopped.

He started receiving the results almost immediately. For the time being everyone, including his enemies were standing behind him. Many countries had already experienced nuclear tests, so the implications weren't anything new.

It was time to make the most important phone call of his presidency. His counterpart's reaction could affect the future of the world.

To make things easier, the other leader spoke English. In the past, they always had a cordial appearance of a relationship. That was despite the lack of trust that came with the territory.

The pleasantries would come first. He debated between beating around the bush or more likely, coming to the point. He decided it was necessary to open up his mind.

"We have something to talk about. It's an extreme urgency and affects both of our nations."

"I always consider what you say as important. I will help if I can."

"It's a nuclear issue."

"We have treaties. We never violate them."

"It's a danger from a rogue group."

"You have my attention."

"We have a domestic problem with some people that are in my country. They possess such weapons. They also claim to have allies in other countries."

"Does it affect me?"

"I don't know. I'm guessing it doesn't—yet."

"Yet?"

"Let's slow down. It all started with a spy problem. One of your spies did a very bad thing."

"We have no spies."

The president sighed and took a deep breath. He knew full cooperation was going to be like pulling teeth.

"We need to cooperate which I'm not seeing yet."

"I'm being friendly."

"That's not what I mean. Ok, let's play a little game."

"I like games. What kind?"

"It's called tell the truth. For the rest of this conversation, you will tell only the truth and I promise to do the same. If at any time, either of us is dissatisfied with an answer, the conversation will end. Agreed?"

"This is strange, but I like it. I will be happy to see where it goes. I agree."

"You have two men that died trying to steal a secret."

"I heard we lost two men. You killed them?"

"No, they killed themselves by stealing something they didn't understand."

"These things happen in this business."

"That's a violation of our unwritten agreement. Our spies are only supposed to steal items that they at least know approximately what they are."

"I admit we have agreed on that."

"Then you agree that the reason for not stealing something unknown is to prevent a tragedy like this."

"I suppose you could say that."

"Imagine a mistake like this on a much grander scale. Many people could be killed. A crisis could develop. Most importantly, it would all be because of one agent's stupidity."

"You want me to agree my man made a mistake? I will trust your judgment and say yes. How about you agree to let us dispose of two of your agents? I know two intelligence officers that have been annoying us for years."

The president said, "That idea is out of the question."

The counterpart said, "Most spies are lousy people. Maybe we can agree to get rid of more."

"The ways you propose are too drastic. I was thinking of something more benign."

"If you're being honest, I'm very interested."

"This will work on two levels. First, you select three known agents you want to expel. We will do the same. All six will be expelled simultaneously."

"So far I like the idea."

"We also know our locations where there is foreign intelligence activity by both our nations. I propose we put a moratorium on three locations for one month. There will be no spying activity whatsoever."

"Who chooses the locations?"

"We can choose our own. I'll let you go first. You choose three and I'll follow suit."

There was a mutual agreement. Both sides agreed to keep in touch until the situation was resolved.

"These people are not ours."

"I never thought they were. The truth is I have no idea who they are."

"Give me details of this next event."

"I don't have a lot. The areas are barren of people. We will be given a longitude and latitude one hour before the detonations."

"How will I find out?"

"I will inform you the moment I get the locations."

That was the end of the call. The president went back to his inner circle to see how they were doing. Each person reported similar activity.

The exception was hot spot areas. There already were tense situations in these locations. These countries anticipated their local enemies to be behind this. They said their military would start deploying on the border.

The president made sure Jim heard all the news. It would be his job to continue talking to the voice and speak about what they believed to be a sensible solution.

Bret and Ani had the most to lose now. If these detonations didn't go off, their lives and those of their friends would be essentially over. On the other hand, any human casualties would likely make an all-out attack forthcoming.

CHAPTER 14

The crews that Bret had notified were working feverishly. The first had begun work as soon as they got the word. Since all of Antarctica is considered international territory, they thought the experiment would not be directly retaliated by any state.

They had previously selected a location in Antarctica that was nowhere near any research stations. It was still close enough to the coast so the weather was bearable. There was very little wildlife in the area and the valley itself was barren.

This group had previously discovered a small valley surrounded by mountains on all sides. The ice wasn't so deep that they couldn't drill through it.

They made calculations on how the land and the layers of ice would limit the blast and the resulting fallout. While this would be a small charge, it still had to be large enough for the powers to take notice.

Most of the work had been done at a previous time. This piece was ready in case the need arose.

The first order was to verify there were no humans remotely near the blast site. They scoured the coast for miles and saw nothing. It was relatively easy to work as the weather didn't vary much throughout the year.

The next portion of their actions was to clear as much wildlife as they could. The only animals were penguins and there weren't as many of them as in some of the other areas. The gathering took about a day and the birds were moved to a much safer place.

They would finally make a surface test charge. This would verify their equipment was in working order. The charge went off and made a small crater in the ice.

They were now ready to fulfill their commitment at the exact prescribed time. They escaped to a safe area where they could monitor the explosion.

The group in the Arctic faced different circumstances because the seas were so rough, a hazard to their sensitive equipment.

They were using an unclaimed island. It was quite remote, and not near any inhabited area. They still had to monitor the area. There were no fishing boats or spy vessels noted.

There was one problem when their test charge was picked up many miles away by government instruments. The scientist there informed the military. Going through channels, the military would send a reconnaissance aircraft to look for anything unusual.

The group could visualize this happening and worked at a feverish pace to complete their mission and get away as quickly as possible without being detected.

Their ship wasn't that lucky. It was spotted by the reconnaissance jet. The pilot got on the radio with them.

"Please identify yourself."

"We are an independent group of oceanographers studying the ocean composition in this area."

"We had a seismic reading which was consistent with some sort of explosion. Did you notice anything?"

"Our equipment registered nothing and we saw nothing."

That seemed to satisfy the pilot. He made several passes in the area and radioed he was coming back.

They knew they would have to sink their ship when they got back. It would be a prime target after the international demonstration. They could still do what had to be done via remote control.

Stan received the word that both weapons were armed and ready. He was also told about the problem up north. There was a request for verification that this would proceed. It was still possible to scrap the mission.

Stan immediately went to Bret. He read the message word for word. This was something Bret didn't plan for.

Time was of the essence. He didn't have the luxury of calling another meeting and getting bogged down in a long discussion of the pros and cons.

Ani was present and she was the only one Bret could ask for an opinion. He discussed it with her along with the government reaction if they identified the ship.

"I would say we have to continue. I've already told everyone we can't be responsible for the fate of others."

Ani said, "This will most likely be the bailiwick of another country. I'm not sure a positive vessel identification would affect matters here."

"You wouldn't stop anything?"

"I don't see why. You're ready to stage another event on the other side of the world."

"The message did say they felt they could scuttle this ship and get to safety by the time of the event."

"Baby, you've gone this far. I don't think you have a choice."

"I don't have much time, but I really need a quick chat with Alex and Lana. I'll be right back."

Bret left Ani and hurried to the lab his friends were working in. He got to the window and motioned for them to come out. They both came out wearing masks. Bret showed his usual attentiveness to their emotions.

"Sorry to interrupt your experiments, but I need a quick word with both of you. I'll only take a couple of minutes."

Alex said, "You're never a bother, you know that."

Bret described the situation. He wanted some final encouraging words from his friends. He told them his opinion, as well as the way Ani phrased hers. He would then have to run over to Stan's work area and get the wheels in motion.

Lana said, "Is Ani now your main confidant?"

Bret understood her tone was one of disdain. He knew he better set the record straight.

"I know what you're thinking. She happened to be there when Stan brought the message and that's it. Why do you think I came running to the two of you?"

Alex said, "Forget it, darling. Bret needs us now."

"I need that opinion from both of you and I'll make the

decision."

They were both in agreement that there was no choice but to proceed. Alex made sure there was an understanding that stopping it now would assuredly destroy any chance they had of succeeding.

Bret thanked them and ran to Stan's work area. Just as with the others, he called Stan into the hall.

"Send out an immediate commercial that the drug is safe to take. Send it twice. Get me confirmation as soon as possible."

"It sounds like a prelude to World War III."

"I hope I'm not doing the wrong thing for us."

"Your hunches have been right so far. I think everyone here believes in you. I, for one, am ready to suffer any consequences from any error."

Instead of letting his staff do it, Stan personally sent the message and awaited the reply. The reply was almost immediate. It decoded as things were ready and all would continue at the designated time.

Stan ran back to Bret where he was just explaining the news to Ani. Now that everyone agreed, it was time for the plan to go forward.

Bret was still fretting. Ani tried to commiserate with him.

"I'm not worried. Don't you worry either. Whatever happens, at least we're in this together."

CHAPTER 15

The day had come for the demonstration. Ani and Bret were sitting in Bret's room wondering how things would go. Ani wondered if there was anything more they could do to give themselves an edge.

She said, "I suppose we're locked into our fate."

"I can think of only one more thing." Bret reached into a drawer and pulled out a statue.

"Who is that?"

"It's Saint Jude, the saint of desperate and lost causes."

"I didn't know you were Catholic."

"I'm not. I've worked him really hard before and there have been good results. I try not to use him often." Bret said his prayer. It surprised Ani that he also said several additional prayers in several languages.

"Wow, you never cease to amaze me. All those languages are impressive."

"It's not just the languages. I tried to cover a prayer for every major religion in the world. I'm just trying to put a few coins in the bank."

"Could you teach me some of this one day?"

"I'm not sure I'll make it that far."

Ani hugged him and started talking positively. She spoke about her dreams to spend the rest of her life with that special man.

"We can't give up, we just can't."

"You have a long life ahead of you. My fate may be sealed."

Ani was trying to cheer Bret up. She was thinking long and hard for a distraction since the contact with Jim (and the main action) would not be until later in the day.

"You want to watch a movie or listen to some music?"

"Not really. You can go ahead if you want."

Bret started feeling a little selfish and realized Ani was hurting also over the way this untidy situation would end. He figured he would do something they hadn't done together.

"How about playing some ping-pong or shooting pool? We can head over to the game room."

"You have a game room?"

"I didn't tell you? I guess I forgot."

They took the elevator and walked to a less used area of the mountain. There was a window looking into a substantial game room.

Ani was shocked at what was available. There was a full-size pool table, ping-pong table, foosball, and chess table. There was a dartboard hanging on the wall. There were pinball machines along the wall as well as a small skeeball machine.

"This is a favorite hangout for the kids. It's an incentive to get their school assignments done on time."

Ani felt like a kid with a key to the cookie factory. She remembered the one game they had at the orphanage was a beaten-up ping-pong table. She practiced a lot and became very proficient.

Ani suggested they play that first. Bret was flabbergasted as she took him apart point by point.

"You're a hustler?"

"I'm not. Honestly, nobody at the orphanage could beat me."

Bret wanted to teach Ani a good-natured lesson. He was the best pool player in the mountain. That was his next suggested game. He started sinking balls, many of which were difficult shots.

"You accused me of being a hustler?"

"They were just lucky shots."

"Yeah, right."

Ani turned the pool cue backward and lightly whacked Bret on the butt. She told him to try another explanation.

"Ok, you caught me. Now watch this."

Bret lined up a few balls in odd positions. He sunk four in one shot. Then he showed her a masse' shot where he curved the cue ball around another. He finally made the cue jump over another ball and sink a third.

"You should've been a pro."

"My eyes aren't good enough for that. It's just fun entertaining the kids with some of these shots."

They started playing one game after the next, cheering each other on. It was like a day at the amusement park. Ani had accomplished what she wanted. She was able to calm

Bret's nerves and have some fun at the same time.

After a couple of hours, reality settled back in. They knew Jim would be calling in early, long before he would receive the info he needed for the nuclear blast.

Bret was chuckling and looking at Ani. He knew Jim was about at the end of his rope.

"Maybe we should try to have a light conversation with him."

"Yes, he's turned into a nervous wreck."

They went to their communication room and sure enough, Jim was calling in. Bret told him he was early. Jim just said he didn't want to take any chances.

"Did you see something in the box?"

"I saw a tiny metal case. It looked like a pillbox."

"I left you some natural calmatives. You need them and they're harmless. Take the homeopathics now and the herbals in fifteen minutes. Make sure you lay off the booze."

"I'm surprised you would do that for me. I guess I shouldn't be."

"So you don't think I'm a complete ogre."

"You may not believe this, but every time my opinion's been asked by my superiors, I've always tried to say something that would help you survive this ordeal."

"I suppose I should thank you."

"It's the least I could do for saving Billy's life."

"We would have done that for anyone."

"I believe you."

They started speaking about Jim's family and some unrelated personal matters. Jim changed the subject.

"All this time, and you still haven't told me your name. I'd really like to stop referring to you as the voice."

"I promise to tell you before this ordeal is over. That is if you don't start a sneak attack and I don't get the chance."

"I hope they don't do that without a warning. I'll do my best to stop it."

The time was getting near the one-hour prior notice. Bret decided to give Jim a little extra time. There were paper and pen ready. Even though Jim was being monitored, he didn't want to take any chances with the message getting garbled.

"Are you ready for the coordinates?"

"Please, let's have them."

Bret read off the latitude and longitude of both locations. He also gave Jim the exact time. The tension was rising as those locations were relayed to the government.

"I suppose I should thank you for working the poles rather than any populated areas." Jim then temporarily disconnected his outside line to his superiors.

Jim said, "While we wait, I'll tell you something I'm not supposed to share. A Jet spotted your ship up north when they were leaving the area."

"They're tracking it down?"

"I don't think so. Last I heard, there are too many small fishing towns close enough in all directions. Their boats are registered, so it seems the passengers either sank it or left it somewhere. They're all far away by now."

The reconnaissance jets were sent up immediately upon notification and the satellites started snapping pictures. The time came for the blast.

None of the participants on the call would know what happened until somebody informed Jim. It was like a bad dream and they would all wake up and find out that nothing happened.

Both poles started shaking and the sound was a rumble, then a roar. It was similar to a train closely passing at a high speed. The detonations were successful.

The information started to trickle into Jim. He spoke to Bret and Ani as he received the facts.

"It looks like you've done it. I can give you a visual if you want."

"Please do."

"The valley in the south had something very unusual. The explosion was limited as you promised. However, the small cloud wasn't mushroom-shaped. It looked more like a dome."

"That will engender some additional research."

"The northern one broke the island in half. We don't know the outcome."

"We anticipated that. The water currents and airflow won't bring any fallout near a populated area."

The new info came in and was good news under the circumstances. There was no loss of human life.

The studies would take some time. Decisions would be flourishing at the mountain long before they were complete.

Jim's demeanor changed once again. He seemed more aggravated than before. "I hope you're proud of yourself. You've caused a lot of problems, not only here but around the world. Even here, you turned me into a drunk."

Ani decided to interrupt.

"Hey Jim, cut it out. We have enough problems without you feeling sorry for yourself."

Then Bret interrupted.

"It's ok Ani. Jim, I'm so sorry if I had anything to do with your adverse health. You'll be fine after all this is resolved. My time is likely coming to an end."

Ani was steaming mad but held her tongue. All she could do was reach over and slap Bret on the back of the head. She wiggled her forefinger at him.

Jim said, "Exactly what were you trying to accomplish with this conflagration at the poles?"

"As I've been telling you all along, I'm just trying to buy time and get my friends out of this mess."

"After what you've done today, I can make no more promises. You're essentially on your own."

"I want nothing except updates. You need to reinforce to your superiors that we have more—a lot more. Any attack on this location will promote a worldwide catastrophe."

"Why do I believe you're too decent a person to destroy lives?"

"We all value our lives dearly. This threat is the only way to keep my friends alive right now."

Jim knew the president would have to make some determinations relatively soon. He just hoped any pressure to end this by force would be resisted.

CHAPTER 16

Everyone was running out of time. The president was going back and forth with his advisors, some in the international community, the Indian Agency, and Jim.

He would increasingly meet at a location that was near the capitol, yet more of a military compound. He used this locale when he didn't want reporters present.

The Indian Agency was relaying messages to the president from the reservation at the subject location. The major liaison was a man named Quentin. He was full-blooded but lived off the reservation.

"My agency is still getting flooded with complaints. There is a man present almost every day. Nobody would care, except he's the same man that showed up with the military platoon."

The president said, "This is a dicey issue. Just let them know there are international elements involved. I'm working as fast as I can, but the situation is unpredictably dangerous."

This mirrored the conversations the two of them had previously. Quentin was also a bit edgy.

"I'm not sure how much longer I can keep this out of the media."

The president said, "Do your best. I don't expect the situation to last much longer."

The president was only taking calls from the most prominent national leaders. Their response to the demonstration was predictable outrage.

His main adversary called frequently. He too wanted more info.

The president said, "Do you remember our game?"

"I do."

"Let's keep playing."

"I want to know everything about these explosions."

"I hope they didn't affect your sphere of influence."

"Not yet, but I still want to know."

The president gave him everything he had. This was basically the point of the negotiations and what little they knew about the weaponry.

"That's it?"

"It's all I have. I swear."

At that time, the president decided to not entertain any more calls from world leaders for the time being. All calls were directed to his advisors who were skilled at deflecting the issue.

Jim had been trying to brief him on his latest conversation with the voice. He wasn't even available for Jim.

The advisors were catching a lot of flak from other nations and then they got together for their daily briefing. The president understood he needed to get an update from Jim and have him force the issue with the voice.

Before speaking with Jim, the president sat down with

someone. He was a mysterious older man. Most people didn't even know his name. All people knew was that he had the president's ear.

The president asked what would be the best course of action at this time. The response was simple, "Let them propose and you can take it from there."

Bret received the communication and knew right away Jim was in a foul mood. Ani had already asked Bret to let her intercede if things got out of hand.

Jim said, "If you wanted to stir up a hornet's nest, you've certainly accomplished that."

"Where are we at?"

Jim said, "Oh, it's not a major concern. We just have four nations ready to go to war with one another. We have Native Americans having a conniption over this affair. The major powers are on alert, and the military is waiting for a call to action. Other than that, it's nothing to worry about."

The talk started getting cyclical. Once again, Jim called for them to abandon their operation and Bret would counter that a plain surrender would never happen.

"You know there's increasing support for military action."

"What about the ramifications?"

"The voices are getting louder that you don't have anything and those demos were a fluke."

"Do you really believe that?"

"I don't know what to believe. I do know that the continued dragging out of this mess is making the situation worse and worse."

Things got even testier as Jim started implying that he was wrong about Bret. He made it seem Bret just might want a lot of death and destruction.

Their voices began to get louder. It was then that Ani held up her index finger in a motion to Bret that she wanted to interrupt.

"Jim, this is Ani. Are you wired?"

"You know I am."

"Then make sure this message gets to the right people."

Ani held up her hand in a motion for Bret to let her do the talking for the time being.

"What is wrong with you people? The folks here have delivered on every promise. They gave you samples that proved to be lethal. They blew up parts of the poles. What more do you want?"

"Now, wait a minute—"

"Wait a minute nothing. It sounds like you're the ones looking for a fight."

"Exactly whose side are you on?"

"That's a terrible, ugly, disgusting thing to say. You know I've always been loyal to my government."

"Which government is that?"

"If we were together right now, I'd knock you out."

"You learned threats from the master, I see."

"The only thing I learned is you're a souse and a kook. Maybe you should learn how to rebalance the scales of justice. If I was an arbitrator right now, these people would be the arbit and you'd be the traitor."

"Name-calling will get you nowhere. Remember, this

side has the final word."

"Unless a complete dolt is making recommendations, I thought it just might be a good idea if a lot of innocent people on both sides weren't killed."

The argument got even nastier. The brash words were flying like buckshot. There came a point where it degenerated into screaming.

Bret began to worry. Not only was the situation getting out of hand, but he was beginning to have concern for Ani.

Her words became more and more random. Her sentences appeared to be patched together.

Bret was becoming convinced Ani was having a nervous breakdown. It was either that or the girl he fell in love with was mentally unstable. Either way, he had to put a stop to this banter.

"Hey guys, stop for a second. I'm supposed to be the enemy, right?"

Jim said, "I guess I lost my temper."

Bret said, "I have an idea, but both of you have to apologize first."

Jim said, "Ok, I apologize."

Ani said, "Yeah, yeah."

Bret said, "Come on, now."

Ani said, "Ok, ok I'm sorry."

Now it was time for Bret to spring a surprise.

"Jim, what if I told you there's a solution that would be acceptable to my friends and me, and at the same time, the president would come out of this smelling like a rose?"

"Now you're talking turkey. Let's have it."

"I can't tell you—"

"Huh?"

"Let me finish. I can't tell you yet. I would have to get an agreement from my friends."

"How long will that take?"

"You have to do something for me first."

Jim started wondering if this was a serious proposal. At this point, he would listen to anything.

"You have to get a guarantee there will be no attack until we've exhausted the possibilities of this proposal."

"I suppose the boss would go for it, but I'm not inside his head. I mean he'll most likely listen but a total agreement is another story."

"That's sufficient. As soon as you get back to me, I'll fill in all the blanks."

After disconnecting, Ani couldn't help but wonder what Bret had in mind. Bret's mind was going in a completely different direction. He just kept staring at Ani.

"Are you ok?"

"I'm fine, why?"

Bret was having weird daydreams. He would think of them as more like day nightmares. Questions were rolling around his mind. Was she really crazy or did she just have a breakdown which was bad enough?

He even got stranger images. Would he have to be on guard watching for her to lose it at any moment? Could they have an awful argument and she decides to castrate him in his sleep?

His love was undeniable. His heart would still pound

when she was near. Bret was true to form. He decided he would stay with her as long as she wanted. She was his one and only.

Ani was still thinking of this proposal that would magically make everyone happy. It was her turn to stare at Bret. She wasn't pleased about being kept in the dark.

"Is there anything you want to tell me?"

"It's a long-winded explanation. I'd rather not give it to you in pieces."

"I guess I have to trust you then. I just thought we had no secrets."

"I have a lot of work to do in a short period of time. It involves everyone here. As soon as I get the complete picture, I promise I'll give you everything."

"Only do that if you really want to."

"I have to get you involved. Your opinions will be invaluable and can sway my final maneuvers."

Bret said that while still wondering about Ani's sanity and unpredictability. He had no choice now. He had to trust everyone to put this desired end over the top.

Bret knew he had to get things in motion and summon all his knowledge, strength, and judgment. One wrong step could mean the end of all of his friends as well as their families.

CHAPTER 17

Bret planned to speak to all the managers individually and then to the whole group together without the children. He felt they all would be more willing to express their mind in a personal setting.

Bret budgeted a very brief time with each individual because he wanted everything completed in a day.

Ani would stay with the children when they all were together. He would ask each person the same questions such as if they're willing to leave peacefully if the government promised not to prosecute.

His closest confidants were Alex and Lana. He left them for last so he could give them extra time if they wanted.

Bret's whole idea centered on his group's terms which were included in "the document." Everyone knew about this document but wasn't familiar with the details. This would be a general discussion. Bret had devised it and was saving it for only a dire emergency.

Bret started with Red Hawk because this mountain was on his reservation. He didn't have to say much. It was almost as if Red Hawk had prepared answers.

"We've been treated badly for so many years, would you

trust anyone? I do trust you. Now that we have a pretty good standard of living, I'd hate to throw it all away by suffering a mass extinction."

"You think that could happen?"

"I have no doubt my people will defend their property like anyone else. That's why we must try for some agreement. I believe you will do the best for us."

"There's no guarantee."

"We've lived that way for hundreds of years, even before your ancestors came here. Guarantees are useless anyway."

Having Red Hawk on his side, meant a powerful ally. He could issue an order evicting everyone at any time if he wanted.

The next person was Wang. Bret felt he would be easy to convince because he had extremely limited choices.

"You know I can't go home. If they deport me, it would be a death sentence. Prison here would be a paradise compared to what I'd have to face over there. Our population is so large, there'd be no place to hide."

"Maybe we can do this without prison."

"That would be a dream."

"You know I'll try my best."

Wang reminded Bret that his country had a leader who basically starved people to death. He made his decision. "Go back to the others. You have my vote. I'll deal with the consequences. Maybe I could practice acupuncture in a prison here."

Carlos walked in with a joyful face and dance. He was always in a pleasant mood and always dancing to imaginary music.

When Bret started asking him about his thoughts, it became the rare occasion that his smile ran away.

"What's wrong my friend?"

"I received word of another revolution in my country. There's heavy fighting in my town."

Bret knew his relatives and friends would get caught in the crossfire because his village was a small one.

"You know Bret, it's funny. They gave my continent a nickname after the disks used on a record player."

"They call it the land of revolutions per minute."

"Could you benefit from going back there?"

"Sometimes they have a good change, but not this time. This revolution will put in a dictator. The man who will take over has a radical hatred of doctors. He blames them for the death of his child."

"It sounds like you have little choice."

"If you could negotiate a brief time in jail that would be a small price for me to pay."

Nkuma walked in with his usual long face. Nobody blamed him because of all the strife in his country and the personal tragedies he faced.

"Sometimes I would like to try to make a change in both my country and the whole continent."

"You were always an altruistic man."

Bret was thanked many times for all he did for everyone. He helped them escape tyranny. This time, he was hugged. Bret was almost embarrassed to ask for the reason. It didn't take long.

"We've done some great things here medically. We helped so many people where I came from. It was bad enough they were starving, but the doctoring was atrocious."

"It's a warm feeling hearing your words."

"It should be. Without you, I accomplish nothing."

"Maybe you could go back."

"You're too young to remember, but there was a great leader back in the 1960s. He was both a president and a devoutly religious man. He fought the encroaching political ideology that was slowly poisoning the entire continent."

"I know who you mean. He was a great African leader."

"Then you remember his fate. He was kidnapped, brought to another country, and killed."

"You think it could happen to you?"

"I'm not afraid to die. I just wouldn't be able to help people anymore. We need to try to get out of this, so I'm with you."

Hans was next. Being of European descent, Bret didn't know exactly how he would react. His country was stable and he violated no laws that Bret knew of.

"I have to be honest. I'm more worried about your reaction than the others."

"Why is that?"

"The others have various reasons as to why they can't return to their homeland. You really don't."

Hans laughed. He tapped the table with his forefinger.

"I thought you knew me better than that. I came here because of the entire movement towards doing away with my form of medicine. The whole union is decidedly against anything natural."

"You feel strongly enough?"

"I'm like you with your beliefs. If I can't practice and research the way I know is right, then I don't want any of their nonsense. I would give up before I give in."

It was a relief as it seemed Hans would not be a controversial factor in the meeting.

Now it was time for Pramesh. Like Hans, he could probably go back to his country and start all over again.

"People who visit my country think we are very advanced. They never go to the countryside where all the poverty is."

Like Nkuma, Pramesh wanted to help his people. He did a lot through this secret group.

"We are bordered by enemies on all land sides. The ocean is no consolation. There's so much religious fighting. My village gets attacked regularly."

"Would you consider going back?"

"Never. No way I will ever return unless I'm deported. Even then, I might do away with myself first."

"Please don't say that."

"Don't worry. I want to live also."

Bret felt gratified that those he spoke to would apparently be supporting his idea in the general meeting. They would still have to hear details regarding the document.

It was the final time for speaking with Alex and Lana together. They were like two halves of a chair so the same answers would come out of both mouths. There were an immediate hug and kiss from both of them.

"My closest friends, please have a seat. You probably know why we're talking and I need your help."

Lana said, "We'll do anything for you. You know that."

"You both understand the situation has become untenable."

Alex said, "Of course. You have a solution?"

"First, I have a personal favor to ask."

They both told him to proceed. Alex told Bret he'd done so much for them. No favor was too large.

"It's Henry. He can't survive on his own. It's unrealistic for him to go with me, so I thought—"

Alex said, "So you thought we could take him."

"I was hoping you would."

Lana said, "Henry has grown very close to our children. They have a deep affection for him. Of course, we'll take him"

Bret was overjoyed because their taking Henry would be a big weight off his shoulders.

Alex said, "Bret, have you noticed something? Henry is speaking better and his concentration has improved a lot. It proves he was normal at one time."

Bret thought about it and came to the same conclusion. He had theorized Henry wasn't born that way. This isn't a smoking gun, but the evidence was compelling.

Now they would speak about the situation at hand. They also spoke about the old days and the way Alex and Lana lived.

"One thing I always wondered was why the two of you would want to leave your country. You had a respected position in the research field along with a nice apartment. It seemed like the government provided you with everything."

Alex said, "We had reasons."

"Maybe you could return."

Lana said, "We are enemies of the state. The secret police would take us in a car and do away with us. We wouldn't even make it to the labor camp. I can't imagine not seeing my children again."

"I somehow feel responsible for your plight. I can't forgive myself."

Alex said, "Bret, let me tell you a story."

Alex took a trolley every day to work. It always followed the same route. He always passed an open field with nothing except an extremely old man, his folding chair, and a tree that he sat next to.

No matter how inclement the weather was, he would be sitting next to that tree. The man's expression never changed. It was neither happy nor sad. It was just a blank expression.

Alex wanted to speak to him. His curiosity had gotten the better of him.

One day, he got off the trolley and walked over to the old man and stood by his side. Both of them looked straight forward at the street, never looking at each other.

Alex just said one word, "Why?"

The old man was silent for a few moments.

"You want to know why? I'll tell you why."

The old man told his story. He was born a healthy baby. To celebrate, his parents planted the tree he sat next to. The tree was like a sibling. They grew together.

He was a normal child. He played sports and had friends. He did well in school. He met the girl of his dreams and they were married. Not long afterward, she presented him with a beautiful baby.

Then the war came. He had to go to the military to fight the evil that was quickly approaching. He would be gone for what seemed like an eternity. Then the fascists came.

"They took my wife, my child, my parents. I never saw them again."

The story was giving Alex a broken heart.

"All I have left is my tree. As you can see, the branches grow sparse, the leaves no more."

"Maybe I can have it saved by a tree expert."

"No. It will die soon. When it dies, so will I."

Alex tried to muster all of his manhood as he began to weep. The old man said, "Now you've heard why."

"I'm sorry for you."

"Now get out of here and let the two of us die in peace."

It was only a short time afterward, Alex passed an empty field with a barren tree.

"You see Bret, the government has been moving in that direction. Lana and I didn't want that to happen to our children."

Bret said, "It doesn't have to be that way."

Alex said, "It will. Just remember one thing; we came from your future."

"I still feel somewhat responsible for getting you out."

"It doesn't matter what happens now. We took a chance. It was our choice."

"Maybe we can keep your family together."

Lana said, "It's a wonderful thought."

"Then let's try. Maybe I can make this document work."

"What else can we do for you?"

Bret repeated that, even in the best scenario, he couldn't leave with everybody else. He outlined something they could do for him. They immediately agreed it would be an easy task.

"Lana, the time is near. I'm going to start gathering everyone."

"Go ahead, darling. I'll sit with Bret a few minutes."

Alex left and Lana wanted to say something personal.

"You know I'll always love you."

"What happened between us in your country was something I'll never forget."

"I suppose we were both lonely. The pressures of life took a toll."

"We did what we needed to do. I just never wanted to hurt Alex."

They both thought about apologizing to Alex. Then Lana made her position clear.

"I could never leave Alex and the children. You know we would never be happy that way."

"I couldn't agree more."

Bret and Lana started walking out of the room.

"May I ask you something?"

"Lana, you know you can ask me anything."

"That woman I always see you with, do you love her?"

"Very much so."

Lana kissed Bret on the cheek.

"No matter how much it hurts, I will do everything I can to help her."

CHAPTER 18

People were gathering as many chairs as they could. They were moving them through the halls to the conference room. It had just enough seating for the managers, the extras would need to accommodate everyone.

Ani had previously been asked to be with the children while this was going on. Bret had given her a copy of the document that everyone would be discussing.

"You sure you don't mind staying with the kids?"

"Of course not. They're all my friends. I don't have to do much. The ex-troublemaker has become my chief disciplinarian."

"Then you'll have time to read through the document. Assuming it's agreed upon, you can give me your opinion later or tomorrow after Jim gets his copy."

"I know it's a dangerous game. I'll defer to your judgment."

"Actually, it's going to be your judgment that helps me decide how to carry on. You'll let me know what you think their reaction will be. This isn't over by a long shot."

The children started piling into the classroom. It was there they would decide the activities during this time. They might even split up into groups.

Ani spoke to her assistant about being in charge of one such group. He relished the opportunity to monitor and direct the others.

They had several choices. They could read in the library, watch a movie in the theater, or play in the game room. They also had a gym with exercise equipment that Ani hadn't seen before.

Ani suggested a vote and the children loved the idea. It gave them a feeling of importance. She let her assistant handle the vote. She was so proud of his transformation from an imp to a leader doing beneficial acts.

The vote came out as expected. Everyone wanted to do fun things. It was suggested they have a party in the theater as there was room to dance in front of the seats. They could play music and have snacks.

Another group wanted to play in the game room. Someone suggested they do both. Ani felt it was fine since both venues were located on the same floor. She decided that she along with her assistant could drift back and forth to monitor the goings-on.

Back in the conference room, it was a bit crowded, but nobody was complaining because this would be one of the most important determinations of their lives.

Bret was surprised everyone seemed to be in a light mood. There were friendly boisterous voices and a lot of laughter. He went to the front of the room.

"Well, I'm glad you folks actually made room to squeeze me in our version of a grand ballroom."

There was some chuckling. He was going to review all the major points of the document. He would skip through the boring legalese.

"Everyone knows why we're here. Our time at the location will soon come to an end."

There were a few groans. One muffled voice could be heard saying we have to stick with Bret. He explained how he wanted to go on and if there were any objections. There were none.

"Is there anyone here who hasn't had a chance to read through the document? Hearing nothing, I'd like to start with the main point. I want them to understand this document is non-negotiable. Anything they want our agreement on can be considered. The only question is, what would happen if they turn the document down. It could mean the end in a bad way. Nobody knows how it's going to shake out. They have to be prepared for a catastrophe. I've tried to reinforce that notion. My best guess is they'll agree to it or ask for some modifications."

Bret wanted to get back to the individual areas. He started with the notion that there will be no prison. He was asked if that meant a full presidential pardon.

"No. A pardon implies a crime was committed. This request is for full amnesty."

Everyone liked that idea. There was quite a bit of skepticism as to whether that would happen. Bret was banking on the threats to pull this off.

The next area would be like a dream come true for the foreigners. It called for an action similar to the witness protection program. All would be given a new identity, including immediate citizenship, new social security numbers, a place to live, a livable stipend for six months, and all adults would be offered a job in their field of expertise.

There was growing doubt. Some compared Bret's idea to an unrealistic fantasy, but everybody still wanted that in the document.

So far, Bret had the unanimous approval he was hoping for. Then things got a little complicated. What if the government agreed and then reneged?

"That's a wild card. They don't know our only form of communication emanates from our transmission base inside here. I'm betting they'll be worried about the codicil outlining the penalty for abrogating any agreement."

The penalty was simply that everything else in the document would be null and void. They'd be risking a holocaust through highly destructive weapons. Once again Bret was theorizing the benefits versus the risks for their side as well.

The next question was a difficult one. It was whether they could have contact with their overseas relatives.

"Unfortunately, that will take a long time. You all must understand, any contact might blow our privacy. As long as they don't work for a foreign government, I don't think the USA will prohibit contact. My advice is to think long and hard about such an action."

An extension of that was who they send and receive signals with.

"I'm glad that was brought up. I don't want to be a traitor. As we have understood all along, they know we are all semi-autonomous groups. The simple truth is they have to fend for themselves."

That was when he was met with the suggestion that they

had to do something, anything to protect these people.

"Stan knows I've recently sent messages for them to give up their good intentions and dismantle their operations before their governments catch up with them. We have to discern that other countries may not be as understanding as the USA. It's up to them now. They know the dangers."

Bret kept reinforcing they had to worry about themselves now. He made an additional hard-hitting point.

"Let's not forget the children."

The stunned group became silent. The silence was interrupted by Red Hawk.

"I'm not leaving with everyone. You all know that I'm going home. No matter what happens, our only chance is to follow Bret."

He was piggybacked by Lana.

"I can't believe some of you. Bret has given up everything to save all of you. Nobody knows that he can't—"

Bret said, "It's ok, Lana."

"No, it's not. Maybe everyone should know Bret isn't going with us."

There was a collective gasp. All imagined different ideas as to what her statement meant.

"Alex and I have no idea what he's going to do. What I do know is he is trying to help all of you survive and what he does is none of our business."

There was silence until Alex spoke. "How about we take a vote? Bear in mind, Bret wants it unanimous or we go back to the drawing board."

Bret nodded and asked if they wanted a secret vote. He

would keep everybody's ballot with him and there would be no hard feelings regardless of what happened. He asked if they wanted to vote by show of hands.

"I trust everybody here. Please let me know now about a vote. Time is running short."

Nobody would dare go against Bret after what Lana said. The group unanimously approved the document in its original form without any revisions.

"We have to break this up now. It's time for me to talk to the outside."

The whole group filed out and back to their quarters. Bret ran to get the kids home and take Ani to the communications room.

"I know you haven't had time to look at the document. We have to speak with Jim now and it's getting late. Could you thumb through it tomorrow morning and let me know? The group approved it."

"I looked a little while the kids were playing. You sure have a lot of nerve."

Ani already had the wheels turning. She didn't want to discuss any details with Bret until they spoke with Jim and had a chance to thoroughly pour over it. When they heard from Jim, this was going to be the usual tense contact.

"Do you want to go first, Jim?"

"The big boss is interested in what you want to do. He specifically said he will consider anything that warrants a peaceful resolution and doesn't embarrass any of us."

Ani said, "You mean anything that won't cost him the election next year."

"Please Ani, don't start with me again. I don't need this."

"Jim, let's get back to business. You see a large envelope in the box?"

"I see it."

"You can open it if you want or read it later. It contains our proposal to end this mess on paper, cd, and flash drive."

"Let me take a look now."

Jim started flipping the pages and shaking his head. He was smirking all the time.

"I see you don't want much. How about we throw in a couple of billion dollars along with naming a state after you and giving you your own micronation."

Bret said, "I don't see how levity helps. You're speaking for the powers that be?"

Ani said, "Forget it, he has a mental block made out of concrete."

"Regardless of what Ani says, will you provide this to your side?"

"I suppose I have to. Is there anything else?"

"Yes, there is. Do not give me a counter-proposal. If your boss has any requests, give them to me separately and we'll consider them. This document itself is not negotiable."

"I hope that's it."

"Not quite."

"This document must be signed by the president and at least a foreign minister from every nation."

"Are you nuts? We'll never be able to pull that off."

"Try."

"I can't believe this. I'd look foreword to Ani's insults

more than the thought of delivering this to the top of the food chain."

"There's always the alternatives. Do you really want to chance another demo, but this time in a populated area?"

"When do you want this?"

"As long as there's no attack, you can take your time."

"I can, but the president has to put this thing to bed sooner rather than later."

Ani said, "Listen, Jim. I know I've been rough on you. It's just my way in this business. Let's be friends."

Jim said, "It makes me feel better that we're hoping for the same end."

After Jim left, Bret and Ani looked at each other. They resisted the temptation to start discussing everything since it was so late. They knew it would be more productive to digest all the facts and speak the next day with a clear mind.

"It's late now. We need to get some sleep. Just finish reading through the document in the morning."

They didn't want any distractions, so they retired to their own rooms. Naturally, Ani didn't listen and read through most of the document before falling asleep.

She said to herself that she couldn't believe the guts he had.

"I guess that's one of the reasons why I love him so much."

CHAPTER 19

Jim was traveling rapidly. He had to make copies, fast. He sent the document in all three formats to the president after making copies. He didn't have to call this time. His phone was ringing off the hook.

Jim was surprised at the president's calm demeanor. He expected a more emotional response.

"Judging by you calling me first, you've had a chance to thumb through the document."

"They're asking for quite a bit from me. It's actually unprecedented."

"Is there anything you want me to tell them?"

"Not at this time. Just sit tight. This isn't happening overnight."

The president knew he had to continue with a logical sequence. He had to deal with the domestic implications and an extremely opinionated group of advisors with input that would be all over the place. All of that would happen before he could approach the international community if this was somehow workable.

Back at the mountain, Bret sat down with Ani to review the document and its implications. He needed her input badly. What she said could impact how the entire affair would proceed.

They sat alone in the conference room. After having so

many people there, Bret felt he was in a cavernous expanse. He was hoping her help would take him out of the abyss.

"You read it through?"

"I sure did. Word for word."

"I think they might go for it."

"I'm not sure they have a choice. There'll be some resistance."

Ani gave the typical scenario since her agency constantly dealt with the executive branch. First and foremost, the president would have to deal with all the implications right here at home. That meant the Native Americans.

"I'm not sure if there would be any spillover to other tribes. Red Hawk is best qualified to help you with this. I've heard rumors of some sort of agreement between many tribes. I'm not sure how far-reaching it is."

"I'll sit down with him after we get Jim's answer."

"The advisor part will be complex. They're different types with different levels of influence."

Unlike some others, this president preferred to keep a small cadre of advisors rather than a room full of them.

"How many do you think he'll speak with?"

"I know of four definitely. He may also have one or more experts to lend any additional info. It could even be Jim."

Bret had to get as much detail as he could. He wanted to know everything she could tell him about each individual. Every detail would give him a better understanding of their potential plan.

"There might be a high-ranking military officer to give his expertise on various possible offensive actions. I'm not too concerned there because his or her opinion won't be asked."

"What can you tell me about the core advisors?"

The first she described was Tom. "He's what can be described as an old-school politician. He's held several elected positions, so he has a good background in the management of people and resolution of divisive political situations. He is in the middle of the arguments."

"What do you mean by old-school?"

"To put it bluntly, he lives by the credo to do no work and you won't get in trouble."

"So you're saying he's a goldbrick."

"While true, in this case, he's a lot more than that. My guess is he'll tell the president to do nothing, sit on his hands. His theory will be that you'll crack or the situation would naturally resolve itself."

"That sounds unproductive."

"You think so? It's been an unofficial and successful method of governing since time immemorial."

"What will be his effect on the president's thinking?"

"Absolutely nothing. He's there to hold hands. I've only met him once and he was kind of charming. That's his secret for success."

The next person would be Mildred, also known as Millie.

"She is an old-time political operative. She has been on the scene for over seventy years."

"Can she really lend a hand?"

"I don't think so. She's a great-grandmother who should have retired many years ago. I heard she sleeps through most of the meetings."

"I don't understand why he keeps her."

"I think it's a reward for so many years of political service. She also has many blind backers."

"It sounds like nobody notices or cares."

"She's like judges who get appointed for life and stay too long. They usually let the law clerk take care of the ruling and write the opinion. When I met her recently, she was really sweet, albeit forgetful. Honestly, she didn't know what planet she was on."

"How will she make a recommendation now?"

"If she's not sleeping, she'll go along with the most persuasive argument. If she is sleeping, the president will just skip over her."

"That leaves two by my count."

"Yes, Scott is the dangerous one. At the academy, he was called the moth."

"So you know him. Why the moth?"

"When he would go out at night, he'd always stand under a light with the rest of the moths."

"It sounds as if you don't like him."

Bret saw she had contempt for Scott. In this case, he hoped she could give an unbiased opinion without anything clouding her judgment.

"He's basically incompetent and says wild things."

"How could he get to such a high position?"

"You would too if your family was the highest single contributor to the party. I mean higher than any large corporations. If they have a choice, it's difficult to get elected without their influence."

"He couldn't be that stupid."

"Oh, no? During a break, a few of us went to that famous place that serves fancy coffee. He said I'll take an open latte. I asked him where he saw that. He pointed. I told him that sign reads, 'Open Late!'"

"Oh, geez, that's too funny."

"You want to hear more? I had an art book with me that day. I was sipping my coffee and looking through it. He looked at one page and said he knew that painting. He was calling it the 'Whistling Mother.' He looked at another. He said that was the 'Mona Lima' by Leonardo Dubinsky."

Bret was hysterical. He couldn't believe this of an advisor.

"If he has his way, you won't even be able to plead Freedom of the Seas."

"I don't understand."

"I mean they'll seize you and take away your freedom."

Bret knew his recommendation wasn't going to be a positive one. He wanted less tongue-in-cheek and more of what she actually thought he would say.

"I know you have an emotional feeling here, but how is this going to translate to his opinion?"

"I'm almost positive he'll advocate for a direct and immediate devastating attack."

"Based on what?"

"For the media, he's a phony pacifist. His real personality is to crush your enemies. I've heard him use an old expression quite often. It's 'kill them all, let the deities sort them out' or something like that."

"I've met several who maintain themselves as political pacifists and were really the opposite."

"So what's going to stop him?"

"I'm betting Myra can do it."

"Isn't that the name of the lady who got you started?"

"It's the same person. At the academy, we all knew she was going to advance to high places. She was so politically astute, so smart, so talented. Let's put it this way. She was persuasive enough to talk me into accepting a lower-paying job than that of a corporate executive."

"You're saying she's the wild card advisor."

"My money's on her. She's way too clever to advocate anything with extreme consequences. She's also practical enough to know the longer this drags on, the greater the danger to this presidency."

"Can you think of any other unknowns?"

"I can think of only one. We call him the phantom."

Bret's curiosity was piqued. Why would anyone in the political arena be known by such a moniker? This would be a potential make or break person.

"Who is this phantom?"

"We call him that because nobody really knows who he is. We've heard he has the ear of the president and is kind of a shadow advisor."

"It sounds if he's privy, you don't know where he stands."

"I haven't got a clue. The expression we hear time and time again is 'when he's around, something always happens.' He always seems to be lurking during tense times."

"I wish I knew such a man."

"He's been known to say, 'I come from nowhere and I go nowhere.'"

"That's interesting. I know someone who used the same expression. Nah, it couldn't be.'"

"There's one other thing. He's never photographed with the president. To my knowledge, no one's ever seen them go into the same building apart or together."

Bret noticed the conversation affecting Ani. As it continued, her voice started cracking. Sometimes she wasn't able to mouth a word or two. He was worried about her. They still needed to get this done.

"So now, with all this knowledge, what do you think they're going to do?"

"I think everything will be just fine."

Bret knew that was a disingenuous remark. He also knew he had to meet it head-on.

"Don't give me that. What do you think?"

That seemed to be the straw that broke the camel's back. The tears started running down her cheeks. Ani got out of the chair and walked to the wall. She could be heard whimpering.

Bret went behind Ani and hugged her.

"I'm sorry, sugar. What did I say wrong?"

"You know I haven't cried in years. It's not your fault."

"Please, I have to know what you're thinking. It has nothing to do with the situation, it has to do with us."

Ani composed herself as she turned around and wiped a tear from one eye as Bret did the other. Her tissue got some use, also.

"I don't know how to say this. I sincerely believe they'll agree to the terms for everybody except you. It will take about a month and then you'll have an accident or something. I can't bear it."

Ani suddenly grabbed Bret and started squeezing him tightly. It turned into a full-fledged sob.

Bret pulled her away and softly asked her to listen to him.

"Do you think I don't know that already? I have other plans."

"What kind of plans?"

"The first thing is to let you go. I'll release you tonight."

"I want to be with you."

"If you go, you will likely get a raise and promotion—a real heroine. Maybe you'll even meet a guy with his act together much better than me. You can keep the infinity ring if you want."

That's when Ani's demeanor turned to anger. She briskly pushed him away. She started slapping him.

"Oh, you big dummy. Can't you see I love you? I love you so much it hurts. I love you more than my own life. You remember that argument I had with Jim? You thought I was crazy, right?"

"I was concerned about you."

"No, you thought I was a head case. It was an act. I decided to stay with you then. Those were coded messages that Jim's area of just collecting data doesn't understand. It was about my phony escape plans."

Bret grabbed her wrists and they embraced again. Now

his eyes started filling up.

"You have to know I feel the same way as you."

"Then why are you sending me away?"

"I'm just trying to do what's best for—"

"I have a problem. I can't betray my country and I can't betray you. I'm staying with you, whether you like it or not. I suppose that means my life has been forfeited. If my life is over, I want it to be with you at the end. Case closed."

"You have to understand, I'm not letting them take me."

"So we'll commit suicide together? I'm not afraid."

"There could be another way for both of us."

"Really? You talk. I listen."

"The alternative is for us to leave separately from the others. It's going to be physically and mentally demanding, always looking over your shoulder. I didn't want that for you."

"You mean we escape? You should know by now, I'm as tough as almost any guy."

"If you're sure, we'll try this the night before everyone else leaves. This is assuming the document is executed."

"I'm curious. They will have a surrounding perimeter for miles. We can't fly, they'll see us. We can't walk out, they'll see us. The ground is solid rock. There's no way we can tunnel through. Are we going to be invisible?"

"It's funny you said that. We were working on something along those lines. It has to do with light refracting off water vapor. Unfortunately, we're still years away. So that's not doable."

"Ok, I'm stumped."

"It will be better if you don't know anything, especially if we're caught. You'll see each step of the way."

"It sounds complicated, but I understand. I like surprises anyway. You're saying steps are in places."

"You hit the nail on the head. If we get through the first few hours, it will turn into the adventure of a lifetime."

"I suppose it will be us alone for the rest of our lives."

"No, there'll be others, but nobody from this group."

"I hate to say it, but this is exciting to me."

"There'll be snags, I can almost guarantee it. The first hurdle is getting an agreement for the others to live some semblance of a normal life after they leave."

"So we have to wait to make our own preparations?"

"No, we have so much to do. It looks like the next few days or maximum a week will be what's left of our time here."

"You know what I'm looking forward to?"

"Tell me."

"I want some real sunshine."

"Why didn't you tell me? I can arrange that before we leave."

"Another surprise? Don't tell me. I want to see for myself."

"It won't be now. We have too much to do."

"So what's next?"

"We'll have to get moving. Are you ready to make a mad dash?"

"Give me your hand. What are we waiting for?"

CHAPTER 20

ret was secretly hoping Ani would refuse to be released. He wanted her to be with him as long as they could, even if it meant the end of their time. They were walking quickly through the hallway.

"Where are we going?"

"We're on our way to the salon."

"Is that so? Another place you forgot to tell me about?"

"I guess I'm slipping."

"The exercise room and the game room, I can understand. Didn't you see me trying to trim my own hair?"

"I missed that."

"It doesn't matter. I can fix myself in my own room as well as there."

"You don't realize we're doing a full-fledge makeover and disguise."

"I didn't know you had that talent."

"I don't. That's Dina's job."

"A pharmacist is going to carve me up?"

Ani had previously spoken about Dina's impeccable makeup and hair. She told Bret there is a difference between a woman who has her hair, eyebrows, and makeup done in a salon and one who has things done by a professional makeup artist.

"I never noticed, but if you say so."

"Believe me, a woman notices. The only thing I can't put my finger on is where a pharmacist learned her skills."

"You're so perceptive. I'll fill in the blanks about that and how she came here."

Dina was a typical example of someone who wanted to be successful, but the meager means of her single mother didn't allow for college.

She got some training and started out as a hairdresser. Living with her mom, she was able to use her salary to pay her tuition for going to college at night.

Dina then got a job at a hybrid store. They had a section for doing hair, but their main thrust was selling and applying makeup. She showed potential in that field.

When she had a break, she would either read her pharmacy books or fool around with a store dummy used for experimenting with makeup.

When she was playfully doing something grotesque with the makeup, a talent scout walked in to buy some items. His wife was a regular customer. He immediately recognized her creativeness.

While his business was looking for acting talent, he knew it takes peculiar skills to be a professional makeup artist.

Through his connections, he got her a tryout at a movie studio. She was able to demonstrate a unique talent for disguises. It's a lot more than hanging a beard on a guy. She was very skilled at disguising someone without anyone being able to recognize the person.

While it wasn't a windfall, the salary was enough to pay for graduate school and Dina was able to realize her first love. She became a Pharm D.

Because her grades were so good, she immediately hooked up with a large pharmaceutical company. It didn't take much time for her to be promoted to a supervisor in the research area.

That's when things started to sour. She noticed a field rep with unusually large sales of a drug she had developed. When she questioned the rep, he was evasive.

She called a few doctors on his route and got similar evasive answers. When she finally called a hospital that bought more drugs than normally needed, she was told to speak to the administrator.

Dina received a one-sentence answer to her query. "Direct all your questions to my attorney."

Now she knew there was something very wrong going on. She called her accounting department and got some payment records. Checks were being issued to individuals instead of businesses.

The people getting this money included that hospital administrator, doctors, and someone who she later found out were in the section of the government agency responsible for approving the sale of drugs.

It wouldn't normally be her business, but if the testing was flawed, it would come back and be thrown on her lap. Her big mistake was following through with the legal implications. Her most dangerous finding was a large payment to a presidential health advisor who also had a large stock position in her company. He could be seen in the media touting one of their drugs.

Management became aware and had to sweep it under the carpet. They didn't know who she was in contact with, so foul play was out of the question. The best they could do was to discredit her.

It was a simple matter to adjust the computer records to reflect her mishandling of lab tests. They would show her incompetence and her falsifying data and test results.

Dina was in a similar position as Stan in that she was falsely accused of several crimes including causing the death of patients. It was easy to get plenty of witnesses to testify against her. Even her attorney told Dina that she was in a hopeless position. She either had to agree to give up her license and never be a pharmacist again or go to prison. It was an easy choice.

When Bret found Dina, he gave her the chance to practice again. She had a chance to study body chemistry and the effects of substances on it. It actually worked well for her because she became more disillusioned with artificial drugs and bought into the thinking of the doctors in Bret's group. She learned they weren't quacks, but instead had more varied and in-depth knowledge than what was provided in medical schools.

After letting Dina know she was needed, Bret and Ani arrived at the salon. Bret said Dina would arrive shortly.

Ani said, "Looking at all this junk, it's pretty impressive. I've never seen a better-equipped salon. I'll take a shave and a haircut, please."

"Ha-ha. Don't worry, Dina's going to give you the works."

Bret reached into a drawer and pulled out a pair of heavy gloves.

"Put these on."

"Are we going skiing?"

"The tips are treated to change your fingerprints. Just in case someone gets suspicious."

"There's no way to change a person's prints."

"We developed a chemical that will make a permanent change. It's harmless. You just have to wear these gloves a couple of hours per day for about a week. You can wear them when you go to sleep if you want."

"What about DNA? They could still do that."

"That's highly unlikely. It would be more trouble for them than it's worth. We could change that also, but we sold the formula to a tech company. This and Dina's magic should be sufficient."

"What's behind that door in the back?"

"That's a photography studio. We'll get to that afterward."

Dina arrived and Ani said that Bret had relayed her story. Although they had seen each other several times, Dina wanted to get a closer look.

She walked around Ani examining her hair and touching various parts of her body. She went to the front and moved her head up and down looking head to toe.

"Are you also an undertaker?"

"Why?"

"You look like you're measuring me for a box."

"That's not a bad idea. Just kidding."

Dina took a pen and paper and made some notes. She looked at Bret and told him to give them a couple of hours together. He then left asking Dina to "ugly her up."

"She's way too girly girl to be a man. She'll look stupid with a beard. Let me keep her as a female."

"Are you going to give me scars like an organized crime figure or maybe I'll look like a mad scientist put me together?"

"It won't be anything that drastic. You need to comprehend the art of disguise. Anyone can buy a fake beard and mustache. Those witty ideas would make you stand out. The idea is to make you blend."

"Where do we start?"

"First thing is to cut those beautiful golden locks. Don't look so sad. They'll be a little less than shoulder length. Women with excessively short hair stand out too much."

Dina pulled out her comb, brush, and scissors.

"Shouldn't it be washed first?"

"No, we don't want it too neat."

Dina started chopping away. She gave Ani a hand mirror so she could see what was happening. Ani found it difficult to say goodbye to her long locks.

"After we're done with this, I'll color your hair. Henna has to be used."

"Why henna?"

"It's all natural. The chemicals in commercial dyes are

dangerous. They may react with the goop I put on your face."

After the cut was finished, it was time to make a mess of Ani's face while the color was setting.

"I assume you won't do a perfect job like on your own face."

"You like my work?"

"I could tell from day one, you were a pro."

Dina's amazing talents were immediately noticeable. Ani's eyebrows were ok but had imperfections. She added some crow's feet and facial lines. Her lips were even made slightly crooked. Not to be left out were a couple of small moles in strategic places.

Before, Ani could walk in a shopping center and every man would turn and just stare at her with an open mouth. Now, she was no longer beautiful. She was still marginally attractive, but would not engender any more attention than the average female.

"How long will this plaster last?"

"Perhaps a week."

"That could be a problem. I may need it longer."

"It won't be. I'll give you a little kit and show you how to touch yourself up. Try not to wash your face."

Dina pulled out a small cosmetic bag. She put several tiny bottles and other articles inside. She finally started writing feverishly on a pad. She tore out the paper, folded it, and put it in the bag. She handed it to Ani.

"Now you're all set. The nice thing is sooner rather than later you'll be beautiful again. I'll be an average looking girl and all alone."

"Don't say that. You're great looking. You have so much to look forward to. You'll have a new identity and your Pharm D license back."

"You're so sweet."

"This doesn't include all the guys that are going to be crawling out of the woodwork chasing you, believe me."

They hugged each other and called for Bret. When he walked in the door, even he was stunned.

"What is that vision of beauty?"

"Oh, shut up, baby."

"You want me to say how lousy you look?"

This time, Dina punched him in the arm. She asked Bret if he wanted any adjustments.

"That's Ani's fault. She taught me the sarcasm. But seriously, your talents never cease to amaze me."

After Dina left, Ani couldn't forget she was still a woman.

"You'll feel differently towards me now because of the way I look?"

Bret pulled her close and put his palm against the back of her head pulling it against his shoulder.

"I'd love you even if you looked like the wrong end of a horse."

"Hey, you're going to smear me."

"I don't think so. That junk Dina uses is stronger than glue."

Bret took Ani's hand and led her through the back door. As usual, Ani was shocked at the professional equipment in the photo room. It had sun guns, umbrellas, large cameras on a stand, and some machinery she didn't recognize.

"That's a hologram machine and commercial embedding printer."

"Why those things?"

"You'll need fancy and formal identification, right?"

"Ah, ok."

Bret set Ani up against a plain backdrop. He told her to make a poker face. He even tweaked Dina's work. Ani had a huge smile. Bret wanted her to make a slight kissy look to make her mouth look smaller.

"Is that tiny walled-off area in the back, let me guess, a dark room?"

"Bingo."

Ani was wondering how the general public would react when they see her. Dina convinced her there would be no reaction from anyone.

The disguise was going so well, the preparation went on.

CHAPTER 21

The president was holed up in his military compound. It seemed everyone there was wearing a uniform except for the government bodyguards. They were easy to spot as they had the prototypical look about them. They all were relatively young and wore a dark suit while sporting sunglasses.

There was a large open area that could be used as a parade grounds. Towers and cameras were everywhere. On one side stood multifunctional military buildings such as barracks.

The other side had a series of smaller buildings. The president and visitors used one for meetings. The others had unknown uses. Occasionally someone would enter them, but this was rare.

A colonel was walking the grounds. He was the commanding officer at the compound. He was accompanied by a major who was recently transferred here to be the colonel's second in command. The major was being shown the lay of the land. They looked at soldiers marching and the way the structures were set up. It was obvious the compound was virtually impenetrable.

"How do you feel so far?"

"I'm a bit surprised at the number of personnel assigned here. I see the semi-hidden rocket launchers. They're almost like overkill."

"You can never have enough resources when protecting the most important person in the world."

As they continued, they saw a civilian walking into one of the buildings. He didn't appear to be any type of official. He was older and dressed in business casual garb. The major pointed over towards the civilian as he entered the building.

"Who was that?"

"I'm not really sure. I do know he has the highest security clearance that can be given to a civilian."

"Shouldn't there be no secrets from us?"

"Normally, you're correct. His anonymity is by presidential order."

"I suppose it's none of my affair for now, but I do wonder."

"My friend at one of the intelligence agencies, refers to him as the phantom."

"What's his purpose here?"

"I believe he's some kind of advisor. He must speak on the secure phone to the president because they're never seen together here or in public."

"I don't understand why he has to be so secretive."

"My agency friend said the most noteworthy decisions are made while he's skulking in the background. He said, when this guy's around, something always seems to happen."

"Well, I won't even guess. Weird."

"Don't even concern yourself with him. We just guard

and follow orders."

The colonel explained there was a secure hideout in the basement of each building. Each had a heavy steel door with an electronic lock. Very few people could unlock these doors. It was expressly for the president during emergencies. What he didn't know was the network of tunnels connecting each one.

The president had a habit of moving from one building to another without the knowledge of his agency guards. He felt certain events warranted nobody's knowledge.

Miles away, there was a limousine approaching the compound. In the back seat, two men were being driven to a meeting.

Their appearance was almost a paradox. They both wore very expensive silk suits, designer ties, and wingtip shoes. They had the appearance of major stockbrokers or large corporate executives. On the other hand, while clean-shaven, they wore their very long, straight hair well past their shoulders. One had gray hair and the other had black hair.

The older man was named George Finectus and he was accompanied by his attorney named Sam. George was a full-blooded chief of his nation. The reservation was in the northeast USA.

George was a particularly interesting man. Not only his appearance was a paradox, but so were his thoughts on life. He was a strict traditionalist in many ways, like his hair length. He felt more comfortable dealing with men in business matters even though he supported women's rights. He had a PhD in business management. He could afford to live anywhere but chose to live on the reservation.

However, he was also a modernist. He understood that the advent of modern communications would allow him to do something special.

Even in enlightened times, the reservations across the USA were separate and distinct. Some might say they were fragmented. They had the same arm's-length contact with one another as they would with someone of European descent.

George had a dream where he could unite them and form an economic coop. Between the ease of modern travel and teleconferencing, he wanted to form the equivalent of a mega-corporation without worrying about government interference.

His agreements started regionally and slowly spread across most of the major reservations situated within the USA. They began with a few small factories. This gradually increased to larger industries. He branched out into the financial sector with banks and even as a hedge fund manager.

Since the records were private per tribe, George could only estimate what the operation was worth. His latest calculations showed assets of over ten billion dollars.

George was personally worth a fortune. Yet, that wasn't his reason. When he was young, he had a voracious appetite for reading history. He had great sadness that so many in his race were languishing in poverty.

His becoming a millionaire was secondary to his wish that all people with a similar bloodline would make a respectable living and be able to afford the same basic luxuries that were common in the USA. Over the years, his constant prodding would gradually bring other tribes into the fold.

It wasn't all peaches and cream. The meetings would naturally morph from economics and business to other areas such as changing the social character of the people involved. For example, George's nation had a constitution. Some areas did not conform to other ways for other tribes.

The biggest problem George faced was the inevitable question of an armed unification. He was a businessman and wanted no part of that. There was no way of escaping the question, though.

George had never hidden the fact that his people had a standing army of 5000. Their need has always been explained that they would support and defend the USA if attacked by a foreign nation.

Now, George had to do his best to limit any abuse of this alliance. Any attempt to use offensive forces in a way that wasn't profitable would destroy everything he built. He believed it then and he believes it now. Still, for the economic alliance to remain intact, George had to endorse the idea of an attack on one would be considered an attack on all.

George had been speaking with Sam about this upcoming audience with the president. He didn't like dealing with those outside of his race other than for financial matters. They rolled around possibilities of the subject matter since they weren't informed of what this meeting was all about.

George thought he had a pretty good hypothesis. Sam, being the typical lawyer, wanted them to be prepared for multiple scenarios. After they pared things down, George pushed a button and lowered the privacy window between the front and back seating.

Along with the driver, Quentin from the Indian Agency was seated on the passenger side. He turned around facing the back.

Quentin said, "Is there anything you want to ask me before we get there?"

George said, "Will you be attending?"

"I don't think so. I wasn't invited. I was just supposed to escort you to the site."

"I don't like this secrecy business. My senses tell me I'll be asked to do something I don't want to do."

Sam reached out and grabbed George's forearm.

"Don't fret, my friend. I'll put a stop to any nonsense."

Quentin's face immediately dropped. He was concerned.

Quentin said, "Gentlemen, we're talking about the president. You have to go in there with an open mind. Please don't assume negative things."

"How can you be so sure if you don't know more than you're saying?"

"George, you know I've never lied to you. I'm full-blooded myself. You're the only man, to my knowledge, that's ever been empowered to speak for other tribes. He's aware of this."

What Quentin said was true. George was so revered and helped so many from all across the land, he was entrusted to speak for all the tribes on economic matters. While they could individually overrule him, he accomplished more in a few years to take a big bite out of poverty than all of their greatest leaders combined.

George said, "I've been known over the years as one who never had an affinity for people of European descent. While some might call it a prejudice, I call it appropriate skepticism."

"Nobody will deny your suspicions. All I'm asking you is to show him the respect you want for yourselves and know he would never bring you here if it wasn't the utmost importance for our peoples."

"Fear not, Quentin my friend. I've been accused of a lot of things over the years, even from my own people. You should hear my wife give me the business."

"Everybody roared, including the limo driver."

"All kidding aside, one thing I've never been accused of is not being a fair man. Do you really think otherwise, considering the characters I have to deal with from the other reservations?"

"I've never heard you speak about your brethren like that."

As cautious as he was, even Sam agreed with George.

"Go ahead, George. You can tell him about the last time."

"Oh, boy. One high ranking guy, a chief, showed up drunk. He did that quite often. He fell asleep during the meeting and started snoring so loudly, I had to yell at him to wake up because he was keeping everyone else awake."

"You really said that in front of everyone?"

"I'm not a man who takes kindly to disruptive behavior. It's disrespectful."

George couldn't dwell on that. He'd had many other incidents. It seems some of them wanted to go along for the ride and reap the benefits without doing the work.

"One guy was never on time. One day, he didn't show up in the morning. During the break, I called his cell phone. It turned out he overslept at a house of ill repute."

"I always thought my people were held to a higher standard."

"Quentin, your family's been off the reservation for too many years. People all over are about the same. There's good and there's bad people. We fall under the same bell curve."

"You never told me you were so—"

"Human? Believe it or not, I'm not a machine. I laugh and I cry, just like you or anybody else."

The limo approached the heavily fortified main gate. No identification was necessary. The military guard took one look in the back and waved them on. The building they stopped at had a metal detector by the door.

"You fellows don't mind, do you?"

"We know the routine."

They left Quentin in the car. The building they were told to enter was one neither the president nor the phantom entered. After passing through the detector, they entered a small lobby with a stairway facing them. At the top of the stairs, the phantom was standing. He obviously had access to the underground passages.

He pointed to the elevator and said they could use it or walk up as he motioned with his hand to come. George and Sam both expressed the desire to walk.

When they reached the top, they were escorted down the hall and led into an office. The phantom entered after them and closed the door.

The office was large enough to have an executive desk along with a bridge table with four chairs around it. The president was sitting at the desk.

After the introductions, the president got up and joined the other three at the table. He smiled as he looked at George while pointing to the phantom.

The president said, "Do you know this man?"

George said, "I don't know his name, but I do know him."

"Do you mind if he joins us?"

George said, "I think he's a good man, an honest man."

George and Sam nodded to each other.

"I feel comfortable. He can stay."

Through the entire conversation, the phantom would do little more than nod, shake his head, and shrug his shoulders.

The president said, "I don't often come in contact with great Native Americans."

"Let me stop you right there. I feel Native American is a condescending and placating term invented by Caucasians. I'd prefer you to refer to me as Indian. Archaeologists have shown my ancestors came from Asia. Indian is not exactly correct, but it's closer than Native American."

"As you wish. Do you know why I asked to speak with you?"

George didn't let on but he had a pretty good idea of what it was related to.

"I would think it's about your illegal military incursion on the reservation in the Midwest."

"Illegal?"

Sam immediately put his hand up and in front of George.

"Please don't play with us, sir. I find it hard to believe you haven't checked with your legal staff. Assuming you did, you already know you've lost every court case in the past with similar incidents."

"Well, you must also know I had nothing to do with this."

"Aren't you the commander in chief?"

"This was an unauthorized action by one of our generals. He did not know his location. Even so, he's been relieved of his duties."

"You didn't allow this?"

"As soon as I became aware, the troops were immediately withdrawn. It won't happen again. I would appreciate you immediately rescinding your complaint to the Indian Agency."

"I'll check with that tribe. I'm convinced it was a misunderstanding. I can't promise anything, but I think they'll go along with me."

"In that case, I'll need more of your help and some information."

"If it's the info you need, why not ask your spies? You have them on every reservation."

"Let's be serious. I wouldn't ask you here if I was able to get the information I require. I also want to limit the number of people who will know about what I'm discussing with you and the info I require."

Sam interjected once again.

"You realize sir that George can't be asked to supply any information I regard as internal Indian matters."

"I only ask because I respect you."

George hated false modesty. That's why he made the spy remark and he had to once again address that.

"I thought you folks imagined Indians as people who sit around all day stringing beads, living in tents, and drinking firewater."

Now it was the president's turn to get a little testy. "If you believe I think that little of a person who runs a billion-dollar enterprise, then you're dead wrong. I certainly couldn't do that."

Being the diplomat that he was, George decided to smooth things over.

"Why don't you come out and ask what you really need, and I'll see if I can help."

The phantom just smiled and nodded for the first time.

"Ok, George, here it is. I need military information about the various tribes."

Sam and George just looked at each other. Sam was getting impatient.

"I told you about internal matters and that's about as internal as it gets. You know we're not under your jurisdiction."

"I knew this was going to be hard to sell. Please don't reveal what I'm about to tell you to anyone."

The Phantom nodded.

The president began to explain the situation without revealing details of the weapons.

"Any sloppy handling of this situation will cause the loss of many innocent lives. That includes those of the Indian nations."

"What exactly do you want?"

"I want to know exactly how many troops the reservations have. I've heard there's some kind of agreement about their banding together. Is that possible?"

Sam quickly said, "I think George and I need to discuss this privately."

"There's an office across the hall. Be my guest."

Both duos broke up and closed their respective doors. The president was able to allow the phantom to talk freely.

"Do you think they'll help me out?"

"It's hard to say. Even if he agrees, it's going to be difficult to persuade the others. I'm hearing they have some kind of conference scheduled soon."

"Does he have the juice to pull this off?"

"I'm not sure. He has a lot of opposition from some that I know will be sitting there."

"What do you suggest?"

"He may need some help."

"I assume you mean Sam isn't enough."

"Sam's a nice kid, but public relations and effective rhetoric aren't his strength."

"How would you like to attend if I can persuade him to take you?"

"I was thinking the same thing."

The other office was buzzing in a completely different direction. Sam was most concerned with George's personal liability and protection.

"You could be opening yourself up to a multi-million-dollar lawsuit from the others in the group. Your reputation could be destroyed."

"You don't think it's wise to tell them the little I know?"

"I didn't say that. It could be worse if Indian lives are lost and they point the finger at you. I can't make the decision. It's all on you. What will you do?"

"I'll see."

When everyone came together again, they sat in the same seats. George spoke about what he knew.

"I've never hidden our troop strength of 5000. I've always spoken about our loyalty to the USA. I, myself, served during the last war overseas."

"I didn't know but your patriotism doesn't surprise me. What about the others."

"I'm not privy to their troop numbers. I can only give you a nationwide guesstimate of about 100,000."

"Holy—I mean I never imagined power like that."

"Let me reinforce the idea that these are not some savages with bows and arrows. These are well-trained men. Most of them are US military veterans and they're plenty tough."

"I have to wonder if they would fight together."

"That, I have no idea. I'm in the business end, remember?"

"That will definitely affect my decision making."

George asked, "Are you planning a war against the

Indians? This isn't the 1880s."

"Don't be silly. I have to consider all scenarios. One of them would be an illegal incursion, as you call it, at the source of the problem. If it happens and everyone understands it's in their best interest to just sit on their hands, we might be able to pull it off without the loss of Indian lives."

George said, "And if they don't?"

"It depends if it's a few unreasonable types. If it blows into a full-scale conflict, I might as well resign. Leadership won't allow us to back off. Many innocent people will die."

"Does it have to happen? Can't you get a peaceful resolution?"

"I'm hopeful of that. This is the worst-case scenario. The international community is involved now, unfortunately."

George said, "I don't envy your situation. I can't promise, but I'll try to persuade them that this is in their best interest. I'll have an answer for you tomorrow, if that's soon enough."

The president was flabbergasted. He didn't understand George's keen sense of anticipation. That's why some people refer to George as a genius. He knew this talk would concern something much bigger than his own reservation, so he called an emergency meeting even before he spoke to the president.

"George, I'd like to give you some help."

"How so?"

"I'd like this man to attend the meeting with you. He can just give prearranged facial and hand signals with his opinions."

Sam almost had a conniption.

"You can't be serious. A Caucasian at our internal tribal meeting? Where do you come off suggesting that? How do you justify such a ridiculous request? I must tell George to refuse."

For the first time, with all present, the phantom spoke. The second he opened his mouth, all were silent because it was such a shock he would say anything.

"Come on, Sam. There'll be all kinds of assistants present. Can you swear they're all full-blooded? I know some of the characters at these meetings. Some have criminal records and you're worried about me?"

George interrupted.

"It's ok, Sam. This is way beyond an Indian affair now. I'll be happy for any help I can get including this man with no name."

They left and returned to the limo. Quentin was waiting and asked how it went.

"It was fine. You'll see things take shape soon."

"You were treated well, I assume."

"The president is a charming man."

That's when Sam raised the privacy window.

"I don't like this. I don't like this one bit. You said you know of this man. I don't. Suppose he's a saboteur?"

"Don't be so dramatic, my friend. I've only seen him on a few occasions. The rumors about him swirl. It's said he can turn the world upside down. Besides, I don't have to do what he says."

"I hope you know what you're doing. If not, they might go back 200 years and ask for you to be burned at the stake."

"If they do, I'll ask them to make me medium rare for the vultures."

George winked at Sam and they both smiled.

CHAPTER 22

The emergency meeting scheduled for the members of the economic coop would take place shortly at a hotel near the capitol. A large double meeting room was set up specifically for George's convenience.

The tables were put in a square fashion so there could be more than twenty participants facing one another at all times. There were chairs placed around the periphery for advisors and other non-participating guests.

The person known as the phantom would speak to George ahead of time to review a set of discreet signals which basically consisted of head, mouth, and hand gestures. They would be facing each other and these would be used only if there was a participant saying something that needed George to opine.

Even though the phantom, along with Sam, sat along the back wall facing George, Sam would save his counseling for the breaks. George was not required to follow any of the suggestions. Should the phantom feel strongly, he would continue with his motion. He might cough to get George's attention. In that case, George would respond with the briefest of nods or head shakes.

Everyone would be so engrossed in the powerful subject matter, that these signals wouldn't be noticed.

The room was set up the night before, so it was locked. Sam had the hotel unlock the room so he could informally reserve their needed three seats and tell the hotel staff if any adjustments were needed.

Sam tipped the chairs he wanted forward. The others could be left for anyone to sit where they wanted. George had experimented with written nameplates at one time. That was a complete failure because there were petty squabbles and unbeknownst to George, there were people present who just didn't like each other. He fielded complaints about everything from elbow contact to body odor. He wouldn't make that mistake again.

Sam watched as the staff set up a table with coffee, tea, donuts, bagels, and spreads. The staff brought everything except cups. He made them lock the door because he wanted to get the cups before the meeting started. There was plenty of time to get what he wanted.

When he saw someone giving directions to the people bringing in the supplies, he flagged him down.

"Good morning. Your people forgot the coffee cups."

"The list doesn't say you ordered any."

Sam had no tolerance for what he considered stupidity. He just walked away from that man and proceeded to the front desk. He asked for the woman in charge of sales. George and Sam had dealt with her before and she was always very accommodating.

She wasn't in her office, so they paged her. When she exited the elevator, she walked towards the front desk. She recognized Sam and greeted him with a smile and a handshake.

"Is everything satisfactory?"

"It depends."

The woman knew something was wrong, so she escorted Sam to her office.

"How can I help?"

"I would like to get an immediate supply of rubber gloves. Of course, we will pay for them."

"We have boxes from housekeeping. There's no charge. I've never been asked for this before. We thoroughly clean and sterilize out meeting rooms for each time the rooms are used."

"Oh, I believe you. It's for the coffee."

"You're right. We really need to put a warning on the urns so people don't burn themselves."

"Nobody was burned. We need them for drinking."

"I don't understand. The cups usually don't get too hot."

"Please come with me."

Sam brought her to the room which she unlocked with her key. She looked around and still didn't understand.

"Try the coffee."

"I had some already, thanks."

"No, I insist."

"If there's something wrong with the taste, we'll replace it."

"The taste is fine, but I'm asking you to try."

"Alright. Where are the cups?"

"That's why I asked for rubber gloves, so we can drink

out of our hands."

She stifled a giggle. "Why didn't you ask the staff?"

"I did, but your man said I didn't order any."

She was horrified. She wanted to know who he was to make sure this never happened again.

"Did he say anything else?"

"No. I guess he assumed since we were Indians we would drink with our hands or perhaps right from the spigot if we were sophisticated enough."

Sam returned to the room. Many of the participants were waiting in the lobby. He told them to be patient for a few minutes.

This hotel had a restaurant, so it only took a minute to get cups. Then the staff started bringing in large trays of scrambled eggs, bacon, and other breakfast items.

Sam saw the woman again.

"We didn't order all this."

"Compliments of the house."

"That's very nice of you."

She winked as Sam and said, "Notice I even had them bring utensils. Now you won't have to eat with your hands."

Sam didn't laugh often, but he did this time. He didn't like contact very much, but he hugged her.

The members started drifting into the room. Sam would consistently get compliments like, "Wow, look at all that food."

Sam always had the same response, "It's with George's compliments."

George even asked Sam about it. When the reason was

explained, George was thrilled.

"That's why I employ you. You're the best."

Sam said, "Perhaps you can someday remind my wife of that."

The large breakfast had a psychological effect. It made everyone relax and put them all in a good mood. George knew it was time to get going.

"Let's finish chowing down and get this show on the road. We need to finish before the end of the day."

This group kept things informal. No recorded minutes would be kept. George would act as more of a facilitator than a controller. There were many diversified personalities and interests.

One of the most important guests was none other than Red Hawk. He came alone and was the sole spokesman for his nation. He knew a lot more about the present problem than even George, but would only discuss the peripheral info that concerned the group as a whole.

"Since rumors are always flying, I think everyone knows this get together has to do with an ongoing situation on Red Hawk's reservation."

He told everyone to keep it simple, if possible. The entire purpose was to get a unified agreement of the coop's response to a series of possible events in just one place.

The people who thought alike had a habit of drifting together. Their opinions would usually match. Most of George's opposition normally came from the southwestern tribes. They weren't the most cooperative and cared less for his "peace at all cost" attitude.

Most of George's allies were from the Pacific Northwest and the heavily populated reservations situated in the northeast. While Red Hawk often disagreed with George, mainly on economic matters, his being a partner was paramount for any agreement George could live with.

Red Hawk was asked for a synopsis of the situation. He warned the group that any action relating to his people had to have his approval. In the absence of that, there was a real possibility of his withdrawal from this group. His tribe was a household name in all the historical texts and they had been granted some of the largest expanses of land.

George made the inflammatory remark that the incursion was a mistake and shouldn't happen again.

He was met with the question, "What do you mean by shouldn't?"

"I met with the president and he assured me he wants to do everything possible to achieve a peaceful resolution. He made no promises."

There were a lot of grunts, groans, and side conversations. The phantom just kept nodding at George.

"What are you asking? We're supposed to sit idly by, while those we have a treaty with are attacked?"

"That's why we're here—to decide our course of action, if any. I must be honest. I am against any mobilization."

Again side conversations voiced a lot of displeasure. The phantom made a motion as if to say "Stay calm and let's see what happens."

"I understand the arguments I'm going to get. They'll be less economic and more about our breaking treaties.

Unfortunately, the two cannot be divorced."

The reps from the northeastern and midwestern tribes were having at it.

"If we do anything that's considered military in nature that would be the end of our marketing and supply lines. We might as well go back to being dirt poor."

"If we don't defend ourselves, there'll be nobody left to produce anyway. It will destroy us either way. I've personally had good relations with the USA. However, there comes a point where you must take a stand."

The phantom immediately shook his head and George reacted.

"Yes, we must be prepared. There are also scenarios where the treaties are broken and there is no loss of life." The phantom smiled.

Throughout the process, George often looked to his side at a perpendicular table. A man, named Earl, was sitting a few seats away. For meetings such as this, Earl preferred to be addressed by his traditional name Chengua.

He was suspiciously silent as the day went on. He was almost like a cat waiting to pounce on its prey. Earl was a chief in the southwest and was almost always in opposition to George.

Earl was different than the others. He could match George word for word and for good reason. He was the single most important individual in helping George develop the empire of extreme wealth.

He held a PhD in economics from an Ivy League university. Brilliant was an understatement. While he wasn't devoted to banks, he almost singlehandedly developed the financial side of this coop.

Unlike many, Earl was educated. He was a strictly free market-based capitalist. On the other hand, he was a former commissioned officer in the army.

Earl loved tradition like his name. However, his remarks could be unpredictable. He would try to do what's best for everyone, yet he hated politicians and would fight with them regardless of political affiliation.

With all his brilliance, he also understood the occasional need to take up arms. He blamed politicians and their plundering of economies for all wars.

The things he especially hated were riots and demonstrations. He knew in his own mind they destroyed rather than produced. He felt most of those involved never took a course in economics.

The main tenet that Chengua lived by was the fact that revolutions are not started by the downtrodden masses. They are started with money and organization. He felt one could learn from exactly who could provide both.

George wasn't the only one waiting for him to speak. Even his detractors appreciated his insight. He didn't disappoint when he decided it was his turn.

"I've listened to a lot of opinions today. They seem to have ranged from going back to the 1880s and waging an all-out war to sitting back and letting the USA violate the old treaties and slowly destroy us the opposite way."

Nobody was daydreaming while he spoke. He had almost as much respect from everyone as George. He came with a different approach than the others.

"I agree with George that everything comes into play. I also agree it serves no purpose to attack and capture a small town while they destroy our families. That's the extent of my agreement."

The phantom shrugged his shoulders in a motion that signaled he didn't know what to suggest next and let the man talk.

"Economies and fighting are always interrelated. My people suffer more poverty than any others in this room. We aren't lazier or lack intelligence. Our type of industry is being choked by federal regulations."

"Aren't we all exempt?"

"That's true. The difference is our economy is strictly based on dealing with companies off the reservation. They are different than the goods and services of the rest of your tribes."

He was making a lot of sense which got George worried. He knew that Chengua would drop a bomb sooner or later. The next portion of his words would explain his idea.

"Everyone here speaks as if we are on the defensive. I believe we have a unique opportunity to make some gains with the government.

Has everyone forgotten that we win almost every case in their own courts? I suggest we turn the tables and make demands. After all, George has the rare opportunity to have the ear of the president. Let's use it to our advantage and make a set of demands that would help our situations greatly. I would begin by demanding the end of regulations for our deals with the outside."

George said, "But Chengua, we know that they're just protecting their deals with the Far East."

"They'll have no war with them over this. I believe the president has a bigger concern right here at home. A disaster here would just about destroy his chances for re-election."

Even the phantom was getting nervous now. He started tapping his foot which wasn't any sort of signal. He then made a motion of slicing his throat and pointing to the door. That meant for George to call for a break.

"Chengua, please hold your thought. It would be nice to take a bathroom break. Let's come back in say, half an hour."

He hit the right spot as everyone flew out the door. The phantom wanted to go to George's room to speak to Sam and George in private.

"Sam, you know the people here. What do you think?"

"I can't say for sure. The way they're giving him attention, I'd say he has a lot of support."

The phantom was even blunter.

The phantom said, "You're not getting out of here without any kind of option that includes mobilization. What can you live with?"

George said, "I think Chengua likely has a good point about squeezing some concessions for us."

The phantom said, "Don't get too greedy. Put in a bunch of nonsense stuff like zoning and monuments and keep it to only a few things. I'll have to run the regulation business by the president."

Sam said, "I don't think Chengua will back down

on that."

"George, I have to agree with Sam. That alone should make him happy. How about you ask for some casinos. They're a great money maker and the president can override any governor."

George said, "He would do that?"

"He won't have to if the governor is from the same party. I think a little arm-twisting will do, especially if it's someone running for re-election. The public loves and supports money-making casinos because it creates jobs. Besides, they can't wait to lose money."

George and Sam looked at the phantom and asked if he could think of anything else for the wish list.

"Yes, one more thing. A request to have a USA funded oil and gas exploration. Enough geologists have said many reservations are floating on oil. If they hit, it's a lot of money. If they miss, you still created a lot of jobs."

"That's a lot of money for the president to front."

"It won't be all his. The oil companies will pay you big money not to develop. They've already done that all along the Canadian border. You really can't lose either way."

George felt he had all the ammunition he needed to return to the gathering. They let Chengua continue. He ultimately said there has to be a warning that the Indians will mobilize all across the continental USA if the army sets one foot on Indian land.

Once again, Red Hawk interrupted.

"You know I have the utmost respect for you. Should the result of your actions cost lives on my reservation, then we will be at war with you also."

"I never meant to hurt you. I only want to help."

"Let my people determine if your help is needed. I understood our military alliance was only for when someone needs and requests help."

The phantom made a motion with his fingers and thumb together repeatedly. He was telling George to speak.

"I think we have to respect our brethren's independence. I started out today with the idea that we should accept the government position and avoid anything that would cost lives. I support Red Hawk's desire for self-determination. I also think Chengua has some great ideas."

"What do you propose?"

"I'm a reasonable man. As such, it's best to come away today with an agreement we can all live with. Red Hawk's view must be respected. I also have some ideas to reinforce Chengua's way of thinking."

George outlined everything he spoke about at the break. Some started applauding as he listed those ideas. However, Chengua wasn't done yet.

"I'm a reasonable man also. If we can get all of this from the government, I am ready to endorse our decision. I still think those putting our military in mothballs are wrong also. We must have a backup plan. Once they attack one reservation, all the treaties are null and void. We might as well starve."

"My idea is not to limit mobilization. It would only be under dire circumstances. I'd like to remind you of a quote by one of your ancestral chiefs. He was a great warrior. He won many victories against the US Army. When it was time to stop fighting, he said something,"

The room was so quiet, you could hear a pin drop.

The quote was, "When we kill a soldier, they replace him with 100 soldiers. When they kill an Indian, there's one less Indian."

There were plenty of gasps and groans. Like always, Chengua had an answer.

"The same chief said something else when he declared peace." Just like George's remark, the room was quiet. "I agree to peace. If even one Indian is killed by a violation of this treaty, I will take many scalps."

There were a lot of nods and groans.

"My friend Chengua, let's write down the things we agree on. I'll get them answered quickly. I think everyone in this room knows this president is a man of honor."

He knew, if the president balked, he would be calling everyone back. He just felt better when he saw the phantom smile and raise both fists in a manner that suggested, "We did it."

The phantom immediately called the president on a secure line with the news.

"There had to be an agreement for you to provide economic benefits or they would mobilize their troops."

"What types of benefits?"

The requests were outlined. The president was surprisingly receptive to everything.

"Most of that is small potatoes. Executive orders can take care of some and my political allies will take care of the rest. Tell them I accept on the condition that they must inform me before they take to arms."

"I think agreement and leaving that reservation alone ensure the domestic mess is just about quelled."

The next step would be meeting with the advisors. He didn't need a consensus from the inner circle, but he had questions that they would have to help him answer. The main sticking point would be the document.

CHAPTER 23

Back in the mountain, just about everyone was in a light mood. Red Hawk had briefed them and there was a renewed feeling of confidence.

Although Bret could never let his guard down, he started spending more leisure time with Ani. They played games in the game room, worked out in the gym, and watched movies in the theater.

Of course, it was always in the back of his mind what the president was doing at the moment. That person would definitely not be relaxing.

The compound had a special bus arriving. The passengers were those who would help the president formulate an opinion which would ultimately determine Bret and Ani's fate as well as how the domestic and international landscape would look.

When everyone filed into the meeting room, it was apparent Ani was very close to getting the correct identification of the contributors. She aced the four main advisors: Tom, Millie, Scott, and Myra. The phantom was notoriously missing.

The general that was attached to the agency was there.

Ani thought it might be a chief of staff. The president's thinking was to keep as few people involved as possible.

Should there be a need for military intervention, it would be an attack with very few options. They wouldn't be facing an entire army which would necessitate a general with more tactical expertise. He was only there to give possibilities and he wouldn't be asked for recommendations.

The only other person Ani missed was Jim being temporarily patched in on the phone. He would field questions for anything his direct contact could help with. Then he would be excused as each person would give their opinion as to how they should proceed.

To keep things orderly, the president insisted only one person at a time give their presentation with any interruptions to be filtered through him.

The president had a specific order in mind. He knew the players involved, so he led off with Tom because he would be the least controversial and worked his way to the most controversial.

"I assume you've all had a chance to review their document. Has anyone not done this?"

There was silence.

"Seeing a bunch of shaking heads, let's get going. I have Jim on the speaker here. Please direct questions to him about his knowledge of the situation. When that's done, he will be excused."

Tom asked what these people were like.

"The voice without a name presents a conundrum. In one way, he's very caring. He gets extremely upset at the thought of humans losing their lives. He even saved my operator, Billy. However, he's provided us with samples of deadly weapons and has threatened to use them again."

Tom said, "What's your gut feeling?"

"He hasn't lied to us yet. I take everything he says seriously. They are not some drugged-up hooligans. They're highly trained professionals. If you held a gun to my head, I'd think they ultimately want a solution where nothing bad happens and we let them walk."

Myra asked, "How is Ani doing?"

"I think she's feeling the strain of imprisonment. We had a pretty bad argument and at times she wasn't very lucid. She's been present for all communications and I haven't determined any of her other statements were made under duress."

Scott asked, "Are you sure he's not bluffing?"

"What guarantees can I give you? My opinion was asked and I gave it."

Millie asked, "Are you able to reason he understands our position and we must do what's in our interests?"

"He said the document would provide us with the best of both worlds."

The rest of the questions were inconsequential and the president decided to end this part of it.

"Folks, I don't want to dwell on this, but time is not on our side. I have a teleconference coming up soon and I have to have some answers for those 100+ foreign ministers."

The president then excused Jim and referred to the Native American situation.

"Does anyone have any comments on the proposal made by George Finectus?"

Scott said, "I sure do. Where do these people come off trying to extort money from us and all they give in return is peace?"

Millie said, "Now now, Scott. When you've been in the political arena as long as I have, you learn to not think that way. You weigh all the possibilities and figure the least costly step forward. I'm old enough to have known Socrates personally and any political solution to anything always involves money transfer."

Tom asked, "This George, can you trust him?"

"He might be the most trusted and revered Indian of all time. He's respected by everyone."

The parties were most interested in what the president thought about their demands. He was point-blank with his answer.

"These demands are nothing. I've been forced during this presidency to accede to a lot more disagreeable things. Protesters and their media friends don't normally go after shenanigans that are positive for the tribes. I have no problem with this, considering the terrible alternatives."

This seemed to put the Native American domestic problem to bed. The only exception would be if an attack was launched.

It would finally become time for the major topic of this sit-down. That was the document. The president had been formulating ideas that he shared with nobody. He still had some problems in his own mind and for that, he needed help.

"You all know they said this document is not negotiable. Any differences must be written as separate stipulations. Legal counsel has advised me with a bunch of technical gibberish. I've been told the bottom line is they know what they're doing."

At that point, some snoring was heard as Millie dozed off.

"Leave her be. I'll wake her if we really need her input."

Ani nailed Tom's way of thinking. He said a lot but basically said nothing.

"There are too many dangers in doing something immediately. We have to wait as long as possible. No matter what you would decide to do, it will have a negative impact. The media will have a field day if it leaks. Let's hold that document. Maybe they'll ask for less."

The president said, "You want me to tell this voice that we're just sitting on it with no time table for an answer?"

Tom said, "You can tell them there will be no attack for now. They're not going to murder a lot of people as long as they have some hope of salvation."

"You have a good point. What's your idea for a time frame?"

"If it were up to me, I'd stall them until after the election."

"But that's next year. I'm afraid that's a non-starter."

"It's your decision, but I've never heard of an election being lost from not making a decision."

Millie would have been next except she was in deep slumber. Therefore, Scott would have the most direct approach. Ani got that right.

"Tom's point about doing nothing to avoid losing an election may be right, maybe not. I do know our allies and enemies alike see non-decision as a lack of leadership. That can lose an election. I would tell them to take this document and shove it."

"So you would prefer an attack? What about the Native American consequences? What about the extended use of these weapons?"

"I think you put too much credence in this guy, George. Most of the tribes hate one another. They have a lot of envy. I don't buy any military cooperation for a second."

"What about those weapons?"

"I personally believe with those explosions at the poles they shot their load. If they had anything else, it would mean their end and the end of their worldwide friends."

"General, do you have a plan if we do attack, as per Scott's suggestion?"

"Not counting the reservation's response, there are several ways. We don't know their food supply or local weapons. We can lay siege with a ground force. Of course, the natives might get restless enough to cause some trouble. The natives would have heavy casualties."

"I want to avoid that."

"We can do several weeks of aircraft bombing to soften them up. Then we can attack where we think the entrances are."

"How long would that take?"

"That's unknown. We don't know how heavily armed

they are. We can use tear gas and flame throwers, but I don't know the insides, so that could mean limitations."

"That could also involve Native Americans. It sounds like it would take weeks, maybe months like your first plan."

"The only relatively sure way to get in and out quickly with no ground troops would be to use MOPs."

"What the heck is that?"

"Oh, sorry. It stands for massive ordnance penetrators. The civilian term for them is bunker buster."

"That's pretty powerful stuff."

"We could peel that mountain like a banana. That would almost assuredly end their operation."

"Casualties?"

"Obviously, none on our side. Unfortunately, they would have virtually 100% fatalities."

"But I've been told there are children in that place."

Scott was fidgeting and finally raised his hand.

"We've successfully put a lid on a similar operation as far as the media is concerned. We could bury this with a little secrecy. Nobody outside this room, except for Jim, is aware children are living in that place. It would be an unfortunate happening, but the quick result and end to the crisis would be worth it."

The president turned beet red with rage. He stood up and leaned over the table, bracing himself with his knuckles. His lips started quivering as his head swiveled making eye contact with everyone in the room.

"I'm going to say this only once. I want no harm coming to any children, zero, zilch, nada. Am I being understood?"

There were no words from anyone, including Scott. They all just nodded their heads except for Millie who was still snoring.

The president saved Myra for last because her specialty was dealing with crises, both home and abroad. She could easily have become an ambassador to any major country but she had previously informed the president of her preference to stay stateside.

Myra was excluded from the Indian experience only because of George's antiquated notion of dealing with men only. It just so happened her front man was Quentin, who was at her beck and call.

"I agree with Scott that we have to act immediately. That's all I can coincide with. I've heard three scenarios, so let's analyze them a bit."

Myra started walking around the room carrying the document in her hand. She just didn't refer to it yet.

"If we do nothing, we have countries waiting for the bomb to drop. They've moved their armed forces to the border with their enemy neighbor. You have a crisis brewing with major allies and their enemies."

"Not good."

"Let me correct myself. I agree with the leadership message. Non-action implies weakness."

"Would you attack then?"

"That's just crazy. Let's look at the possibilities. You attack, they set off weapons, and people die, you're to blame. Native Americans mobilize, they take over a few towns, and we crush them, with heavy loss of life, you're to blame.

Children are killed from that group and it gets leaked, you're to blame. The list goes on and on."

"Ok, ok. I see your points are valid."

"If you do this, I'm afraid the best-case scenario is to get impeached. You certainly couldn't even run for dog catcher, let alone president."

"Do you propose a solution? You haven't mentioned the document."

Suddenly, Myra started shaking her copy of the document in the air. She waved it at everyone's face.

"You see this so-called document? It's a piece of garbage."

She walked over to the wastebasket and threw it in. Everyone was shocked including the president.

"You sign this thing and there'll be no more explosions, no more uprisings, no small country wars, and big shots wiping the sweat off their brows. You'll not only get re-elected, but you might also win the peace prize. You'll also have to get the other countries to sign it to flex your power."

"Now that sounds good. I'll try it."

Myra could see the wheels turning in the president's mind. He was partially daydreaming of being a celebrated hero. He was also thinking about other realities.

"What about these criminals holed up in those mountains? We just let them go?"

Myra said, "They're not criminals. They really haven't broken any laws. Did they kidnap Billy? They had to take him in order to save his life. They most likely just want to live out their lives as productive citizens."

The president said, "What about the voice?"

Myra said, "He's too dangerous. Let him go and have him meet with an accident in about a month?"

The president said, "You don't see any scenario for attack?"

"Sure I do. Then they unleash crazy weapons and millions are lost. Of course we have to crush them."

"What about that agent, Ani?"

"She's a good agent. I recruited her. She's also expendable and she knows that."

"If there's nothing else—"

Scott said, "I also know her. I don't trust her. She could sabotage our whole effort. You must give Jim misinformation to relay or we could be headed for disaster."

It was Myra's turn to get red in the face. The president saw her anger. He could almost see the steam coming out of her ears. He just wasn't quick enough to stop her. It's possible he wanted someone to put Scott in his place.

"You want to talk about Ani? Let me tell you something. I love that girl as if she was my daughter. If she gets killed, I'll go home and have a good cry, but personal attacks have no place in a meeting like this. If you want to discuss the skeletons in everybody's closets, feel free to meet me in an office down the hall so we can clear the air."

Most people wouldn't take him on like that because of his powerful family. This time, the people saw fear in his eyes. Although the president had to be poker-faced and a mediator, even he was secretly proud of Myra's action.

"Ok, that's it. I have some thinking to do."

The president sat thinking and then looked out the

window to verify everyone boarded the bus. He waited until he saw the bus leave.

The president walked out and down the hall and stopped by an office. As he opened the door, he saw the phantom sitting behind a desk.

"Was the speaker working ok?"

"I heard everything, word for word."

"What can you tell me?"

"I'm glad you're doing this for George. It's the right thing."

"And the others?"

"Please don't be upset with me, but your man Scott is a dodo."

"You know why he's there. I had no choice. What about the document?"

"I agree with most of what Myra said."

"You don't agree with what?"

"That voice person. Don't lay a hand on him."

"Isn't he dangerous?"

"No more than you and I. If you kill him, the others will find out one way or the other. You have a major catastrophe."

"I see what you mean."

"You have to go out of your way to keep him alive at all costs."

"Ok, what else do you have a problem with?"

"I suspect you feel distaste for letting the others go. All they're asking for is new identities and a small stipend to get them back into the swing of things."

The president said, "What if they leave and become

foreign agents."

The phantom said, "My friend, you missed something. They asked for immediate citizenship. That means they are all foreigners and persona non grata in their old countries."

The president nodded. "True, I missed that."

"If you do this for them, they'll never take a step out of the USA."

"Anything else?"

"Don't worry about foreign signatures. Get as many as you can, but this is all window dressing. These people could care less about any signature except yours."

"I'd like to make some demands."

The phantom said, "Just have them sign that they will never leave the USA and never have contact with any foreign government. That's important. Maybe put other minor things like keeping a job and paying taxes. They'll be happy to sign anything like that."

"It looks like things are finally coming together. I'm still a little concerned about the foreign ministers and the major powers."

The phantom patted the president's hand and said, "You're famous for your powers of persuasion. Just lay the charm and emphasize that their cooperation will ensure peace for quite a while."

If the phantom was right, their side of the equation would essentially be completed. The president knew full well, there was still a chance a country might make a rash decision and try to hunt down who they felt were accomplices. In this case, all bets were off.

CHAPTER 24

Jim made his usual trek through the woods to give Bret the scheduled update. This time Alex and Lana would be joining Bret and Ani in the room.

Jim now felt he could take the gloves off. There was no harm in giving out his understanding of things. The only areas would be anything he was specifically told not to share.

Bret asked, "Is there any news?"

"I don't have a whole lot. I'm friends with a colonel who runs the compound where the boss has a lot of meetings. I'm not privy to anything official yet."

"He knows something?"

"He did mention a bus came and went carrying several people. He recognized a couple of them as his advisors. When they were leaving, he said they all seemed jolly except for one guy."

Ani said, "This sounds like the president is close to making a decision. I bet the others are going to give their input and that will be it for the domestic side. If the unhappy guy is Scott, that's good news."

Bret wouldn't share the fact that he knew more info about certain things than Jim because of Red Hawk. It wouldn't help nor hinder the situation, so Jim was still on a need to know for both sides.

"I hear voices in the background. Are we being joined by anyone?"

"They are invaluable help. I probably should have had them present all along, but so be it. I can ask them to leave if you want."

"It's fine. I believe the boss has some kind of meeting scheduled with the international sector."

"It seems you'll be coming back very soon with either good or bad news."

"I think that's likely. Our time together is fast coming to a close. Funny thing is I feel as if I've come to know you as more than just a voice. I suppose, in other circumstances, we might even call each other friends."

That would get to Bret. Seeing his sad expression, Ani passed him a note saying, "Don't fall for it. He's baiting you." Alex reinforced that notion by grabbing Bret's arm and wiggling his index finger back and forth.

"Life plays tricks. Maybe someday, but that's not likely. Believe it or not Jim, I sincerely wish you and yours the best of everything."

"I hope they spare you."

"I hope you go easy on the juice."

"I haven't touched a drop since things started taking a turn for the better."

Lana asked for Alex and her to be excused. It became apparent nothing important was going to happen today.

"Listening to the others and what Billy told me, it seems

just about everyone there has some sort of foreign accent. Do you mind telling me why? I just hope they're not enemy agents."

"You know I can't give you identities. I will give you my word that none of these people would harm the USA. They're all good people, decent people."

"If they do anything bad afterward, you know I'm the lowest person on the food chain. The powers that be would find a reason to railroad me."

Ani said, "I'll put in a good word for you."

It was time to end this mutual admiration society. The clock was showing the time the president would have his final discussions before making a decision.

A bus pulled into the compound loaded with foreign diplomats. There were no heads of state, but everyone present held a high position with the authority to negotiate. These represented the major countries. The president would focus on them.

The diplomats were herded into a place that looked like a theater. It contained a lot more seats than needed. There was a large screen that was set up to facilitate a teleconference for those who couldn't make it. The president would stand at the podium with the cameras facing him.

This wasn't going to be the typical speech making they were used to. There would be no grandstanding, no gerry-mandering. Everything the president would say would have to be done in pieces to allow the translators to do their job.

He immediately met fierce resistance to the document. The comments were biting at times. They were somewhat repetitive.

"Why don't we just give them a slice of our country?"

Some were more realistic such as, "We have many world funds. We could easily afford to buy them off with perhaps a billion US dollars."

"I have told all of you money is not one of their main interests. The USA will take care of any funding. The problem is their safety."

The more totalitarian nations were more adamant about that. Their thrust was, "We have defectors all over the world. If any of these people are from my country, they are considered criminals and must be extradited."

That's where the president drew the line. His usual mild manner turned fiery.

"You all know extradition is out of the question. If they are jailed, it will be in the USA. If we get an agreement, they will be freed in the USA. If any other nation sends what we determine are hit squads in our country, they will be immediately arrested and we will start closing consulates."

He knew he needed to continue because it became obvious the saber-rattling was affecting the attendees.

"It seems some of my friends here have forgotten the immense power these people have. They demonstrated it twice. I think it's a small price to pay."

He expected the response that came.

"We have never given in to peace as a result of threats. That's a very dangerous business. It also sets a bad precedent."

The president finally had some of the allies speak up.

"Most of those situations have involved the desire for

national sovereignty. This is different. I can't believe we're ever going to meet a situation like this again."

"What about the people involved with the polar predicaments? It seems this will just repeat itself."

"I have been assured that those located in the USA have instructed their worldwide counterparts to abandon their projects and dispose of their assets. It's your choice if you want to pursue anything that runs contrary to your laws on your soil. I, personally would leave it alone as it may have no effect."

Then came the question the president couldn't avoid.

"How do we know the money you provide them won't be used to destabilize our country? They could try to overthrow their former governments."

"The short answer is we don't know. If it is acceptable, we can put that as one of our stipulations. They just need to be protected from reprisal from some of the more fanatical governments."

"We are not fanatics. We get our authority from our deity."

"I apologize if I offended you. Please understand these people have given us no indication that their individual beliefs translate to a major upheaval. They have not given us any indication of political, religious, or any other extreme belief."

Unfortunately, questions and petty squabbling were getting out of hand. The president felt it best to start winding things down.

"I have to remind everyone that diplomacy normally

takes months and years. I don't have that luxury. There must be a speedy decision. I have no illusions about getting 100% agreement. Today, all I want is one of three answers from each of you: we will sign the document, we will not sign the document, we will take it back to our head of state and give you an answer within twenty-four hours."

Aids passed out pens and papers with the three answers. Attendees were instructed to fill in their country's name and circle one answer.

"For those who will sign now, please bring your copy up-front with your signature, title, and country you represent."

There were a few stray comments especially directed towards USA policy. The president had a good answer.

"What guarantee will you give us that they will stay with you and never return to our nation?"

"We're ahead of you on this. That's already on our list. These are intelligent people. They know any defiance from these requests will be like signing their own death warrant."

A bunch of countries saw no reason not to sign. The USA was assuming the responsibility of any future recurrence of the individuals already. They acknowledged that their participation would be looked at kindly by the subject people. They felt a signature might possibly avoid a conflagration in their own country if things were to get out of hand in the future.

It was a surprise there were so many signatures as more than half signed before leaving the meeting. Another quarter of the nations assured the president that their signature would be forthcoming before the twenty-four-hour deadline. They just required the head of state to execute anything this important. The most important signatures were those received by all nuclear powers, friend and foe alike.

After everyone was safely out of the compound, the president made a beeline to the building where he met with his advisors. He went up to the same floor as the prior meeting and stopped in an office. Seated there was none other than the phantom.

"You heard?"

"Every word."

"I'm shocked so many agreed with this document. I hope the mountain people accept it as enough."

"Believe me, they will be as happy as a pig in doodoo. Your acceptance is first and foremost."

"What about all those requested stipulations?"

"They're nothing. That voice couldn't care less about the various nation's internal laws. Their hidden identity is what matters most. If you're a man of honor, you'll give them that chance to integrate back into a society free from those dystopian nations they came from."

"It'll be tricky since their signature will be their new identity. We won't be able to execute that until after their release."

The phantom said, "They won't renege. Anyone who does, just remind them that you will release their identity to their former country. You'll see an immediate signature."

"I've decided to sign their request. Special accommodations have already been made to siphon the witness protection similarities resources. They will have job offers waiting.

We could probably use those brains with government work if they want. It will only be a matter of their agreeing to our requests."

"I trust the military will be nowhere near the reservation?"

"I've taken care of that. There will be a couple of greeters by that mountain who'll direct them to the buses. We will also honor that agreement regarding the lack of debriefing."

"It sounds like you have it all covered."

The president said, "We even have their new names and biographies ready. Their social security numbers will have to match their approximate ages, but we've freed up so many, that it shouldn't be a problem."

"What did you do with their living areas?"

"They will be spread out all over the country. They won't get anything fancy, but it will be a decent home. The money they get will be the same as the formal witness program."

"What about their real records? They need to be safeguarded."

"I'll have those or at least what little we know. I'd like you to keep a copy of their vital statistics and their new information. I need someone outside the government to have this in case we have an internal problem."

For unknown reasons, the phantom wanted to get this information as quickly as possible. The president thought that was no problem.

"I've decided to personally greet them at the processing center where they'll get their new lives. They'll be taken there right after they surrender, so to speak. You go there and I'll make sure they have a copy waiting for you. You'll be referred to as a courier. I'll be there. If there are any problems, we just won't speak."

"You'll give them a little pep talk? I love the idea. I don't think you'll regret it."

The phantom still had reservations about the plans for the voice. The president was evasive when speaking about him. He knew that any decision to do away with the main person in this whole affair could provoke the world into a fiery, destructive war.

CHAPTER 25

It may have taken a few days, but it was worth it. Jim's car was speeding. His heart was racing. He finally had some news for the voice. It was much earlier in the day than he was scheduled to talk—a time when most people are just having breakfast.

Jim screeched to a halt on the side of the road. He walked to his usual path carrying an attaché case. When he hurried through the forest, Jim sensed his sometimes friendly voice knew he was there. It was just an intuition.

Jim was impatiently waiting for his communication to be answered. It buzzed a lot more than usual. Could something be wrong?

When the call was answered, it wasn't the voice and it wasn't Ani. It was Alex.

"Where's my contact?"

"He isn't available. If you would like to wait, he'll speak with you shortly."

"What about Ani. Can I speak with her?"

"She's not available either."

Jim began to worry. Something didn't smell just right. He wanted to find out about her right away.

"Is she ok? I mean, is she sick or has something happened to her?"

"To my knowledge, she is in good health. I wouldn't worry."

"I have some very good news for your friend."

That was a relief for Jim. He didn't want to find another fly in the ointment. Any harm coming to Ani could torpedo the whole deal.

Jim just decided to sit and wait. Even though nobody was around, he clutched the handle of the attaché tightly. Old habits are difficult to break.

He started hearing a rustling noise in the forest. It being too thick, he couldn't see anything. He was praying it wasn't a bear. His head reared back as he saw a human figure walking towards him.

A man exited the forest carrying two glasses.

"You look thirsty. How about a cold lemonade?"

Jim didn't know what to say or do. He just gathered himself and took the glass.

"Strychnine or arsenic?"

"You're so melodramatic. You want me to taste it first?"

"That's ok."

"Perhaps I should introduce myself. My name is Bret and I'm the voice you've been talking to all this time."

"Aren't you afraid we'll find out your real identity."

"Go ahead and try. You'll find nothing about me."

"What about the glass? Fingerprints?"

"That'll do you no good either. You're welcome to take the glass as a souvenir."

"I forgot my manners. It's really nice to finally meet you."

"Likewise. I see you have something for me."

"Before we get into that, where's Ani?"

"She's safe and making wisecracks as usual."

"Bret, why don't you just release her now."

"Jim, do you believe in dreams coming true?"

"I never thought about it much."

"Well, I do and I had a heck of a nightmare. All my people were massacred because I was premature."

"So you're not letting her go?"

"It won't happen yet, but it will be soon. I've been honest with you all the time. When she leaves here and gets back to civilization, Ani will be safe and sound."

That brought a smile to Jim's face. He never gave a thought to the cryptic comment. He couldn't believe he was talking to his primary adversary and they were conversing like two old friends. They sat on two large boulders next to the box.

"I was wondering about something. How did you pull off doing this on a reservation? It almost cost me my job."

"The simple answer is, we did a lot more for these people than the government ever did. We were essentially invited."

"You don't want to give me details of your operation, do you?"

"Come on. You know better than to ask me that. You can direct those questions to Ani."

Jim opened his case and showed the contents to Bret. There were signed papers, CDs, and flash drives. The main stack of papers were separated from a few pages via a partition. That would take a lot more time than examining the stack that was three inches thick.

"The good news is the president's signature is on your request and it has been notarized with a government seal."

"I sense some bad news coming."

"It's two things. We couldn't get all the countries of the world to sign this. You can appreciate that's next to impossible. We did, however, get all the major powers on board. A lot of less significant nations are there too. Everything you wanted will be done for you and your friends the same day you leave."

"What's the second problem?"

"I have a list of stipulations. Like your document, this list is non-negotiable."

Bret started looking at a cover page listing the nations that are included and those excluded. He said they looked pretty good on the surface.

He then started looking at the requests form the other side. He tilted his head and shrugged his shoulders.

"On the surface, I think this is doable. I still have to pass it by my people. I'm pretty sure we can work with this. I'm assuming you want them to sign this when they're sworn in as citizens with new identities?"

"That's the plan."

"You understand everyone has to thoroughly read what's being signed and compare it to this original."

"Of course. We can have a lawyer present and assigned to all of you."

"I don't think that's necessary."

"I suppose I should get going."

They got up and Bret started walking with Jim on the path to the road. Jim hesitated and was actually concerned for Bret.

"You know you could be ambushed. You better go."

"We constantly monitor everything. Remember your military charade? The forest is clear, as is the road for several miles each way."

"I should have known you're precise about everything."

As Jim was leaving with his car, they both waved to each other. While Bret was walking back, he was thinking about the talk he just had. Bret sometimes had a habit of speaking to himself.

"They bought that business about the countries of the world. Nobody's going to leave the good, old USA."

He was confident that no one had ever had their new identity in this program blown, except for a couple who outed themselves.

The demands from the other side would be easy to convince his people to go along with. That requirement regarding foreign governments and staying in the USA would be child's play. None of them wanted to leave. If people wanted a vacation, there're so many beautiful and entertaining places in this country, they could find it all here.

Ani was waiting by the entrance. He nodded, put his thumb up, and smiled. Together, they trotted to the conference room.

This time it was overcrowded because the children were there. They all waited with bated breath. Bret was shocked.

They all started clapping in a show of their appreciation for everything he did for them.

"Well folks, we did it."

There were screams, hugging, and crying. Some of the women ran up to Bret and kissed him on the cheek.

"Settle down everyone. There's a few kickers here."

It was suddenly noiseless. Everyone had gone mute. They knew it wouldn't be a walk in the park.

"I hope no one has any second thoughts about staying in this country. We didn't get all the countries on board, but the president gave us everything we asked for. Also remember, nobody has ever had their identity blown in the program, unless their brain was the size of a pea. I want you to appreciate the great favor this nation is doing for us."

The cheers erupted again. Bret held up his hand for silence.

"They're asking everyone to sign a bunch of requirements. I've looked them over. There's nothing there that will change your lives, but I'll go over them one by one. Now's your last chance to object."

As he read each one, there was unanimous approval. When he was done, he had one last comment.

"In the next few days, we will be forced to leave our home. It isn't much and it's a bit claustrophobic, but I've come to love it like any other home. Just recognize the fact that this is that price we have to pay for liberty. See you all later."

There were some sniffles and tissues were drawn. As each person filed out, Bret received hugs, kisses, handshakes, and other symbols of appreciation. Even the children did their part.

The child that was once a problem held all the children back. He waited for the adults to leave except for Bret. He then waved his hand in the air and the children spoke in unison.

"We love you Bret and we'll never forget you."

It was Bret's turn as the tears started rolling down his face. They all hugged and kissed him before they left.

Ani was waiting in the hall. Bret grabbed her hand and they started walking. He escorted Ani to her room. Ani wondered what the schedule would be for the rest of the day.

"Got anything planned?"

"I suppose we're entitled to a celebration or something like that. Relax a bit, I'll be back."

As Bret walked through the halls, he was saddened to see the labs sitting idle as people started getting ready to destroy records. They would start making plans for their unknown future.

It was a bit later that Bret was walking down the hall carrying a wash bucket. He was holding it by the handle as it appeared to be a bit heavy. There was a towel draped over the top. He reached Ani's door and knocked.

"Room service, mademoiselle."

"You may enter, monsieur."

Ani looked at the bucket and started laughing.

"If you came to wash my floor, you forgot your mop."

"I always forget something. Since I have no mop, how about we go on a picnic?"

"There are no public parks around. You mean by the box next to the forest?"

"I know a better place."

"I'm guessing it's another one of those rooms you forgot to tell me about."

"Nope. Let's take a walk. You'll see."

They took the elevator to the top floor. At the end of the hall, they made a right turn and there was a heavy door, much thicker than the other doors. Since this was a remote part of the operation, Ani hadn't had occasion to see this.

Bret opened it and there was an unfinished area. It was a cave that they never developed. He gave her a flashlight.

They started walking. Ani noticed some white paint marks on the walls every time they came to a fork.

"Are those directions?"

"Exactly. They mark the way to an emergency exit in case of fire or another calamity. There's one I don't know about that Red Hawk uses."

They could have easily gotten lost if it weren't for the marks. They came to a fork where Bret diverted from his route.

"Aren't we supposed to go the other way?"

"Red Hawk has his secret passage and I have mine."

After a few turns, Ani noticed a light in the distance. They kept getting nearer. It was obvious that this was some sort of way to get to the outside.

They got to the end and Ani was astonished. There was a steep drop on one side and a small field on the other surrounded by the mountain. It was very private and had incredible views. Facing out, one could see two extremely high waterfalls.

"This place is incredible. It's so private."

"Have a seat on the grass. There's no insects at this altitude. We don't need a blanket."

They sat and Bret uncovered the bucket. There were sandwiches and wine.

Ani grabbed the wine and read the label.

"Romanée-Conti? Are you kidding me? This bottle is worth at least ten grand! You even remembered red wine glasses."

"How did you learn so much about wine?"

"The academy had specialized programs. We were going to be put in situations where we needed to be semi-experts. We had to choose a few and this was one I chose. I guess I'm an oenophile."

"Sorry about the bucket and the food. It's the best I could do on such short notice."

They ate and drank everything there. A half bottle each made them feel no pain. Ani laid on her back. Her eyes were closed and she wore the widest grin.

"What are you thinking?"

"Oh, it's just the first time in my life I've been really happy. I can't describe what it feels like to be part of this."

Since nothing lasts forever, the grin suddenly disappeared from her face. Bret noticed something was wrong. He wanted to know.

"I always think something bad will happen. I'm not usually that lucky. I'm worried about them. They've all become my friends, even the ice queen."

"They'll do just fine. They're promised jobs and a place to live."

"What about Henry? He can't survive on his own."

"He can't come with me. He wouldn't make it. He's become very close to Alex, Lana, and the kids. They promised to take him."

"It would be a burden for them."

"They're close to being saints. They'll never throw him in the garbage."

"He's so different than everyone else here. Where did he come from?"

"I knew him as a child."

Bret's adoptive parents were poor but they scraped up enough money to take vacations in the country. They thought the fresh air would be good for everyone. They could afford a house there which was really closer to a shack.

The area was sparsely populated and the shack cost little to rent. Bret was so unspoiled that he just liked to wander around. He spent most days exploring the forest.

The closest house was down the road a ways. Bret would walk and see this youngish man sweeping and cleaning up. It turned out to be Henry. The widow who lived there gave Henry a room and board in exchange for doing some menial duties.

Every day, Bret would stop by and they would talk a bit. Even with his mental limitations, Henry was able to teach Bret simple things in life. Bret never understood when Henry would start speaking like a college professor once in a while. It didn't matter as Bret had deep respect and affection for him.

As time flew by, Bret's parents stopped going there. For many years, he thought he wouldn't see Henry again.

During one of his jaunts, Bret decided to go back to that area of his childhood. If nothing else, he wanted to say hello to Henry once again.

He drove to the neighborhood. Although dilapidated, the shack where he stayed was still there. When he drove further, his car skidded to a halt.

In front of him, stood the ruins of a house that was completely burned. He raced from the car and looked around with a pounding heart. There was nothing remotely salvageable. He thought the worst.

Bret continued driving to the next neighbor who was quite some distance away. An older woman was sitting on the porch. Bret jumped out of the car and strolled along her walkway.

Before he even made it to the steps, she reached over and patted the seat next to her, inviting him to sit. She had a friendly demeanor.

"Sorry to bother you, but that house down the road."

"It went up in flames. Gas leak or something. What a shame."

"It's not being replaced?"

"Not for now. The widow took the insurance money and moved on."

"What about the man who lived with her, Henry?"

"Yes, the retarded man … We saw him rummaging

through the rubble. He took some linens, tools, and a shovel and disappeared into the forest."

"He's still there?"

"I think so. Some of us put a garbage can near the front. We leave food in there for him and keep the lid tight so animals don't get at it. Every morning the garbage is neatly wrapped and left for us to take away."

"I knew him when I was a child. We rented the old shack down the road."

"I think I remember you. Ned or Ted or something."

"I'm Bret."

"Oh, that's right."

"So Henry is surviving. I hope he knows how."

"Funny thing about him, he could talk like a smart man sometimes."

"I wonder why."

"He wandered here one day. Nobody knew where he came from. I heard he was an engineer or something. There was an accident. He lost part of his leg and it really scrambled his eggs."

The engineer part piqued Bret's memory. He recalled Henry building a little footbridge over a stream in the yard. Bret asked why the bridge wouldn't collapse if he stepped on it. Henry said, "Material resistance."

Bret didn't understand the words, but never forgot them. When he was older, he looked up the terminology. It means something about the forces in a bridge. It was listed as one of the most difficult mathematical and physics courses a structural engineer had to take. Henry was a real brain at one time.

Bret thanked her and drove to the forest. He wanted to see if Henry was still alive.

Walking a ways, he didn't see much except a few scraps of paper. When he got near his one-time favorite pond, he saw a makeshift tent. There was nobody around. He noticed the way it was braced took a specific type of knowledge. He also saw a trench dug inside. The military taught that so one could protect himself from the elements.

Bret sat near the remains of a campfire. After a few minutes, he heard a familiar uneven gait. He looked up and Henry was staring at him.

"What you want?"

"I was looking for you."

"What you need me for?"

"I'm the boy who spent summers here many years ago. I'm Bret."

"Bret?"

"Think Henry, think."

Henry was thinking and then he broke out in a smile.

"Yes, yes, Bret. You the boy who always talk to me—a very good boy."

"Why do you live here?"

"Don't wanna hurt no more."

"How about you come with me?"

"No. Don't wanna hurt no more."

This discussion would go in circles for a while. Bret tried to say how bad it was where Henry was living and Henry kept giving him the same answer. Bret finally tried it a different way.

"What if I told you there's a place with friendly people. Everyone would like you. You would have a bed and food. Most of all, there would be no fires."

"Sound good, but nobody want me. Nobody love me."

"Well, I do. Have I ever lied to you?"

"No, you good boy."

"You're coming with me, even if I have to carry you."

"Promise if I don't like, I can come back here."

They left and Henry would never come back.

"That's how Henry made it to the mountain, Ani."

"What a sad and beautiful story."

With that, they both fell asleep on the grass. The wine helped them sleep the entire afternoon and evening. This was actually something they needed. Later, Ani poked Bret.

"You know it's the middle of the night?"

"It's ok."

"I think we just wrecked our body clocks. We won't be able to sleep at night for a while. We'll want to snooze all day."

"Actually that's a good thing. When we leave here, we'll be up all night. You'll have to catch a long nap that afternoon."

Since it was getting chilly, they knew it was time to head inside.

"Hey, don't throw out that bottle. I may never get to drink that stuff again. I want to soak it and save the label."

Bret said he would make sure Henry did exactly what she asked. Ani didn't know his planned destination had more of it.

CHAPTER 26

This was the penultimate day for anyone to live inside the mountain. After tomorrow, the only thing the interior would be good for was echoes. Everybody, including the children, were making final preparations to leave their home forever.

When Jim showed up, he anxiously waited for the final acceptance, rejection, or modification of the demands from the government. Today, Bret answered from inside.

"I've gotten verbal approval from the folks regarding all of your requests."

"I trust you reminded them any violation by even one person will result in the whole group getting it right between the eyes."

"They know the stakes. I don't think there's an individual who has any reason for that, unless the government reneges. We both know what that would mean."

"The buses will be ready right after dawn. If things work out, we should have them processed before the end of the day."

"They'll start coming out after breakfast. I think business at this location will be closed by noon."

"Before I forget, there'll be someone with me to expedite the process here. Don't worry, he'll be in civilian clothes."

Ever suspicious, Ani wanted to know who he or she was. She was really doing this to aid the people who were also her friends.

"Who is this? I don't want any surprises as long as my butt is going to be on the line."

"It's someone you know very well. Jeff from the agency."

"Ok, I'll explain it to Bret."

Ani told him that Jeff was in the same section as she. This was a different area than Jim and Billy. It seemed they wanted to keep this within the agency to stymie leaks.

When everything ended, Jim left with "see you tomorrow."

Lately, Bret had become less definite. He still made it sound reasonable to not arouse suspicion.

"See you around."

Bret made his own final preparations. He took Ani back to the photo lab, opened a drawer there and pulled out some items that looked official.

When he handed them to Ani, she started looking at them. She saw that they were her new forms of ID. There was a driver's license, memberships in a few clubs, and a booklet.

"Whoa. Wait a minute. A phony passport? If they catch us with these, they'll lock us up and throw away the key."

"Who said anything about it being phony?"

Naturally, Ani was bewildered. It wasn't her passport, so how could it not be phony?

"I better explain. I have a passport from the same country. If you look closely, you'll notice it's a diplomatic passport. It is real as any other."

"But how?"

"I can see you were only in domestic counterintelligence. Many of the smaller countries have economies ready to go belly-up. If you give a large enough contribution aka aid, you'll be given citizenship and diplomatic status."

"Don't the power people just steal the money?"

"You once told me, regarding those responsible for doing away with that pedophile orphanage director you don't question people like that. This happens in all walks of life."

"I get it. So what happens if we ever leave this country and customs questions us?"

"They can't. They can't even search us. The most they can do is deport us. Even if they contact this issuing nation, there will be a record of us as part of the diplomatic corps. It's all very neat and 100% legal."

"I guess it's all ok, except that horrible picture of me."

When they left, they stopped at Bret's room. He grabbed two backpacks and gave one to Ani.

"Go pack any essentials you can fit. I already put some snacks and water in yours."

Ani looked through the bag and noticed something strange. She felt a heavy metal object.

"A gun?"

"You do know how to use it, don't you?"

"I could pick my teeth with it. But why?"

"You have to be prepared for anything. You'll see

throughout the day tomorrow. Your flashlight has enough juice and extra batteries."

It was time for Bret to leave and start saying goodbye to each person individually. He advised Ani to sleep as much as possible since they would be leaving right after sundown.

Ani was sitting in her room reading a book. She finished packing her essentials including the small disguise kit that Dina had given her. She heard some footsteps outside her door and a knock.

"May I come in?"

When the door opened, it was Lana who entered. Ani was shocked, to say the least. Lana's eyes were puffy and red as if she had been weeping. She said Bret just told her goodbye.

Lana stood within a couple of feet of Ani but now said nothing. They were staring at each other in silence. It was extremely uncomfortable.

Lana suddenly lunged at Ani, grabbed her upper arms, and pulled her close. She kissed Ani on the cheek and whispered in her ear.

"Please take care of my lovely, dearest Bret."

They released and Lana wiped her eyes and nose. For the first time since they met, Lana actually smiled at Ani. Ani had hoped this day would come and they could be real friends.

"I think I understand. Don't worry. It will remain our secret forever."

Lana lost her smile and said, "Good."

As Lana was walking out the door, she stopped while

straddling the threshold. She turned her back towards Ani.

"I think we'll not see each other again."

She closed the door behind her and walked away like the good soldier she was.

After Bret said his goodbyes, he grabbed a nap. Ani had also been sleeping. When the sun fell from the sky, Bret went to Ani's room.

"Did you get any rest?"

"A few hours."

"It's time, young lady."

"You sound like the warden being ready to escort me to the electric chair. Where's the priest?"

"If things work out, it might actually be a fun adventure for you."

"I'm pumped."

They went up to the top floor and made their way to the same door that they used for the picnic. They retraced their steps, only their walk was much further. They went far away from any of the white-painted marks and were descending very steeply. They went down quite a few stories.

"It's spooky here. I'm waiting for the bats."

"I've never seen any. We'll come to a stopping point pretty soon."

They reached the point of an almost vertical drop. There were about a dozen large cans of oil as well as a heavy rubber box that resembled a life raft attached to a power winch.

"We're going down there?"

"We could climb down, but it's a little too steep, making it dangerous. We'll line the side and bottom of the rocks and dirt with oil to make the rough ride a bit smoother."

They started descending. The ride was quite bumpy and reeked of oil. After an additional several stories, they landed softly. Bret cut the line and destroyed the craft.

"We can walk ahead for a bit. There'll be a sharp turn and after that, you won't need your flashlight for now."

"That's weird. I was pretty sure we were far underground and it's almost pitch black out."

"You'll see."

They turned the corner and saw a blue lighted exit in front of them. They walked through and Ani stopped. She laughed and slapped the side of her head.

"Of course! That's the one thing I never thought of."

After a few feet of rock, there was a fairly wide body of flowing water. Sitting there was a docked submarine. There was a bright blue light emanating from the water. It was that way as far as they could see.

"What's up with that lighted water?"

"It's bioluminescent algae. They're usually found in saltwater, so I have no idea how they got here."

Bret stowed the backpacks in front of the seats which were in the middle. The engines were behind in the rear. They boarded and sat up top because the ceiling was pretty high.

"It's a little cramped, but it's set up so we can sit side by side."

"There's something unusual about this tub. Tell me about it."

"I will as soon as we get into open water. Let's get going."

They started moving in the plenty wide waterway. Ani noticed the engines were almost completely silent. She figured they were electric.

The beauty they passed was just as breathtaking as any outdoor scenery. The blue light flickering off the stalactites and stalagmites gave a rainbow effect. It was almost like a strobe.

It was a longer ride than Ani expected. They were riding for about an hour and Ani pointed up.

"The ceiling is getting lower."

"Yes, we'll have to submerge."

They sat inside and secured the top. Bret was constantly looking at the instruments.

"How can you avoid hitting the side if you can't see?"

"It's no different than any sonar. I could put it on auto-pilot but I'll wait until we're free of this place."

They rode for another hour. Bret was almost positive they went so many miles, they cleared any military perimeter.

"We're going to hit the river now. It's wide and deep. You'll feel a surge when we get into the current."

The current jolted their heads back and the increased speed was easy to feel.

"They won't see us. It's very dark tonight. We can stay close to the surface and use the periscope. It slides to either side and has night vision."

"That's a skinny scope."

"It's the same type used in the Middle East for peering around corners when the soldiers are looking for terrorists."

"Is it my imagination or are we moving really fast?"

"No, it's actually happening. I put electric car engines in this old tub, as you call it. This might be the fastest sub in the world, especially with the strong current in our favor. With the spare engines, we can go ten to twelve hours at full speed. It's just about as fast as a car. I'll put it on auto for now, but you can steer later if you like."

"I'd love that."

"By the way, I never asked you what that coded message was in that fake fight you had with Jim."

"You mean when you thought I was nuts? I just let them know I didn't trust you and I would escape the night before the end."

"Wouldn't Jim understand it?"

"No, it goes right to that guy, Jeff. He's one of my superiors and we work in a different unit than Jim. He collects data; we do the spying."

"Aren't they looking for you now?"

"Not where I told them I was going."

Ani had known routes where she could escape. They knew she had to go a back way so she wouldn't be chased.

"I told them the north country."

"That's pretty dangerous."

"That's why I sent that message. Tomorrow they'll search for me and keep searching for a few days. They'll get tired of it, thinking I got killed by a bear or fell down a ravine."

"You really think they'll give up?"

"Sure, why not. I have no family. They'll just delete my records and poof, no more Ani."

"Sugar, you're so resourceful."

"No more than you, baby."

After a couple of hours, they raised the periscope. They both took turns. Ani was really excited.

"Look, there's a couple of deer."

"Anything else up there?"

"Not a thing—no aircraft, no civilization, no nothing."

"We're getting near our destination. In about an hour, we can sit up top for the remainder."

"I can't tell, but it seems we've gone really far."

"We've crossed three states already and the end isn't close."

They came to a point where they could surface. Ani had gotten her thrills driving the tub. When they released the top, it was quiet as a mouse. One could barely hear the engines and the force of the propellers.

"It's so quiet and romantic. If it wasn't for the excitement and tension, I'd say we should camp out."

"I'm afraid we'll have to leave it for another time."

They started slowing as Bret pointed to a small clearing ahead on the right. It was only a few feet and after that was a dense forest. They docked against the dirt.

"Last stop, everybody off."

Bret unloaded the backpacks and a few extra survival supplies. Ani wondered whether this was just a stop or if they were really moving on, and what about the sub?

Bret took one of his many remotes and started the sub. They watched from the shore as he drove it to the middle of the river.

Two whines were heard for a few seconds. Those were

anchors. He hit a switch and two muffled explosions could be heard. Bret had scuttled the sub.

"Is it deep enough?"

"It's at least thirty feet. Nobody will find in for maybe 100 years."

They turned and Bret pointed towards the woods.

"Are you up for a hike?"

"I can absolutely keep up with you. How far?"

"Should be about ten miles."

They started walking using their flashlights. They made sure they were attentive to any sounds. If they heard anything, they would kill the lights even though they were dim night vision lights. Their guns were sticking out of their belts with chambered bullets. They had to be ready because this was wild country with wolves, coyotes, bears, and mountain lions.

"We've gone about halfway. How about we take a break, sugar?"

"If you're tired, ok. Let's just sit."

"We'll be traveling through the morning. I know you're in good shape, but I'm always worried about you."

They rose and walked again. They finally arrived at a clearing. They couldn't go any further. The clearing ended at a mountain lake.

"Do we have to swim now?"

"Just watch."

A motorized platform started moving from the woods into the clearing. It was difficult to see at night. There was a camouflage tarp covering it and its contents.

"The trees are so thick, even a satellite photo won't pick this up."

Bret uncovered the platform and it was hiding a helicopter. He straightened out the blades and checked it over.

"Does this thing really fly?"

"It better. I took it up last week and serviced it. Believe me, it flies like a dream."

"If you want me up in that thing, it better fly like a wet dream."

Once they were up, Bret hovered not too far from the ground. He directed the platform to drive straight into the lake.

"It's so heavy and low, it'll nicely be covered by water."

They flew away. The route was through a ravine between mountains. He made sure his altitude was low so no radar could pick them up.

Bret said, "Does it scare you to fly this low?"

"I'm assuming you've taken this route before."

"As we get towards morning, there'll be a lot of air traffic so we can go higher and blend in."

They started approaching a small airport and dawn was only a short time away.

"Is this the end?"

"Not nearly."

They landed smoothly in a field near the runway and started walking. Bret pointed to a small jet and said they would be taking that.

"What happens to the copter?"

"It's sold. The new owner will take it today."

"Take it where?"

"He'll try to get it out of the country. If he anticipates any border problems, he'll just part it out. The individual parts are probably worth more than this big old machine anyway."

They boarded the jet and took off. They weren't flying long when daybreak made its appearance.

They were flying for a few hours when Ani queried Bret for a hint.

"We're going to stay with Essi. She's really nice."

Ani looked at Bret with a tinge of jealousy.

"And exactly who is Essi?"

"I've known her for a long time. Believe me, you'll like her. We'll be flying for a few hours. Get some sleep."

Everything within the flight rules and regulations was legal now. They had free contact with any tower and the jet was registered to a third party. Bret even filed a flight plan.

The sun was shining bright when most people were having breakfast in this time zone. Short of engine trouble, things should go smoothly. Both Bret and Ani were confident the government wouldn't be looking where they were nor would they ever.

Still in all, Bret knew this was just the beginning. Erasing the trail would take a lot more doing. He hoped Ani would be up to the task and not tire of him. Essi would provide them with a temporary hideout.

CHAPTER 27

While Bret and Ani were cruising in their jet, Jim arrived at the reservation. Right after dawn. He was accompanied by Jeff in the same car. They were trailed by two buses. The drivers wore civilian clothes.

"I know we're early, but we can wait by the box where I had communications."

"The fog is so dense I can't see past the first tree."

"It's ok. I've taken this walk so many times I could do it blindfolded."

They left their car and Jim directed the buses to park along the side of the road near him. He wanted the doors on his side of the road since there was heavy fog and crossing the road would be a danger to the children.

They started walking through the path. The trees were close on both sides. Well before they got to the box and point of contact, they heard some rustling in the trees on both sides. It seemed unusual as the wind was calm. Jim determined those were either animals or humans. He decided to stop and look around.

"That's so strange. They weren't scheduled to leave yet."

"If these are humans, are you sure they're those who are

coming with us?"

"Right now, I'm not sure of anything."

Jim called out, "Hello?"

A human figure got closer. As he became visible, Jim and Jeff were both shocked.

The man was wearing camo fatigues and carrying an automatic rifle. He was accompanied by a large, mixed-breed dog.

"What the … what's going on here? Who are you?"

"My name is unimportant. This is our land. We can dress and patrol it as we like."

"You must know my business here."

"I do. Those are our friends who live there. Unlike you and your military, they were invited."

"I have peaceful intentions. They are just going to be evacuated. Do you understand?"

"I understand my people have been lied to for over 150 years. Our men are here to make sure that doesn't happen in this case. We're here to protect our friends from any nonsense."

"We don't carry any arms and there are unarmed civilians on the bus. What good does it do after we leave your territory anyway?"

"Yes, you can do terrible things later. Our duty is to protect our friends while they exist on our land. After that, our conscience is clear."

The three men started walking together. They passed quite a few men dressed the same way. They were given an icy stare that would send chills up a person's body. Even the dog didn't have a pleasant look.

"How many guns do you have pointed at just two men?"

"We haven't even chambered any bullets—yet. For now, there's just about 100. If you force us to fight, we can quickly deploy 2000 more."

"I don't understand. Are you looking for a fight? I had to jump through hoops to negotiate a peaceful end to this."

"Let's just say I don't like surprises while on my land. The men are trained well enough. They won't do anything bad, if not provoked."

They finally reached the box where they would meet the former residents of the mountain. The man with the gun stepped back.

"I will walk away now so you can speak to the people comfortably. I'll be out of sight, but know well, I will be watching from a short distance."

What Jim and Jeff didn't realize was the retreat had nothing to do with comfort. The armed man didn't want to be recognized by anyone leaving the mountain, especially the children. The man was Red Hawk.

Jim and Jeff waited patiently. The fog was thicker than ever. Then they heard the distant sound of twigs cracking. If it wasn't the armed men, it was assuredly the beginning of the exodus.

As the sounds got louder, faint visions appeared in the fog. Jim could only think of a typical zombie movie where images would come from the fog and attack normal humans.

The first person to appear was Dina. Jim did do all the welcoming.

"Welcome back to civilization, pretty lady."

"Do you really think I'm pretty?"

"You're not pretty, you're gorgeous. Just follow the path I'm pointing to and you can make yourself at home on the bus. There's a cooler and cold drinks in the rear."

Dina bounced along thinking this was the first time in years someone paid her a compliment. She said to herself, "I wonder if he's married."

Other singles were coming out as well as couples. Jim was surprised at the number of couples emerging with children. He was overjoyed that the children would live to see another day.

One small girl, who was little more than a toddler, ran ahead of her single mother and jumped on Jim. She squeezed him tightly, kissed him, and whispered, "Will you be my daddy?"

Jim blushed a bit but was smiling from ear to ear. He held her in his arms, petted her back, and whispered in her ear while his eyes welled up.

"Don't ever worry, my sweetie. Nobody will ever hurt you as long as I'm alive. Somehow, I'll find you and protect you."

Jim had a premonition the night before. He envisioned a child that he would feel close to, coming to him. He always kept something with him that was very dear.

He reached in his pocket and pulled out a small gold chain with a tiny heart. He gave the piece to his child when she was an infant. She never made it to double digits.

Being a single father, Jim was crushed by her death. His

daughter was his whole life. He never got over it. This time, he felt some strange affinity towards this girl.

Her mother walked up and asked the girl not to bother the man. Jim wasted no time.

"I want her to have this. If they allow me to know your new identity, would it be ok if I called on the two of you?"

"I'd like that very much. I'm not really a criminal, you know."

"That's the furthest thing from my mind. Let's talk on the bus. My friend here can take my car back."

The boy that was once a problem and then became Ani's right hand, walked up to Jim. He shook his hand and said, "There's so much I need to learn. It would please me if you were my guide."

"We'll see, young man. I'll try."

It was incredible the way Jim was turning from a greeter to a personal friend to each person in the group. He kept looking at Jeff and Jeff just smiled and nodded his approval.

It was unrealistic for him to contact everyone. The easiest way would be to give those who wanted to be in contact his personal info except the little girl and her mother. Jim would try his best to contact them. He would fiercely guard their secret.

The short conversations made the process a little slower than anticipated. The people kept coming out. It seemed there was no end to the march.

For the first time, a larger group emerged. There were five including three adults and two children. One of the adults walked with a visible limp. It was Alex, Lana, Henry, and the children.

Alex said, "We're the last. We'd like to stay together."

"I didn't see Bret. Where is he?"

Lana asked Henry to bring the children to the bus and said they'd be along shortly. They left and the conversation continued. Alex looked a little down.

"I'm afraid Bret isn't coming."

"But I don't … he said … why not?"

"A very bad event happened. Bret committed suicide last night."

"I can't believe it. This is so awful. I just learned his name."

Jim now understood why Bret had told him his identity and fingerprints would do no good. It made sense.

"I was beginning to think of him as my friend."

Lana said, "We all lost a good man whom we won't see again."

"At least we'll do an autopsy and give him a proper burial when we go inside."

"I'm afraid you can't do that either."

"What do you mean?"

Jim was starting to look suspiciously at Alex. He didn't like what was transpiring. He knew that any deviation from what was expected would get him a tongue-lashing and might even cause his side to terminate the deal.

"All the weapons will be set off shortly in the interior. The entrances are sealed, so there is no danger to the outside. You may be able to go inside in another hundred years or so. Earlier would be fatal."

"That's dirty pool. The agreement was—"

"The agreement said nothing of the government being able to examine the contents inside. This was done with the express agreement of the owners of this land. It was their suggestion."

"You weren't supposed to detonate anything."

"The agreement was in an open-air area and exposed to the general public. Besides, after walking into a reactor, there's really not much left of Bret for you to autopsy or bury."

Jim knew there was little he could do. The president wouldn't risk a war with the reservations and he couldn't chance unleashing destructive weapons who knows where.

"I never thought this would happen."

"You believed the Native Americans would let you just walk in? Believe me, it's better for you this way."

"Ani had no clue? By the way, where is she?"

Lana said, "She escaped last night. It was quite depressing. Bret took it hard."

"I did not know about her coming out. This might even be a more serious problem. Harm coming to one of our agents would immediately invalidate the agreement."

Jeff tapped Jim on the shoulder. He motioned with his hand to walk a few steps away. It was clear, he wanted a private conversation. Jim excused himself. Jeff spoke in a quiet voice as not to be overheard.

"Don't worry about Ani. We have things under control."

"I do not know about her getting out."

"Jim, she spoke to you in a coded message. You're in a

different section, so you didn't understand it. She said exactly when and what route she would take. She went up north."

"But that's brutal country."

"She's trained in survival. The standard procedure is to get pretty far away and wait a few days in case she was followed. We'll start looking immediately upon leaving here."

"What if you don't find her?"

"It doesn't matter."

"What? I don't follow you."

"If we don't find her, it means she didn't survive. If she emerges, we'll deal with her."

"You mean as in no longer needed or eliminated? Why?"

"I'd rather not say. She outed herself by giving her real name. She should've known better. Ani knows the penalty."

"What a shame, so young."

Jim and Jeff walked back to Alex and Lana. They wanted to complete things and get going.

Alex and Lana gave one last look at their former home. While all four walked along the path, Lana was thinking about the children.

"I wonder where they're going to stick us. I hope it isn't an area with a lot of crime, you know, the children."

Jim was sympathetic. After the experience with the little girl earlier, he understood their concern.

"I wouldn't fret about it. I have some experience with this program. The accommodations are nicer than what you may think. The idea is to keep it up nicely, you have to work. Welfare is not an option. You folks impressed me as the type who's been used to working long hours your entire lives."

"I like to garden and my husband likes to make things in his spare time."

"Can I ask you something personal? It has nothing to do with the operation."

"I suppose it's ok."

"That woman with the young girl. Can you tell me something about her?"

"I can't say her name. She's a typical story. Married too young, abusive ex-husband, put herself through medical school. We all love her daughter. So sweet, so polite. Are you interested? She's an ex-model."

"I'd like to keep in contact, yes."

"My husband can stay with the kids. Let me ride with you and them. I'll see what I can do."

They got on the bus and Jim immediately took the little girl and sat her on his lap. Lana sat with her mother and spoke for a few minutes. She reached across the aisle and tapped Jim. He looked over and Lana just smiled and winked.

They exchanged seats and it was a new beginning for Jim. Before he sat, he went to the coolers in the back. Jim was searching for something. He started getting miffed when he couldn't find it, so he walked to the front to speak to the bus driver.

"There's nothing back there for a child—no straw, no sippy cup, no nothing."

"This ain't a restaurant."

"Hey, watch it, buddy."

"What do you want outta me? I'm just a driver."

"Ok, I'll tell you what I want. In a couple of miles, you're going to see an ice cream store. You're the lead bus. I want you to stop there. That kid is getting an ice cream cone, whether you like it or not."

"Don't bark at me. I'll stop."

"Better yet, I'll buy everyone on both buses ice cream, including you. Maybe it'll sweeten you up. Does that float your boat?"

"Well, I do have a weakness for ice cream."

That would be the first positive experience for the almost new citizens and hopefully not the last as they will be confirmed in a short while.

CHAPTER 28

Bret and Ani stepped onto the front walkway of Essi's house. It was a small home and pretty old. Still in all, it was well kept. The lawn was mowed and there were no weeds around the bushes.

"What do we do if she's not at home?"

"I know where the key is. She's probably there, so we can just walk in."

"You don't bother to knock?"

"No, we have a special relationship."

They walked in. The furniture was old, but it was clean as were the floors. It was easy to see a neat person lived here.

"Hello?"

A woman came darting out of the kitchen. It was Essi. Although she was older, her pretty features made her seem like she might be Bret's older sister.

After the hugs and kisses, Ani's formal introduction went well. The two women seemed to be at ease speaking with each other.

Although it was early afternoon, Essi insisted on getting dinner going. Everyone sat down with a soft drink. Essi's curiosity got the best of her.

"Have you known Bret long?"

"Not very long, but I guess long enough."

The idle chatter continued through the afternoon until dinner was ready. Although the food was delicious by any standards, Ani wasn't very hungry.

Essi noticed Ani didn't look quite right, even for a stranger. Her eyes were red and puffy. Her face looked flushed and she kept clearing her voice.

Essi got up and walked over to Ani. She said she wanted to see something. She put her hand on Ani's forehead.

"You have a fever. I bet a sore throat too."

"It hurts a little. It's not too bad."

"You're sick. Probably some kind of virus."

Bret didn't say much. He knew Essi learned a lot about natural remedies from him. He thought it would be best to let Essi take over.

"March into the bedroom, young lady."

"I think I'll be ok."

"You better listen to Essi or she'll carry you there."

By now, Ani was feeling pretty lousy. Essi stripped her and stuck her in bed.

She then got out her noxious potions. It consisted of elderberry syrup, olive leaf extract, vitamin c, homeopathic virus nosode, and some other supplements.

"Do I have to choke down all that stuff?"

"It's all-natural and harmless. Just take it. You'll be better in a couple of days."

With Ani incapacitated, Bret had a chance to do some chores. He did the shopping and some small repairs around the house.. He would check on Ani, but Essi chased him away a few times until she was sure there was nothing contagious.

Essi had the exclusive task of providing care. She brought scheduled remedies along with toast and hot tea. After the first day, Essi examined Ani after changing the sheets. She even stroked Ani's hair. The bond was quickly moving along just like with Bret.

It was quite remarkable, after a couple of days, Ani felt so much better. Essi sat at her bedside to keep her company.

"I'm amazed that junk really works. You should've been a doctor."

"Thanks, but I prefer to do other things besides play golf."

"I feel so much better, I'd like to get up."

"Maybe some fresh air would do you good. Let's sit on the back porch."

Essi grabbed a blanket for Ani and they headed for the lanai. Ani didn't think the blanket was necessary, but Essi didn't want any drafts yet. They sat outside, and the weather was beautiful. Ani partially laid back in the recliner and Essi sat with her feet up on a footstool. There was a lot Ani wanted to talk about.

"May I ask you something?"

"Sure, why not."

"Are you Bret's mom?"

"Well, yes and no."

Of course, Ani was perplexed. As it turned out, Bret came to Essi as the product of the old story about the baby on her doorstep.

"I see that ring on your finger. I assume he gave it to you. I gave it to him as a child and told him to give it to his one and only. Love is infinite and lasts for the eternity."

Essi was very young, still a teenager. It was a difficult decision, but Essi wanted to keep him. There weren't many questions asked when he went to school, so she was able to pull it off.

"What was he like? I mean as a child."

"He was always very special. He was a normal boy, things like having friends and playing sports. He did other things that set him apart from the others. For instance, other children would be playing but sometimes he chose to take food to seniors who weren't able or couldn't afford it instead of playing with the other children."

"It sounds like he was sensitive to seniors."

"He was sensitive to everyone less fortunate, but he especially felt bad for them. He wondered why they spent their life working and were abandoned in the last years."

"He has quite a heart."

"He was precocious. He'd sometimes ask uncomfortable questions like why healthy welfare people collect money and seniors can't afford a decent meal. When I told him maybe they can't get a job, he said there was help wanted signs all over town."

"He had you there. How did you handle it?"

"I just said it was politics and we shouldn't discuss this at home because it's so divisive. Anyway, as a teen, he started a garbage recycling company. That's why I say he was so special. He even helped animals."

During her last sentence, she was pointing at two large boulders in the corner of the yard. Ani asked what they had to do with anything. Essi said it's another part of Bret's moral character.

Under the first boulder was a puppy. "A local German Shepherd breeder was selling a litter. We were poor, so that was out of the question."

"There was a very sickly male puppy. The breeder was going to put him to sleep. Bret wouldn't hear of it. He begged the breeder and the pup was given free of charge. The breeder said he won't live long. Everything's wrong with him. Bret took him anyway. The poor thing only lived for a few weeks. We never even had a chance to give him a name. Bret buried him under the rock on the left. The whole first night, he wouldn't leave that rock. I could hear him crying and talking to the pup."

"That's so sad. What about the one on the right?"

"We used to take Bret to the country in the summer. It's all we could afford."

"Yes, he told me about the handicapped man he used to talk to."

"I believe his name was Henry. When they weren't talking, he'd spend all his time in the forest."

Bret mentally mapped different routes. The day came when he heard movement behind him. He turned and froze when he saw a large male German Shepard staring at him. Although its ears didn't stand, being a purebred was unmistakable. He had a one-inch bald spot on his back and a peculiar checkmark in his color pattern on top of his head.

Bret was so frightened. Was he sick? Was he vicious? Bret started to walk slowly. The shep followed him, never coming closer than a few feet. Bret would walk, so would the shep. Bret would stop, so would the shep.

Bret was still unsure, so he walked to the exit. The shep came to the edge of the forest and sadly looked at him. He wouldn't step foot out past the trees.

"We asked the neighbors. There were so few residents, they knew every dog. Nobody ever heard of him. It was like he came out of nowhere."

Bret returned almost every day and the same dog was there. The same events happened—walking, stopping, and never close enough to pet.

The day came when Bret didn't see the dog. He was by his favorite pond and playing with the frogs when he heard footsteps. He turned and two men were facing him. They wore orange jumpsuits and had chains hanging from their wrists.

Bret didn't understand they were obviously escaped prisoners. They looked menacing enough to scare him.

"Hey, kid, you got any money?"

"Please mister, don't hurt me."

"Forget it, he has no dough."

"Please, mister, don't hurt me."

"You know, he's kinda cute. Hey, kid, you wanna be nice to us?"

Bret didn't know about pedophilia either.

"Please, mister, don't hurt me."

The first convict took a step towards Bret. Suddenly, there was a low-pitched growl and a bark. That dog was out of sight. Like a flash, the shep bolted at lightning speed. He hit the convict like a truck, knocking him down. He was biting hard in several spots as the other convict ran for his life.

The bleeding one freed himself for a moment and took off. Rather than chasing him, the shep positioned himself between Bret and the no-goods with his rear pressing against Bret.

That was the day the dog left the forest. He followed Bret home. Bret made a stink about keeping him.

"Bret asked for so little, we couldn't turn him down. The dog stayed with Bret for the rest of his life. Even going to school, he was waiting for Bret the entire day. Nobody could move him."

"What was his name?"

"Bret called him Micah. He carved an inscription on his rock marker, over there."

"May I look?"

Essi nodded and Ani made her way to the bolder. As she looked at it, Essi could see from behind Ani was wiping her eyes.

The carving read BE STILL TREES, DON'T WAKE MY MICAH.

Ani came back sniffling.

"What a powerful story. You know I hardly cried at all before I met Bret. What about the rest of the family?"

"It's complicated and boring. Are you sure you want to hear it?"

"I want to know every detail, please."

Essi was widowed. She was married early and they lived barely above poverty.

"We argued a lot in front of the kids about money. That was a huge mistake."

"So you have other children."

"I'll get to that. He was a good man. He worked two jobs sometimes, trying to make ends meet. We bought this house in poor condition and we made it look nice."

"It sounds like you weren't happy."

"I guess the money pressure was too much for him. He developed other interests if you know what I mean. Except for one of them, the other women didn't mean anything to him. He resented Bret for siding with me."

"So he passed away, and that was it?"

"Not at all."

Essi never bothered to have her name included on the deed. Before he died, he changed his will and left it to his other two kids along with his sister. Bret and Essi were left nothing.

"I assume you contested it."

"Who's got money for a lawyer? Bret told me to forget it. He'd make things right."

Essi assumed she could still live there until one day she came home from shopping and all the furniture was missing. There was a FOR SALE sign on the lawn.

"I was going into the street. He left no money and I had none."

Bret knew his family would never sell him the house.

The jealousy was too deep. He easily set up a third party to buy it and transfer the deed to him.

"I was wondering how you could be in the same house from when Bret was a child. Why were the others like that?"

"I don't know. I tried to be a good mother. I sacrificed everything."

"You had to be good because of the way Bret is."

Essi's daughter was a selfish girl. She was told so many times as a child that she was a princess, she actually believed it. She married for money and used Essi for babysitting and there was little other contact. She was so selfish that on a trip to France, she made her husband fly her to Belgium just to get chocolate.

Essi tried to teach her grandchildren the right way to be. Feeling good about yourself is fine. It's not fine when you step on others to get to that point.

Essi felt it was important to have courtesy, consideration, and politeness. She saw too many times a child walking ahead of a senior with a walker and slamming the door in their face. She made it a point to teach them to respect anyone that was in authority such as parents, teachers, police, and firefighters.

The final argument started when Essi told her to turn off her cell phone. If she wanted to visit her mom, she didn't need to be constantly texting. It went downhill. Her daughter wanted no crazy ideas for the kids. She finally forbade Essi from ever seeing the children again. Her last words were, "I can't wait for the day you're euthanized. I'll pull the switch myself."

"That's horrible."

"I was so broken-hearted. It's been years. She won't accept or return my calls."

"You had another son. How was he?"

"Since he was a boy, as my New York friends would say, he just didn't get it. He was spoiled more than the girl. Bret called him an amoeba … he would just open his mouth and you people would stick money and food there."

He only thought of partying. No matter what Essi taught him, he would do the opposite. He's been arrested so many times—forgery, grand larceny, selling imitation watches with the designer name on them—the list goes on and on.

"Does he make money?"

"He has a job. They gave him a title and pay him nothing. Most of his money goes to the bookie for gambling."

"How does he live?"

"I used to give him food and money."

Every time he visited Essi, he parked and opened his trunk. He expected her to fill it with groceries and give him an envelope. There were times Essi lost a lot of weight because she couldn't afford food for herself.

"Where was Bret?"

"He was away. I didn't tell him. He came home often, but I was self-conscious about taking so much from him. I told him I was dieting."

"I didn't know people like this existed."

"It got so ridiculous. Bret threw me a birthday party. Of course, he paid for everything because they refused to contribute. For my other son to show up, I had to drive two hours to pick him up and the same after it was over."

"You had to chauffeur him for your own party? Geez."

The end came soon after. Essi finally understood she wouldn't be around forever and he had to learn to stand on his own two feet. Essi broke the news to him and he flew into a rage. He started beating her. He knocked her down and kicked her. Essi was screaming, "Please have mercy!" All he said was he didn't need her anymore. It was to no avail. Like his sister, it'd been years and he wouldn't return or answer her calls.

"What did the police say?"

"I didn't tell them. I went to the hospital and said I fell down the stairs."

"And Bret?"

"I could never tell him and don't you say anything either. He might kill him."

By then, Ani was fuming. She couldn't take it anymore.

"If anyone ever hits you again, don't tell Bret, tell me. I'll take care of things even better than Bret."

"Thanks, but I won't see either of them ever again."

"That leaves your sister-in-law."

She was the person behind a lot of the misdeeds. Essi tried to have some empathy because she was mentally un-balanced. That didn't take away from her making up untrue stories about others, especially Essi. She too, was jealous of Bret.

Essi couldn't prove it, but she was pretty sure her husband's sister was the one who convinced her brother to change his will. Her conniving ways were always meant to divide and conquer.

"I suppose there's still a chance to see them?"

"Not after what I'm going to tell you."

Bret was summoned to have a meeting with his brother and sister. The aunt, as she usually did, eavesdropped from behind the door. Essi was right. She was the instigator for this meeting.

Bret's sister did all the talking because his brother, while educated, had the brain of an immature pea.

"We were discussing that mom isn't going to be around forever and we need to make arrangements."

"You mean a funeral and burial?"

"We don't want that. It's too expensive."

"Huh? You want to cremate her against her wishes?"

"There's another alternative."

The ignorant brother just kept nodding his head. That's when things turned ugly.

"The local medical college has a big need for cadavers and pays top money. We could save a bundle, make a bundle, and let them chop her up. She wouldn't know the difference."

Bret was so filled with rage, he got nauseous and wanted to vomit. He held that back.

"Now listen carefully. That means both of you and that woman who's listening behind the door. If I find out anything bad happens to mom, even if she's swallowed by an earthquake, I'll know where the finger gets pointed. You're all going to be looking over your shoulders for the rest of your lives."

"Is that a threat?"

"You're so right. Why don't you call the police now and we'll air out all the dirty laundry. I know the skeletons all three of you have in your closets. If you're ready, let's rock and roll."

They were all stunned and speechless He opened the door, the aunt fell on her butt, and he walked out, slamming the door behind him.

"Bret actually told you this story?"

"He felt I had a right to know what was going on. I cried and cried for the rest of the day. I knew at that point I only had one child."

There was a small table in between Ani and Essi with a box of tissues on it. Essi grabbed a couple and looked away from Ani as she wiped her eyes and blew her nose. Ani wanted to know what the matter was. Essi started to stutter. Ani told her to relax and explain what she was feeling.

"I feel so alone. I know you and Bret will be leaving soon. I can feel it in my bones he's never coming back. I know that'll be the end for me."

"Hold your horses. Let's take this slow. There's a simple solution for your misery."

"I should do away with myself?"

"Don't ever say that again—not even as a joke. Are you interested in the solution?"

"You know I am."

"Why don't you come with us?"

"Oh, no. I could never burden Bret that way and I don't want to interfere with your relationship."

"Why don't you let Bret and I figure out those dilemmas."

"You would have me?"

"You're not reading me very well. In my short time here, you've done more for me than anyone else in my life. You've become the mommy I never had."

"You're going to tell Bret?"

"No. You're going to tell him and I'll be sitting right next to you. Now give me a big smile."

Finally, Essi's face lit up.

Later in the afternoon, Bret returned with a bunch of bags. He went for tools and groceries. He wanted to put them away but there was other business to attend to. Bret was still holding the packages when he saw Ani and Essi staring at him. The way they looked, it wasn't going to be anything good for him.

"I'm getting the vibe that I'm not going to get a fair trial. Are we going to skip it and take me straight to the executioner?"

Ani wasn't in a joking mood.

"Sit down, genius. Your mom has something to say to you."

"Bret, err … I mean to say … err—"

Ani couldn't take it anymore.

"I've invited your mom to come away with us."

"She told you she's my mom? I can't take her away from her home and her other children. I'm not sure she would want that."

"Essi, look at me and forget about him for a second.

If you had a choice, with no ifs, ands, or buts, what would you want?"

"I want Bret!"

"Mom, I dreamed about the day you would say that. It's going to be a tough trip. I hope you're up to it."

"I hope you two youngsters can keep up with me."

Essi ran out of the room and came back with a bottle of champagne. She has bought three bottles, one for each child when they got married. Her daughter got one and her other son just took his and drank it.

"I want to celebrate with dinner. I cooked something special."

They drank and had a great evening.

"Oh, I meant to tell you ladies, Niz is stopping over tomorrow."

Essi beamed because he would pick up packages from Essi that were left by Bret.

"That's so nice. I always look forward to seeing him."

Ani was a little confused and asked who he was.

"He's a friend of mine. We sometimes do business together. He's very friendly. I think you'll like him. He'll be here in the morning if nobody minds."

Essi was excited. When Niz stopped over, she made coffee and they talked for hours. He was in her age range, maybe a little older. They had a lot in common.

Bret had to verify Essi's passport was the same as the other two. He was ready as Niz would have much of their travel plans with him.

CHAPTER 29

The doorbell rang and Bret answered. It was Niz. He was the same man Bret would meet at the airfield to discuss the sale and purchase of Bret's merchandise and discoveries for his clients.

After the hugs and kisses, Ani was introduced. "So you're Niz. I hear you're very accomplished."

"Thanks, but I'm just an average older guy."

Bret said, "Believe me, Essi will agree he's far from average." Bret opened a bag with plastic cups and poured Niz a cold drink. "I hope you ladies don't mind if Niz and I sit on the back porch. We have some business to discuss."

Niz took his drink and they sat in the back. On the chair next to Bret was a corrugated cardboard box. Niz said, "I hope your trip here went well."

"I think you perceived all along, it was more of an escape than anything."

Niz said, "That's why I assumed you were going to the place you always dreamed about. I've been there before. It's a nice country."

"You seem to always know everything."

"Here are some travel arrangements I took the liberty of

making for you. There'll be a driver and limo waiting for you at the first stop. Here's a business card for a real estate person at your final stop. He's a good friend and will help you get a place to your liking."

"There's a slight change of plans. My mom will be going with us."

There was a sudden cracking sound of plastic breaking. Niz squeezed his glass too tightly and the drink's remnants spilled onto his pants.

Bret snatched some tissues from a box he had on-hand. "Are you ok?"

"I'm fine, I was just a little surprised. That's all."

"Good, about the money—"

"I've set everything up. I trust you've given the people you were doing this for the access codes? Their accounts have the name of a financial planner. He will help them out. I see you've given them quite a nest egg."

"I wanted to give them a new life."

"The story you told me was quite impressive."

"I figured your government connections would help."

"And where is the money for you?"

"I wanted things for them. I'm not important. I'll get by somehow."

"I knew that would happen. Don't be angry, but I siphoned off a little of their money and set up something for you. The info is on the back of that business card. Worry not, they still have plenty."

"I trust you gave extra to that couple with the two children and the crippled man?"

"Of course."

Bret and Niz went over the figures for each person. When they took a break, Niz leaned back in his chair, took a deep breath, and sighed while looking towards the yard.

Bret said, "I remember you told me at the airport how you knew me so many years, you could tell when something's wrong. I know the same about you."

"It's really not anything wrong. When you told me you were changing everything and in essence retiring, it made me start thinking."

"I know you worked very hard all your life."

"Where does it all end? I'm well into retirement age now. Sure I have good health, but I wonder for how long."

"You're strong as an ox. I know you will live a long, long time."

"I want to tell you something, Bret. It's been many, many years since I've gotten any enjoyment out of life. I was thinking maybe it was time to go, just like you."

"What about your business? You offer a service that can't be replaced easily."

"I thought of that. You're the only one I could discuss this with. I've made arrangements."

"I get the feeling there's something I should know. You've been holding back on me, even with all the years I've known you. Now I want to know."

Niz started choking up. Bret had never seen him in a weakened state like this before.

"You know, I was married once."

"I never realized that."

"She was very young, much younger than me. We did everything together. We laughed, we cried, we danced, even though I was a lousy dancer."

Bret knew there was something bad coming, so he asked no questions. He was a good listener.

"When she became pregnant, I was the happiest man in the world. I was walking on air. She died during childbirth. Just too frail. I feel that somehow, it was my fault."

"That's ridiculous. You did everything you could. You're an excellent person. I won't let you destroy yourself like this."

"I don't know, but she gave me a child. He was a beautiful, healthy boy. I knew I couldn't be a proper father. You know the way I traveled and such."

"You gave him up for adoption?"

"No, I loved him too much from the day he was born."

"It must've been difficult. Babysitters and an occasional governess tend to be so informal."

"That's exactly right. The state getting involved would've been a bigger mess. He deserved better than that. He deserved a better father. Once again, I wanted to stop that."

Niz thought back to that time in his life. "A hard decision had to be made, and I gave the situation a lot of thought. I came up with a solution. It wasn't a perfect solution, but I had to chance it working out. I knew a couple (through business) that were childless. They wanted to adopt, but the agencies were reluctant because of their age. They weren't just wealthy, they were ultra-wealthy. Yet, they didn't act it. If you dressed them the same as a poor person and met all of them on the street, you couldn't tell the difference. They may have been the nicest people I met. I offered them a choice. They could bring the child up as their own with one condition: I would be the boy's uncle and have unlimited visitation. We concurred that, when the time was right, I would tell him the truth. We all thought the best time would be someday after college, and I had the responsibility of choosing that date."

"So you told him?"

"The situation was bizarre, to say the least."

Niz decided his son should know immediately after college since he was quite mature. He was really nervous, but he knew it had to be done.

"I don't want you to hate me but, even as your uncle, you know I love you and I have something to tell you."

"You're going to tell me that you're my dad."

"How did you know?"

"I figured it out a long time ago. Uncles are good to their nephews, but not as good as you."

"I thought—"

"Listen, Dad, have you ever looked in the mirror and at my picture? We look a little too much alike. By the way, I love you more than ever."

Niz was getting emotional again and Bret kept the box of tissues handy.

"I've been grooming him to take over since then. He's officially got the business. The clients know him and like him."

"You think he can handle it?" Bret asked with a grin.

"He can always call on me if he needs anything. Besides, he's smarter and nicer than me. He has no serious vices. He's a special young man."

"I'd love to meet him."

"Oh, maybe someday. He's always busy. You understand," Niz said with a smile. It was almost time to rejoin the ladies. He always enjoyed speaking with Essi, and Ani hit it off well with him. "By the way, what's in that box?"

"It's my prized possession. I don't need it anymore. I want you to have it."

"The thing?"

"You got it."

"But it's priceless."

"I don't care. You can keep it, donate it, or sell it."

"I know how you cherished it. I don't know what to say."

"It's no biggie. I'm entering a new stage of life."

It wasn't only this that was given to Niz. Early on, Bret figured out his mountain situation was hopeless. As such, he started bringing things of value home during his secret trips. Included were some of the deadly weapons. He trusted Niz would know what to do. He wanted Niz to have all of it.

They tied up a few additional loose ends and rejoined the women. There wasn't a lot to reminisce. Niz wanted to tell the women about one thing. It was how Bret and Niz met. The subject came up and that's all he needed.

Niz said, "Years ago, I was doing things I wasn't proud of." He purposely left out that he was a fence. "Although it was dark, I took a walk. The crime was high in this country. I was accosted by two large hoodlums. I made the mistake of resisting."

Essi could be seen getting a bit upset. "Did they

hurt you?" she asked.

"You could say that. They were giving me a terrible beating. I was bloodied and semi-conscious. As fate would have it, a very young man was taking a night walk. It was Bret. When he saw the mugging, he sprang into action. I never saw a display like that. Perhaps only in the movies. When you're outnumbered like that, it's almost impossible to fend off two big assailants, let alone what he did to them."

Bret interjected, "I didn't do much. I just got them off you and slapped them around a bit."

"Slapping them around wouldn't have disarmed the one brandishing a knife."

"I needed to disarm him. It was nothing, really."

"If it was nothing, why were they running away with one screaming that you broke his nose and the other groaning you broke his jaw?"

"I guess I was a bit intemperate in my youth."

"Ladies, this man saved my life and I'll never forget it."

Ani was looking at Bret with glazed eyes the whole time. While Niz told the story, she kept playing with her infinity ring. She felt the eternal infinity that Essi was talking about.

Essi just said, "That's my boy."

They later sat down and discussed Bret's plans. Niz already knew he couldn't speak out the details. When they spoke about the happiness of all three of them going, one could see the sadness on the face of Niz. He would certainly miss them.

They would be leaving in two days. That gave Essi a day to put together any memorabilia and do some light packing.

It would be an all-day drive to the airport because it was in a different state.

"I have an idea. Why don't I drive all of you to the airport?" Niz volunteered. "Then I can feel better about saying goodbye." Bret put up his hand and shook his head. He wanted Niz to begin relaxing in his retirement. "I insist. I'm not doing anything for the next few days. If you're worried, I'll let you chip in for gas."

Bret started laughing. He knew the second his wallet came out, Niz would violently slap his hand. Essi had another reaction.

"Leave him alone," Essi interjected. "If Niz wants to take me to the airport, he can."

Ani picked up on Essi using the word me. "Baby, I think it would be nice if the four of us went together."

"I guess I've been outvoted. I can pick everyone up in the morning."

Essi immediately jumped in. She was very demanding. "You're staying right here and I won't take no for an answer."

Niz stepped back and saluted her. He was hoping for that all along. "How can I turn down two days of Essi's gourmet meals?"

Essi was hoping there was a fourth airline ticket in the package. That was not to be. It had to remain nothing more than a fantasy for her.

Packing day was a little more work than Bret thought. He had most of what he needed but also had to get the house ready for sale.

Niz told Bret not to worry. He would get rid of the contents and have it sold by a local real estate broker. Since Bret was the owner, he signed a power of attorney to allow Niz to conduct the sale. Niz also said he would go through the remaining contents. If he thought there would be anything Essi would want, he would contact Bret and ask.

Ani walked into Essi's bedroom as she was packing to see if she could help. Ani already had what she needed ready to go. She saw Essi going through photos and other memorabilia. "There's a lot there. Do you want me to stuff some of it in my luggage? I'm taking the bare minimum, so I have room."

"I'm really done with clothes, shoes, and toiletries. Maybe you could take a few things for me."

Essi saved Bret's first pair of booties. That was the only bulky thing. The difficulty came with the photos. Essi asked Ani to help her decide.

Together, they chose to keep all of Bret's pictures. The quandary was what to do with her other children's photos as well as that of her husband.

It was thought best to take a few of the children just as a remembrance of better days. She would also keep her wedding picture.

"What will you do with the rest?"

"Tonight, I'll burn them all in an old pot."

"Are you having second thoughts of leaving?"

"No, no, no. I'll stay here and never see anyone? What to do in life is problematic. I want nothing more than to be with you and Bret. He'll tell you I'm like a mule, my decisions are final."

Once all of that was done, each person's luggage was left by the front door. They all had to go to bed early because tomorrow would be a long day.

They left early. The ride took all day as they crossed two states to a major international airport. Bret sat in the front with Niz and they took turns driving. They all gave a ceremonial wave to the home they would never see again.

Bret wondered if the others would like their first stop. Only Niz knew where it was. The women would find out at the airport.

The car was over-the-top with bells and whistles. It had a TV and a hidden bar in the back. The women took turns dozing while sitting in the overstuffed seats.

On more than one occasion, they were followed by law enforcement. There was a tinge of paranoia. Niz told them not to be concerned. "Can't you see all the police cars with flashing lights and their prey? Today must be quota day."

When they arrived at the airport and parked, they checked-in. When Ani saw the country they were flying to, she was curious. "We're going to live here?"

"It's just a trail-erasing stop," Bret answered.

Niz collected his hugs and kisses. They all waved goodbye. It was time to start a new life.

CHAPTER 30

The beginning of their international flight was fairly smooth. Then a storm was forecast ahead and the pilot made a diversion. The storm grew in size and intensity, so the pilot made a landing on a Caribbean island. He would wait out the storm for several hours.

Essi was curious because she had never been outside the USA. She hadn't even flown before. She showed her naiveté when she asked Bret, "Does this hotel have toilets?"

"You've been sheltered for so many years. I'm sure it'll be fancy. Your son would never let you stay in a place like that."

Bret and Ani would have a more serious conversation.

"I'm wondering why you chose South America."

"It's close and a very good place to disappear. I'm sure you've read how people go there and can't be found by their governments."

"You mean like fascists after the war?"

"I get the rhetoric. Really, there are actually some good people who were persecuted and tried it here. They've never been found. It's just another step in erasing the trail."

The boarding announcement was made. They were informed the weather had cleared. After takeoff, the pilot announced he would try to put the pedal to the metal and make up some time.

The flight was long and tiring. When they landed in the capital city, all three had some renewed energy. They proceeded to baggage claim.

Essi had remembered Niz saying he ordered a car. As they waited for the bags, she looked around and tapped Bret.

"I think there's a man there holding a sign with your name."

Bret asked Ani to see if he was their driver. That way, he could carry the heavy bags. Ani returned with the man.

"He said he's not a driver, but he came for you."

Bret scratched his head. He didn't exactly understand what the guy meant, but so be it.

The bags came and the stranger insisted on carrying two of the bags while Bret carried the third. There wasn't much dialog as they walked to the car.

As they exited the terminal, standing in front of them was a stretch limo. The driver grabbed the bags and the man they met sat in the back, opposite them.

Essi was amazed. There was a bar with food and drinks along with a TV. She spent a lot of time just looking around the car. Bret wanted to know which hotel they would be staying at.

"We're not taking you to a hotel. We'd like you to be our guest at the embassy. We don't often get such high-ranking government officials."

Bret and Ani looked at each other. He just shrugged his shoulders. It sounded like a stunt Niz cooked up. He knew they would have to play along. Essi was savvy enough to keep her mouth closed except for innocent chatter.

"You're very late. The ambassador was getting concerned. I'm one of the assistants. When we arrive at the embassy, we'll review your itinerary."

Bret and Ani again raised their eyebrows. Their ride through downtown was dotted with scenic old buildings with classic architecture.

The embassy looked similar to a brownstone except much bigger. They stopped in front as two of the staff took hold of their bags. They entered and saw an impressive foyer with classic art.

"One of the staff will escort you now. I hope your quarters will meet with your approval. You can meet me in the parlor when you're rested."

The bedroom was a sight to see. Even the French provincial furniture was amazing. Essi said, "I feel like a queen."

Ani was more direct. "Ok, field marshal, what's your plan?"

"I have none. Let's just go with the flow."

They walked downstairs, even though there was an elevator. It seemed they wanted to take the whole episode in. The assistant was sitting in the parlor.

"Unfortunately, the ambassador will be tied up for dinner and a good portion of tomorrow."

Bret figured he'd play the game.

"That's too bad. I was so looking forward to meeting him."

Ani gave him a strange look. She thought he would do

his best to avoid seeing the ambassador.

"He wanted to meet you also. He has a solution. There's a formal reception tomorrow night at the grand ballroom downtown. He'd like all of you to be his guests. There'll be over 100 attendees."

Ani watched Bret open his mouth to change feet and started giggling. She also knew there was no way Bret could turn him down.

"Will the American ambassador be there?"

"Why yes. Why?"

"You realize I'm traveling incognito. He might recognize me."

"I doubt it. He spends most of his time at these affairs chasing women."

"None of us have formal clothing."

"We can take care of that tomorrow. The ambassador asked me to give you a tour of the city. They have wonderful boutiques and such downtown. We can just put it all on the ambassador's expense account."

Ani rolled her eyes and shook her head. Essi was excited to go. They were tired from the trip and wanted to sleep. Tomorrow would be a crazy day.

The tour was given in the same stretch limo. They passed art galleries and museums.

"I know you can only stay a few days, but next time stay longer. We can go to all these places."

The shopping took longer than the tour. Bret's tuxedo was easy. They would alter it and he'd get it in a few hours.

Many of the female places showed daring evening gowns

with a lot of exposed skin and glitzy sequins. Bret shook his head. He didn't need Ani to attract attention.

"I want you to know my wife and mother are very conservative dressers. They want to be covered up."

"Certainly. There's a great place with those kinds of gowns. They are by designers, so they're not inexpensive, but they can take whatever they want."

Bret wanted a matronly look. He could barely make Ani look average. Unfortunately, Essi was still quite attractive and looked a little too good also. So be it.

They came back and finally met the ambassador. He was an older, balding man with a round stomach. He was more than polite being very soft-spoken and friendly. He was the type that engendered respect.

As they spoke, Bret was careful to remind him that his trip was secret. He was absolutely understanding.

"I apologize. I would advise you to take care during this affair. Since these are important people, they have a habit of imbibing too much and becoming a little too annoying. They're quite harmless, but let me know if anyone gives you difficulty."

They all were dressed to the teeth. Ani couldn't help but admire how nice Bret looked in a tux. She wagered him that at least one woman would put the moves on him tonight.

Essi was in the same boat. She looked much younger than her age and Bret worried it would be open season on her too, not to mention the uglied-up Ani.

When they arrived, they saw formal attire everywhere. Many people were standing as they waited for the attendants to perform the valet parking.

They were escorted inside by the ambassador. There were huge chandeliers everywhere. The event took place in a hall that was reminiscent of the large catering halls used for weddings. There was no way to remember everyone's name they would be introduced to. There were just too many people.

They were sort of glad they went because the food was sumptuous. There was everything from cold shellfish to meats with rich wine sauces. There were even local dishes which were a bit spicy but delicious just the same.

The ambassador's predictions were right on the money. Dina's disguise and Ani's matronly gown had minimal effect. She was still easily the prettiest woman at the affair. It was only a matter of time before the American ambassador put the moves on Ani.

Ani had to cover her mouth so she wouldn't laugh in his face. In his attempt to chat her up, he was using the oldest, worn-out clichés.

"I'm the USA ambassador. What's your name and where have you been all my life?"

Ani was prepared. She mustered up the lowest and deepest voice she could and gave him her answer.

"My name's Ralph. I was told this was going to be a costume party."

He dropped his glass and was visibly shaken.

"Well … err … I'll see you later."

He disappeared while tripping and almost falling.

Bret wasn't as lucky. While Ani and Essi were mingling with people, he took a break and sat at a small table with two chairs.

An older woman stumbled over and sat next to him. She wasn't quite drunk, but it was evident she was floating. She had diamonds and gold dripping off of her. For sure, this wasn't costume jewelry. It was all real.

She grabbed his hand.

"My name's Muriel. I've been watching you."

"Really?"

"You're quite handsome."

"Thanks."

She suddenly grabbed his thigh.

"Why don't you come home with me? I'm quite wealthy, you know."

"I can't do that."

"I'll buy you a new car."

"I don't need a car."

"I'll get you girls."

"I don't want any girls."

"Then I'll get you boys."

"I don't want any boys."

Essi saw what was going on and poked Ani.

"I'm afraid my son is floundering over there. That sow, I'm sorry, I don't like calling people names."

"Well, I like calling people names. We better go save him before that old syph drowns him."

They both paraded over to the small table. Bret had a look that yelled "Help me!" on his face. Muriel and Ani were shooting bullets out of their eyes at each other. Then Ani grabbed Bret's hand.

"Come along now Bret, mommy has to take you home and change your diapers."

Muriel stuck her nose in the air.

"Well, I never—"

"You should get around more then."

Bret flew off the chair. He started whispering to Ani about this woman.

"We're not supposed to be attracting attention. She could screw us up."

"You want me to let you go home with that succubus? I would, except she probably has diseases that haven't been invented yet."

"Alright, let's leave. My mom has a headache, right?"

Essi and Ani agreed. Bret went to the ambassador and explained. As before, he was understanding and summoned his driver. They were able to leave without getting noticed.

The next morning, the assistant that had originally picked them up saw Bret in the foyer and asked to speak with him. They sat down with a younger man that was built like the ambassador and bald with a paunch.

"We need a favor. I understand you're leaving tomorrow."

"Yes, we're flying out."

"I took the liberty of canceling your flight. I'd like you to accompany the courier here to the next capital via train. The airport there has been clamping down on people, even with diplomatic passports. The courier will get you through customs at the train station."

Ani was standing by the door. She didn't want to interrupt in case this was private. Bret took the tickets and left.

He met Ani in the hall.

"Are they planning another reception for us?"

"Hardly. We have a change for tomorrow. We'll be accompanying that courier you saw by train instead of air."

"Ah, the proverbial courier aka spy."

"I almost forgot the business you were in."

"I hope this trip isn't too much for your mom."

"She's a real trooper. She can sleep a lot."

"I'll make sure they treat her right."

Ani was acting more like the mother every day instead of the reverse. Their closeness grew every day. She was extremely protective of Essi and would be a great guardian in the future.

CHAPTER 31

The foursome was dropped off at the train station during the morning. They proceeded to and sat in the waiting area for the boarding call. The courier kept an attaché case by his side.

Ani wanted to take a walk and look at the train. She saw a modern train with clean sides. When she was close, Ani peered through the windows and saw something she didn't approve of. Her protectiveness towards Essi was kicking in.

While walking back, the boarding announcement was made. Ani intercepted the other three as they were walking towards her. She asked the courier to walk separately for a moment.

"I understand we won't arrive until tomorrow."

"That's correct."

"Those cattle cars have six-across seating. It's small and cramped. There's no way Essi can take a trip like this in that kind of seating."

"Worry not. A club car has been reserved."

Since the definition of a club car had a different meaning in various countries, Ani decided to wait and see what it meant.

They walked past the crowded cars to the rear. As they were walking, the courier and conductor waved to each other. One could see they were acquainted. They came to the final car. As usual, Ani was feisty.

"Are we looking for the next train or do we sit on the back ledge?"

The courier wasn't used to Ani's dry humor. He pointed to the door.

"We wouldn't do that to you. We can enter here."

They gawked at what they saw. The car looked like a full-sized recreational vehicle, only much larger. The front had a stocked bar and a TV. Going back there was a couch facing a kitchen table and several chairs. Still further back, there was a bath across from a kitchenette. The back door opened to four bunk beds, two on each side.

Everyone felt Essi would be more comfortable on the bottom and not climbing a ladder, but Essi said, "I haven't slept in one of these since I was a kid. May I sleep on top?"

The courier said he would be happy to sleep on the couch. Essi said, "Nonsense, you take a bunk. We're not that private."

Bret and Ani both nodded. They walked back and saw a large paper on the kitchen table.

The courier said, "That's a menu for all of the meals. I made sure they gave you an English version."

As the train left, Ani and Essi agreed this trip was the best vacation either one had ever taken. Bret was more taken by the countryside after they left the city. He was still thinking about being followed. He realized that the trail was getting too cold for even the best intelligence agencies.

The trip was fantastic. They saw lakes, rivers, fields loaded with flowers, and strange animals. The food was gourmet level.

The next morning, reality set in as all good things come to an end. They pulled into the station and headed towards customs with their bags. Bret got in a rather long line for customs questions and inspections. The courier pulled Bret off the line and said to follow him.

"I don't have time to wait on lines. You can all follow me."

The courier led them to a door next to customs. Behind it, was a room the size of a conference room. A man in a uniform was sitting behind a desk. He seemed to have the rank of a military officer.

The courier told the others to wait and he went to the desk. They couldn't hear what was being said, but it appeared to be a friendly conversation. There were occasional gestures to the door on the other side of the room, bypassing customs. Both men also pointed at the entourage as they were talking.

After a few minutes, the courier waved for the group to come to him. Bret began to pull out the passports, but the courier waved his index finger back and forth as if to say it's not necessary.

They all went to where the pickup area was. The courier and another man waved to each other, approached, and shook hands. He would be their next driver.

When they got into the new limo, it was just a

normal-sized car. Bret thought how unusual it felt to actually ride in a regular car again.

The driver was pointing out different areas of interest in the city. He said the ambassador got a call from home asking that your group be treated with the utmost respect.

"He wondered why someone on your level would be coming to a forsaken country like this, but he knows not to ask questions. There is actually a lot of culture here, arts, museums, and the like."

Ani wanted to know what the ambassador was like. The courier laughed.

"He's like no ambassador you ever met. A real contradiction. He's more than friendly. He's a traditional sort, yet modern. He doesn't delegate much, preferring to do such things as tours and entertaining himself."

Essi said, "He sounds like a special man."

"Very much so. He's older, but acts younger. You'll know how special by just looking at him."

Since the trip had already taken a day and a half, it was getting late. There would be time for a quick bite.

They all noticed how similar the embassy was to the last one, both inside and out. Even the bedrooms were decorated the same way.

"You can sit inside while I bring your luggage up."

They sat down in, what they termed, the salon. One additional man was reading a newspaper. He put the paper down and started chatting. He spoke about the weather and even local sports. He was too well-dressed to be a low-level employee.

After a minute of chat, he said, "By the way, I'm the ambassador."

The description of nice was insufficient, to say the least. He also fit the unique physical description. He was wearing designer clothes and his appearance was flawless right down to his manicure. The most unusual aspect was his facial appearance. He wore a pencil thin mustache with slicked-back hair. More than an ambassador, he looked like a movie star from the 1930s. His manners were impeccable.

The ambassador started describing an itinerary for the next day. They included a tour with a stop at an art museum. The evening would include dinner and a musical show with dancers doing their own choreography. He finally asked their permission or if they wanted any changes. The women looked at Bret and he gave his resounding approval.

The next day, the ambassador didn't disappoint. Even in casual clothes, he looked like a mannequin. After the museum and lunch, it was time to rest up for dinner and the show.

The restaurant would compete with any five-star place. Between the ambiance of old art and a roving violinist, they couldn't believe how well they were being treated.

When it was time for the show, things started to change. While it was entertaining, Essi didn't seem to be enjoying it that much. The ambassador looked at her. He suspected something was wrong. As always, he was dignified but interested in the time she was having.

"What do you think of their dancing?"

"It's ok."

"Just ok?"

"I'm sorry, I forgot my manners."

"No, you were right. They're no better than ok. For professionals, that's unacceptable."

"I didn't mean to disappoint you. What do you think?"

"You know what I think? I think we should leave and go to a private club I belong to. It's mostly dancing and I think everyone there is better than these stinkers."

They all opened their eyes wide. An impolite remark like that was so out of character for him. Everyone was enthused, though. The ambassador wanted to make sure it was ok with Essi.

"When we get to my club, I'd like to dance with you."

"I haven't danced for a while but I'd love to."

They drove over to the club where a man wearing a uniform was identifying people who wanted to go in. He immediately recognized the ambassador and let the group pass.

Bret and Ani danced first. They knew all the basic steps like most people and didn't embarrass themselves. It was clear the people here were all pretty good dancers. There was a variety of music with all different dance steps.

When they came back, the ambassador put out his hand for Essi to hold and come with him.

That's when the shock came. They started dance with a variety of steps. They gradually morphed into more complex areas. They were doing steps in sequence like they had danced for years together.

The dance got so crazy, the ambassador started flipping Essi, rolling her over his back and between his legs. He threw her and she landed on her high heels in a position that was only done by professionals.

During this display, all the people cleared the floor and stood in a large circle. There were screams, gasps, cheers, and applause. It was a display that only pros normally performed.

Ani punched Bret in the arm pretty hard.

"Wow, what a pair of dancers. You're holding out on me again."

"Mom has danced before, you can see that."

"That's like saying I've eaten before. Don't talk like an accountant with info that's 100% accurate and absolutely useless. Come on, fill in the blanks."

When Essi was a teen, she belonged to a dance group. They weren't only dedicated, they were talented. She was so talented, she was selected to dance on a famous TV show in front of a high profile band. They showed selected couples dancing while the music was playing.

"Why didn't she pursue it?"

"You know the old story of getting married young, then the kids, then the mom stuff."

"She still could've taught with her talent."

"She did for a short time."

"Why'd she stop?"

It seemed, Essi became disillusioned. Her main problems were with the mothers. Some of them just wanted babysitters so they could spend less time with their kids. The children were mostly good kids. It was hard dealing with a situation where the child had two left feet and she was told by her mother she had so much talent she could dance professionally.

No matter how much she tried to be soft, the entitled mothers wanted no part of the truth or they would be on their phone with their lawyer.

"There were so many incidents."

"Sounds like something forced her out."

"Exactly, she had enough."

One of those types brought in her overweight daughter. Essi explained she could learn many things, but the mother insisted on ballet. She also insisted her daughter play a lead part in their shows because of her talent, even though Essi knew her talent was non-existent and she didn't have the body type.

After all the threats, Essi reluctantly agreed. One of the standard moves required the female to jump on the male. Essi knew that this would be a problem as the best boy dancer was quite frail. Even another mother asked Essi why the girl's mother would do that to her.

The worst possible scenario played out. The girl knocked down the boy at full speed and landed on top of him. He was badly injured. Fortunately for Essi, the boy's mother knew the story and actually sued the other mother. She lost, of course.

"That poor girl was so distraught, she never did any kind of dance again."

They all returned in the early morning hours. They all had a great time, but Essi was zonked. Bret and Ani thought it best to let Essi sleep as late as she needed. They would just spend the later morning in the impressive garden in the back.

The next morning, Ani sent Bret ahead. She would join him shortly. He was walking through the garden and came to a trellis with two benches under it. The benches were facing each other.

On one bench, sat a middle-aged couple. They smiled and Bret said good morning. They immediately spoke English with a heavy accent. They introduced themselves as Max and Ina.

Max asked, "So what are you hiding from?"

Ina exclaimed, "Max!"

"It's ok, he's running just like us."

"I apologize. My husband talks too much."

Bret was stunned. He wondered why he thought that and asked.

"When you've been running as long as us, you recognize others doing it too."

Since he had nothing to hide, Max explained his situation. They were both scientists in a country where the head of state was concerned about scientists defecting. It didn't take much to be exiled to a labor camp. They knew others who tried to get out but had a bad ending.

Ina said, "Our best friends tried, but disappeared. We assumed the secret police caught them along with their children."

Everything sounded familiar to Bret. Many of his associates were in the same boat. Then Ina said something that startled Bret.

"I miss them so much. Lana was my best friend."

"Did you say, Lana? Does she have a husband named

Alex and they have two children?"

Ani came over and heard the conversation. After stuttering, he introduced her as Sally. They continued.

"I know two people like that. They might be alive and safe."

They went over details of their family and other factors of the town all four came from. It was obvious they were the same Alex and Lana.

"How long will they keep you here because I'm leaving soon?"

"My wife and I were promised a lifetime if we wanted. We have no place to go."

As Ani and Bret walked away, she said, "Sally?"

"I couldn't give your real name and I always call you sugar, so I was thinking of the first word that came to mind starting with s."

"I'm glad you weren't thinking of stupid."

"Still the jokester."

"Can we help them?"

"I didn't want to bother Niz so soon, but I guess the embassy can give him a call and put me on."

Bret went inside and asked to speak with the ambassador. He knew Niz had set his stay up and could be located.

"I'm sorry to bother you, but have you spoken with Niz?"

"Do you need to speak to him? I can get him on the phone if you like."

Niz was called and the ambassador excused himself after a few pleasantries. Niz was concerned something went wrong.

"Are you alright?"

"I'm fine. I need to ask you something. You remember those two people I was especially friendly with?"

"With the kids and the butler?"

"Exactly. I've met two old friends of theirs. It would be nice if they could speak. They could call here and ask for Max, the caretaker or Ina, the maid."

"Say no more. I'll see what I can do."

Bret left the room and thanked the ambassador. The ambassador asked Bret to wait.

"I'm taking a trip for a couple of days. Would you like to accompany me?"

"Where are you going?"

"Antarctica."

The first thing Bret thought was the fallout. He asked what area it would be. Fortunately, it was on the other side of the continent.

"I can't stay long. Are there flights to the next destination I told you about?"

"Oh, sure. Between the tourist excursions and scientific needs, there are a few flights each week. There are plenty of empty seats."

Bret's mind was going a million miles per hour. He concluded that any trace of a trail would certainly die with a trip like this.

"We would need heavy coats."

"We have plenty and the airport store where we land has even more."

"Then it's a deal."

"Good. Be ready to leave tomorrow morning."

Bret sought out the women. When he found them, he broke the news.

"We're making a slight diversion from our next stop."

Ani snorted and said, "I don't even know where we were going in the first place. So where is this, or is it another surprise?"

"No surprise … We're stopping at the South Pole."

The women gasped, but more and more they thought along the same lines. They were ready for anything.

The next day, the flying weather was perfect and they made it to their destination without incident. There was an adjacent building with rooms that doubled as a motel.

The next two days were filled with visions of icebergs, seals, penguins, and whales. Music was always playing on the loudspeakers both inside and outside. It was funny watching the ambassador and Essi dancing together with winter coats and heavy boots.

They were all packed and ready for their next leg of the adventure.

They were surprised that it was a large commercial jet. They thought it would be more of a transport jet.

As they were ready to leave, Ani looked at Essi.

"He's wonderful, isn't he?"

"He's a nice man."

"Just nice?"

"That's about the size of it."

That deflated Ani's idea of a romance. When she told Bret, he said it didn't matter. The ambassador had already confided in him he was a lifelong bachelor and wasn't about to change.

Away they flew.

CHAPTER 32

The Pacific Northwest had one of its common overcast and rainy days. A rental sedan was driving along a semi-rural road. The area had been farms, but in the last decade, several nice gated communities dotted the road. They sold well because this area was only about half an hour from the major city.

The thirtyish driver turned into one of these places and up to the guardhouse. The development was about seventy percent sold and had an active sales office.

The guard gave his standard query regarding the house he was going to. There was a way around that.

"I'm going to the sales office. I'm interested in purchasing one of the homes."

He drove past some of the completed houses as well as the clubhouse and tennis courts. While they weren't high-end homes, they were Victorian style and attractive with small properties.

Since the guard was out of sight, he bypassed the sales office and looked for an address he needed to visit. He turned down the correct street and saw a small ranch style home next to a larger two-story home that wasn't completed. The rest of the block was unsold lots.

Since it was a weekend, he knew there was a good chance the occupants were at home. He pulled in front of the ranch and parked. The man walked to the door and rang the bell. Within a few seconds, he heard uneven footsteps. The door opened and it was Henry.

"What can I do for you?"

It was incredible how much Henry's speech improved. He then acted like a home guardian.

"I'd like to speak to Alex and Lana."

"There's nobody here by that name!"

Henry attempted to close the door. The man stuck his forearm through the jamb to block him.

"Go away and leave us alone."

Lana was standing on the side hidden by the door. Alex was on the other side and not within view. She took the knob from Henry and exposed herself.

"What do you want from us. I can't ask you in."

The man grabbed his lapels and pulled his jacket apart.

"I need to talk to you. You can see I carry no weapons and nobody is behind me. If I wanted to do something sinister, you would've been finished already."

Lana brought Alex over. He had a heavy lamp in his hand for a weapon.

"You won't need that."

"Just in case."

Lana said, "Please attend to the children, Henry. We'll be sitting on the porch."

They sat down and all were on edge. The couple was

complimented on the furniture even though it came with the house. That attempt to put them at ease didn't work. Alex was direct.

"You want something. Tell us what it is."

"You seem worried. I have some good news."

"So a stranger comes here and decides to give us good news?"

"Let's be frank. Do you know some old friends by the names of Max and Ina?"

Both were shocked as they looked at each other. For now, Alex would be speaking to the man.

"Maybe yes, maybe no."

"Please don't be coy. I'm trying to help you."

"Is that so? I don't even know your name."

"Forget about my name. I'll play it your way. If you did know such people, they've been found. They're in hiding but in good health. They want to talk to you."

"So let them talk."

"They're not here. I wouldn't advise using your phone which may be monitored."

"It can't be done, can it?"

The man reached in his breast pocket. He came out with a cell phone.

"You can use my phone."

He reached out, and Lana also reached to take it. Suddenly, Alex put his arm in front of Lana.

"Just a minute."

"Where I came from, it's common to sabotage a small unit like that. Sorry, I can't trust this."

"I suppose you're right. It's probably not a good idea for any calls in this area for tracking purposes."

"We're at an impasse."

"I have a suggestion. There's a large mall about ten miles down the road. We can all go to the parking lot. I'll make the call and put you on. Does that work?"

"I just don't know. I can't—"

"I didn't want to say this … Niz and Bret sent me."

Alex scratched his cheek in thought. He looked at Lana and she smiled.

"Excuse my manners, but I'd like you to walk away for a couple of minutes so I can speak with my wife."

The man walked to the street and leaned against his car. He stayed outside as the rain had stopped.

"You were smiling, why?"

"Darling, I don't want to live like this anymore. It's bad enough we don't have Bret. Talking with friends would make our lives a lot easier. He couldn't know Niz and Bret unless it was legitimate. Don't you agree?"

"As always, you're making complete sense."

They motioned the man back and told him they agreed.

"I'll go inside and let Henry know we'll be gone for a bit."

Alex had one more bit of caution. He pointed to the car in his driveway.

"They've given us a leased car. We will take two separate cars."

They left the house and stopped in a parking area of the mall where there were no other cars.

They all exited their cars. Lana's normally calm demeanor was tried. Her hands were shaking. The man dialed his cell and got through to the embassy. He asked for either Ina, the maid, or Alex, the butler. Ina came on.

"Hello, Ina? I have someone here who wants to speak to you."

Lana took the phone and started speaking their foreign tongue. After about thirty seconds of crying, Alex spoke to Max. The conversation was all benign as they couldn't speak about serious topics yet.

When they were done, Alex shook the man's hand and Lana hugged and kissed him.

"You can keep the phone. Don't worry about the bill. All I ask is when you're not using it anymore, you destroy it."

With that, the man left. The couple returned to their home and found all was in order. They discussed old times the rest of the day.

The nighttime was a different story. Alex sent Lana to bed at their normal time. He then took a pencil and paper out of a drawer and sat at their dinette table. He spent several hours writing and using a hand calculator.

Lana was worried the following morning. Alex went to bed much later than midnight. When Henry and the children were done with breakfast, Alex suggested Lana sit with him so they could review what he did last night.

"I was thinking about Max and Ina. I started thinking of ideas and running some figures."

"They would need to be safe ideas."

"Bret taught me well about immigration here and private ownership of real estate."

"To be safe, we can call them every couple of weeks for the next few months. We can't leave the USA, but we can invite them for a vacation."

"It can't be close."

"The USA is a big place. We'll find a city to meet. At that point, we can invite them to stay. It'll be easy because we're citizens."

"They would need jobs."

"We can help. If we sponsor them, they could get a green card. Then it's just a wait for citizenship."

"Where would they live? This is such a small house."

"I have a plan. I looked at the numbers. Bret gave us enough money to pay for college for the children. We have enough to buy this house for very little. It's only a rental from the government."

"How does this help Max and Ina?"

"I called the sales office early this morning. The unfinished house next door is stagnant because the deal fell through. They offered a huge discount if we took both houses. We have enough money."

Alex showed Lana the figures.

"We could have the bigger house with four bedrooms. Everyone, including Henry, would be set and he could have his privacy. We could give this small house to Max and Ina."

"Alex, you're a genius."

"With them working in their professions, they can pay us back. This house is more than big enough for them."

In such a short period of time, Alex planned the future for seven people. There was little chance such a plan could fail.

In the coming year, it would come to fruition.

Lana said, "I wonder if there will ever be a way to thank Bret."

What she was really thinking was whether she would see Bret ever again.

It might take a few years, but it would be a good bet that someway, somehow, they would all see one another again.

CHAPTER 33

Bret's next leg on the journey was approaching the runway. Even Ani was getting fatigued at so many stops.

"I would think you've completely lost any lingering trail by now. I'm worried about Essi. She looks so tired."

"I was concerned about both of you. I'll let you in on a little secret. Maybe it'll make everyone feel better."

"You already know I like surprises."

"This is our last stop. I hope you like living here."

"I've never been here, but everyone says great things about it. I do have one question though. Why here?"

"I thought about it a lot and it checks the most boxes: common language, stable government that doesn't overreach, thriving economy, everybody minds their own business, etc."

This would be the first leg where they were completely on their own. They had to use a taxi and stay in a downtown hotel.

After resting for a couple of days, Bret wanted to go to the bank and brokerage house to check on their funds. He would worry about finding a job after they all had some rest. He asked the women to enjoy themselves. They could go shopping or anything else.

Before leaving, Bret called the real estate number on the card he had. Since Niz knew the man, he should be trustworthy. His contact turned out to be out of town and he made an appointment several days later.

The bank, brokerage, and real estate were all within walking distance. Bret hurried to the bank first. He wanted to draw some money so his traveling companions could have some fun. He was shocked at the amount of money in the account. Niz really took care of him.

When he went to the brokerage house, he was assigned a financial planner. He didn't understand why and asked the person who looked up his account.

"I'm not sure I need someone like that. My finances are modest, at best."

"He's here today and will answer your questions."

A middle-aged man came out and escorted him to an office. He was dapper and wearing an expensive suit. Bret asked him the same question he asked before.

"I wouldn't exactly call your position modest. I'm always available to help you manage this. I recommend at least once per month."

Niz had set him up with a sizeable amount of stocks, bonds, hard assets, and money market funds. Bret signed the needed papers and went back to the hotel.

All along his walk back, he thought how things changed so quickly. He went from being a pauper to having money in just one morning.

Bret waited for the women at the hotel. He had to change his thinking for the immediate future. The plan was to rent an apartment. He thought he would have the real estate guy show him nice buildings that were affordable. He now believed he could actually own something.

The ladies returned fairly soon. Bret was beaming.

"That was fast."

Ani threw her palms up.

"The walk was great, but it's hard to have a good time when your pockets are empty."

"I'll take care of that."

Bret reached in his pocket and pulled out a fistful of currency. The women were stunned as he divided it up. Ani was shaking her head.

Bret said, "Do you think you can have fun now?"

Ani said, "I don't want to be nosy … aw, forget it."

The next couple of days were filled with shopping, museums, and other attractions. The time to get serious came too soon.

Bret walked over to the building that housed the real estate office. Usually, they're located in a storefront. This one was several floors up with other offices on the same floor.

He looked at the directory in the lobby. There was no name like the business card. Fortunately, there was a suite number on the card. He took the elevator up and walked the hall.

"Let's see. Jalko Realty, Jalko Realty."

There was nothing by that name on the floor. The suite he was looking for showed a blank door. It seemed as if the former renter had abandoned it. The door wasn't locked, so Bret knocked and walked in anyway.

A man was sitting at a desk. The office was barren except for a desk, two chairs, a file cabinet, and a laptop on the desk.

"Excuse me, I'm looking for—"

"You must be Bret. I'm Jalko. Niz sent you. Have a seat."

Bret kept moving his eyes around the meager settings in the room. He didn't know what to expect here, but it wasn't this.

"If you're looking for a fancy office, you won't find it here."

"I apologize if I was so obvious. It's just—"

"You weren't expecting a hole in the wall. Perhaps I should explain."

"Really, it's ok."

"Listen, I run an unusual realty. I only cater to a very few people like Niz. There's no advertising, no pictures."

"Ok, I get it."

"Niz said you want privacy."

"I originally wanted an apartment, but I think I can afford a nice home."

Jalko looked through some listings on his laptop. He zeroed in on several areas.

"It's difficult to get what you want in the city or the suburbs. They all have small properties. We have several choices."

"I don't want to be a pain, but let's see."

They started discussing areas.

"One area is past the suburbs and gets a little remote. It's very private and you won't see your neighbors. Of course, you will see large spiders, snakes, and other nasties."

"That might be a little too much wilderness for my female companions. Anything else?"

"We can go to a smaller town. You have to realize the cities here are quite spread out and they're far away. There are some nice cities, just the same. Those smaller towns are quite nice also."

"It might be good. My girlfriend and mother have fallen in love with this place. I'd like to exhaust the possibilities here first."

"That leaves us with coastal properties. They're bigger and very private. It's difficult to see them from the road. Knowing this would be a possibility, an arrangement would be set for you to take a look from a boat. You can get a nice tour of the harbor also."

"I'd love that. Is it ok to bring my two companions along?"

"I'm pretty sure the boat has room for all of you."

They discussed the early morning meeting time and Jalko provided the boat slip number. Bret said he would take a taxi early. He didn't want to be late.

"No, it would be my pleasure to drop you off at the dock. It's part of my commission."

Bret headed back to the hotel. Essi and Ani were sitting in the lobby. People-watching can be fun also. He told them the news. They both got excited as Ani tilted her head.

"Aren't coastal properties very expensive?"

"I told him what we can afford and he seemed to think we can find something in our budget."

Essi said, "As long as I'm with the two of you, I can live

in a shack. I've been there before."

"I promise one thing. My mommy will never live in a shack again."

They all wondered if they could find a place where they could settle down. Tomorrow might be the day.

CHAPTER 34

The next morning, the happy trio walked out of the lobby into the street. Sure enough, Jalko was waiting inside his car. They all jumped in and Bret made the introductions.

"You folks picked a fine day for boating. The weather couldn't be better. I'll leave you just a short walk away from the slip."

Essi said, "You're not coming with us?"

"I wish I could, but I have another appointment. They have your name and they have a list of shore homes for sale. I hope you see something you like."

They reached the downtown docks. It was quite a sight. It was loaded with restaurants and touristy shops. Essi loved the bright variation of colors each store was painted with.

Jalko pointed them in the right direction. There were so many boats and piers, one could easily get lost. The good thing was the slip numbers were orderly.

Bret waved goodbye and yelled out, "I'll see you soon."

It was a longer walk than anticipated and they passed most of the smaller craft. The piers and slips were getting much larger. They stopped at the number they were given.

There was only one unit moored there. All of their

mouths dropped. It was a yacht. It wasn't an ordinary yacht owned by the average wealthy person. This ship was huge. It was the type that would have many crew members, multiple bedrooms, and tons of amenities.

Bret asked his partners to wait while he spoke to someone. It was obviously a mistake. Even if it wasn't, there's no way they had enough money on them to pay for such a rental.

Bret walked up to the normal boarding point. He saw a crew member giving instructions and orders to other crew members. He assumed he was the equivalent of a chief mate even though he was sort of youngish.

"Excuse me."

"Can I help you?"

"My name is Bret. I—"

"We're expecting you. Please come aboard."

"This is a little embarrassing, but I'm not sure I can pay for something this elaborate. Perhaps you have a smaller cruiser?"

"This is all we have. I believe you're paid up through the day. Come aboard and enjoy."

Bret waved for the ladies. They walked up and they both chorused, "Wow." The wow factor wasn't all. Two mates brought up a chair to assist Essi and carry her aboard. She waved them off.

"I'm not crippled, you know."

They wondered how many people were invited to this. Bret was thinking if the other passengers would mind passing the shore homes. Then he thought maybe they were also looking for real estate.

The chief mate started escorting them to the rear. The stern of the yacht looked like a party area. It had an outdoor kitchen and a music setup with large speakers.

"The fridge is full and there's food everywhere you look. Once we leave, I'll have someone serving you. In the meantime, help yourself."

Bret and Essi were sitting and taking it all in. Ani exhibited her exploratory nature and spoke to the chief.

"I've never been on a bridge before. Do you think the captain would mind if I took a look?"

"We're pretty informal around here. I think you can look around. The captain and first officer are there now."

Ani walked over to the elevator. Since the views were too precious to miss, she opted to take the stairs. She got to the bridge and opened the door. There were the two officers and a third man sitting behind them. They all had swivel chairs.

"I don't mean to barge in, I was hoping you wouldn't mind if I looked around."

"Come right in. There's no charge."

The voice she heard from the third man sounded familiar. He swiveled around and she put her hand over her mouth. She was so stunned, she was silent. Ani ran out of the door and started screaming.

"Bret, Bret, get here on the double!"

Bret, fearing something was wrong, left Essi with the chief. He also opted to skip the elevator. He saw Ani leaning over the top.

"What's going on?"

"It's Niz!"

Now Bret was moving so fast, he tripped a couple of times and bruised his knees. He limped into the bridge area.

"Welcome to the Niz Water Taxi and Real Estate Touring Company."

"You dirty … I almost broke my leg running here."

There were the usual hugs. Ani knew right away that they wanted some time alone together.

"I'll go check on Essi."

When she told Essi, her hand went to her forehead with glee. Essi hadn't smiled this much since leaving her home. Ani explained that the men needed a few minutes together and would be here shortly.

Bret and Niz went down to a meeting room. Bret wasn't often speechless, but he had to work to utter his words.

"Why didn't you tell me? Oh, forget it."

"How do you like my raft?"

"I was hoping for something a little larger than this rowboat."

"I have some news. Your close friends are now in contact with their old friends. They have job offers and their kids are in school."

"I don't know how to thank you."

"Some other info, I have confirmation that a name has been added to the accounts of all your associates. I think that wraps up our duties with them for now."

"This has worked out better than I thought. What's the idea of giving me so much money?"

"I didn't give it to you. You earned it. Besides, how were

you going to eat? Photosynthesis?"

"What can I say? It's nice to know my mommy won't starve."

"Enough of this. Let's go see the girls and take a ride."

"One last thing, this phantom that's always seen with the president, fits your description. Is it you?"

Niz smiled and winked like Bret had done when speaking with him earlier.

"Never heard of him."

It was unnerving when they went to the ladies and Essi practically jumped into Niz's arms. To say that their greeting showed a slight sign of affection was an enormous understatement.

The tour of the harbor was quite scenic. They saw everything from fishing boats to naval vessels on the water and small homes to large buildings on the land. The sea was nice and calm.

Niz wanted to take some time looking at homes. He went up to the bridge with Bret and said where to go. Although there was a captain, Niz left no doubt who was in charge.

Bret noticed a shoulder-mounted rocket-propelled grenade launcher standing in the corner. There was a bag of shells next to it.

"What's the artillery for? You expecting trouble?"

"It's just here in case of an event. We often go into the open ocean and international waters. It's always better to be prepared."

They cruised up and down the coast in both directions.

Anything available had a "for sale" sign on the dock as well as the front of the property.

The homes were great for anyone who liked opulence. They couldn't imagine what the exorbitant prices would be. Niz assured them the prices would be doable numbers. They saw one really nice one they all liked.

"It depends if you like these areas."

Bret asked, "You don't like it here?"

"Every area has at least a plus and minus. I'll call and see what the story is."

Niz got on the phone. He sounded disappointed.

"A previous offer was accepted by the owner. However, the deal may fall through if you want to wait."

They all really wanted something they could move into almost immediately. In the meantime, they would go back and see Jalko about the others.

"Honestly, the girls aren't that enthused about the others, Niz."

"That was my impression also."

Bret and Niz walked back to the girls. Essi spoke about being confused. Even Ani was unsure. Niz broke the ice.

"I have an idea. Let's worry about these places tomorrow. Is anyone hungry for lunch? I know a great place. It's a few hours away."

It was very clear they would go wherever Niz wanted. Riding on this yacht was like a vacation itself. Niz made the call upstairs and the yacht turned.

Much to everyone's surprise, the yacht headed out to sea rather than along the coast. Nobody asked any questions.

Another adventure was starting.

Niz put out a couple of fishing poles to add to the ambiance. At the high speed they were traveling, they were unlikely to hook anything and they would cut it loose anyway.

Just over an hour into the open sea, their relaxation was disturbed. There were five short deafening blasts from the horns.

Niz jumped up and asked the women to go downstairs to a bedroom of their choosing. Essi was confused.

"Is there something wrong?"

Niz said, "It's just an exercise, sort of a drill. There'll be gunfire and the sound will be too loud for you."

Although Ani would've wanted to be part of the action, she saw Bret motioning with his head to the door.

"Ok, let's go down and let the boys have their fun."

Bret said to Niz, "Is this really a drill?"

"No. Nklomo pirates."

As they were walking, Bret remembered a story Nkuma told him about his youth. His village was near the sea. It was often occupied by pirates since the government had little control. He mentioned pirates with the same name.

These were particularly savage as they killed Nkuma's father for no reason. They would take hostages when they were at sea. When the nations stopped paying, they found it easier to take the spoils and kill the hostages.

This led to the nations clamping down, forcing the pirate groups to leave. Nkuma told Bret the same group got drunk and their tongues slipped. They were headed for this area "so they could never be caught." Bret knew any fight would be to the death.

Bret and Niz were running up the stairs because it was standard procedure to disconnect the elevator.

"Can you outrun them?"

"I can, but I won't."

"What about the navy?"

"Can't. Diplomatic problem."

What Niz meant was these pirates were given sanctuary by a nearby island nation. That nation allied itself with a major power who just happened to be an enemy.

The mainland didn't want to get their military involved for fear it would cause a major incident. They would hope one of these attacks would solve the problem via a private enterprise.

"You mean like mercenaries or maybe you?"

"I'm afraid so, Bret."

They entered the bridge and Niz directed Bret to look at the screen. That would give all the information.

"Do you see that big blip on top? That's the mother ship. Those smaller blips on either side are circling the yacht."

"They're trying to surround us. Those boats usually have six to eight men with rifles. They'll try to board."

Niz sent out the alarm and quite a few mates came on deck carrying automatic rifles. A large hatch on the bow slid open and a platform underneath began to rise. It held stationary twin .50 caliber machine guns. The chief mate took up the position. Everyone wore ear protection with a microphone so they were all in contact.

"Wow, that's pretty heavy artillery."

"They're long-range guns and armor piercing shells. We should be hearing from the mother ship soon."

Like clockwork, Niz turned on the radio and the message came in. Niz would handle the conversation.

"You are our prisoners. Our men will board soon. Anyone who resists will be killed."

"Pirates, recall your boats. We are well able to defeat you."

There was no answer. As the boats got closer, it became apparent they would have to intercept the small craft. He told the captain to go for the closer craft on the port side.

"Bret, I know your special desire to preserve human life. You can go down below. I won't think less of you."

"We've been through too much together. If Niz goes to battle, Bret goes to battle with him."

Niz smiled and hugged Bret. He pointed to the RPG and bag of grenades.

"We'll go outside. Prop it up on your shoulder. I'll load it. If I tap you on the head, just aim and pull the trigger. The grenade will do the rest. This can stop a tank."

While outside, Niz told the mates with small arms to start firing warning shots. Although they were out of range, he hoped they would turn around.

The opposite was true. One could see the flashes of fire coming from the boat even though they were also out of range.

"This is stupid. I don't have time for this."

Niz sent the order for the chief to open up with the .50s. They were so powerful, they shook the yacht something fierce. It was felt by the women. Essi was shocked.

"Wow, what's that?"

Ani knew this was serious now, but she had to keep Essi calm.

"It's just the boys enjoying their toys."

Up top, Niz gave Bret the tap on the head. Between the RPG and the .50s, the engines were ignited and the explosion ripped apart the boat. There was no more gunfire from the boat.

"Ok, hard around and let's get the other one."

They got to the same range and the results were the same: warning shots, return fire, .50s fire along with an RPG. As before, there was nothing left of the boat.

"Let's head inside and deal with that big garbage scow."

Niz grabbed the microphone and contacted the pirates.

"Pirates, your boats have been neutralized. Now you can surrender."

The pirate said, "We will destroy you."

No sooner they sent that message, two large fireballs could be seen in the distance and a large boom was heard a few seconds later.

"Stop engines!"

There were two cannons fired. They fell well short of the yacht as they weren't nearly close enough. Niz didn't know the host island had fitted them with cannons.

"Pirates, those cannons are useless. If you do that again, I will make the ocean around you flat. No one will know your ship ever existed."

Niz gave the order to open up with the .50s. Bret was

puzzled.

"If we're out of range, aren't they also?"

"Yes, but the tracers from the .50s might scare them into surrendering or at least thinking it over. Those cannons will be dangerous if we get much closer."

Niz guessed wrong. Another two flashes of light and the ensuing boom happened again.

"Let's get this over with and give them an angel. They're not ruining my lunch. Get into position."

The chief mate was removed from the area. As the yacht turned, Bret noticed one of several ten-foot tubes next to the .50s start elevating from the front. It reached a forty-five-degree angle and stopped. The captain said it was locked in.

Niz sighed, took a deep breath, and put his hand on the captain's shoulder.

"Ok, go ahead and splash them."

There was a hissing sound from the tube and smoke started coming from both ends. Then a loud crack was heard and a missile was fired. It went slowly at first, then gained speed as it went out of sight. Niz looked at Bret.

"It'll be over pretty quickly. What a shame."

"You mean the loss of life?"

"No. Anti-ship missiles are so expensive."

There was a huge explosion in the distance that dwarfed what happened with the cannons. Flames were visible and large plumes of smoke went high into the sky.

Over the speaker came screams. Much of the yelling was unintelligible. They could hear some things like "the ship's in pieces, they're drowning, somebody help us."

Niz reached over to the speaker switch and turned it off.

"And that's that. Resume our lunch heading. You can also send a message to the navy to pick up and arrest any survivors."

Niz told Bret they could see the women now. As they were leaving the bridge, Niz turned his head back to the captain.

"And take your time with that message."

As they left, Bret was baffled. He always knew Niz as a humanitarian. He never had such a cold and callous disregard for human life. Bret knew these were murderers, but it still seemed strange.

Bret knew, one way or the other, Niz had some sort of personal stake in this, but he wouldn't ask. If and when Niz wanted to talk about it, Bret would be ready to listen.

When they went down, the ladies were already on deck. Ani whispered to Bret.

"Was that really a drill?"

"No. Pirates."

Niz rushed over to Essi. He wanted to calm her and even give her a sedative. "I hope we didn't scare you too much."

"Oh, no. I found it quite exciting, except next time I'd like to participate."

Ani just slapped her head as the men were astounded. Niz took Essi's hand.

"Essi, you're quite a woman. I hope everybody is still hungry."

Ani came with her dry humor, "I'll eat anything that

won't eat me first."

Even Bret joined in, "I can eat a leopard and enjoy every spot."

Another hour and it would be chow time.

CHAPTER 35

Niz took everyone upfront to the bow and pointed to a barely visible highland in the distance.

"Our lunch is on that island."

Ani, ever the wise guy cracked, "It looks wild. Do we have to hunt for our food?"

This time Niz gave it back to her. "You won't have to hunt. The cannibals are friendly and will give us all we need."

Essi didn't understand the byplay.

"Are there really cannibals there?"

Everyone loved her naiveté. They all gave her a group hug and explained the joke.

As the yacht neared the island, they were intercepted. Another smaller vessel with a mounted machine gun approached from the distance and blew its horn. It was still distant and there was a faint vision of a man on deck. Ani poked Bret as he pulled out a pair of binoculars.

"Another little shootout?"

"I doubt it. He's wearing some kind of uniform. He must be an officer because he has epaulets"

The vessels pulled alongside each other and Niz conversed with the uniformed man. They saw Niz gesturing and pointing in the direction they came from. It was almost assuredly regarding the pirates.

The officer kept nodding. He finally signaled to the bridge with a wave that the captain should proceed.

The yacht neared the docks. Music became audible. The town was barely visible from the docks and required a short walk.

There was a sizeable number of larger cruisers. Those slips weren't long enough to accommodate this ship. The yacht suddenly veered and the giant slips with other yachts were on the side. They pulled alongside another mammoth of similar size.

As they disembarked, they noticed an occasional small jet passing overhead. They started walking and the music became louder. They reached the edge of the town and were shocked.

There was one main street with stores, bars, and restaurants lining one side and a narrow beach lining the other. Every commercial place was wide open with no doors.

They saw live bands playing on every street with different kinds of music such as rock, jazz, calypso, and even a classical string quartet. People were dancing in the streets. There was raucous laughter everywhere.

There were no cars, just small electric vehicles that looked similar to golf carts. Niz explained cars weren't allowed. He pointed to a lot where the carts were kept.

"If you need to take one, go ahead. The only requirement is to hook up the charger when you're done."

Niz pointed to the end of town where there was a park

with tennis courts, a large swimming pool, and even bocce ball. Bret put his arm around Niz.

"I never imagined a place like this existed. It's a real fantasy."

"Most don't know about it. There's no advertising and you can only come here by invitation."

"You were invited?"

"I don't need to be. I have friends here."

"People seem always happy."

"They should be. There are very few rules. The penalty for breaking them is permanent banishment. You know nobody wants that."

They continued strolling. The women's heads were swiveling around trying to take everything in at once. Then they heard a voice yelling from one of the restaurants.

"Niz, Niz!"

Niz told the trio to sit at a large round table on the edge of the beach. It was right across from the restaurant. He walked over and greeted the man. He was about the same age as Niz. There were handshaking and hugging.

"Where have you been lately?"

"Busy, busy, you know."

Niz explained that his friends were hungry and they would like to eat at his restaurant. He pointed to the table.

"Tell them not to move. You can go and sit with them. I'll give the table the works."

Niz smiled and joined the group. He told them food is on the way. Before Niz finished speaking, a waiter appeared with two large pitchers of a local punch. One had alcohol and one didn't.

While they were drinking, two young ladies in bikinis walked over and kissed Niz and Bret. Ani and Essi sounded like an angry chorus.

"And exactly who are they?"

Niz said, "I really don't know. People are just friendly around here."

Essi said, "I hope they're not too friendly."

Ani leaned back. She held the table with both hands as the bench had no back. She looked straight up at the sky with her eyes closed and wore a big smile. Essi was curious.

"What are you thinking about?"

"I was dreaming that I could stay in this one spot, never move, and be content for the rest of my life."

"Many people say that when they come here."

Ani looked at the buildings that ran parallel to the main road. The stores went about two blocks deep and behind them were four and five-story buildings for the length of the town. Behind them was a mountain.

"Those are for living?"

"They're a few hotels, but mostly condos."

"I'll bet they're expensive."

Niz looked around and pointed at a few of them.

"They're incredibly high. The hotels and condos that get rented are booked for two years."

"Oh, well. There goes that fantasy I was having."

"Ani, if you really want to stay there a couple of weeks, I'll speak to one of the owners and see what I can do."

Ani jumped off the bench, ran around the table, and

kissed Niz. He was doing a good job of collecting kisses today.

While everyone was dancing, Essi said, "Maybe Niz can take me dancing someday. I'm not very good."

"I'm out of practice, but I guess I can teach you a few steps."

Essi glared at Bret and Ani as if to say, "Don't you dare open your mouth."

The food then appeared. It was shocking as two waiters brought giant round platters. They had a sampling of so many things from raw shellfish to fried local fish to steak in wine sauce. They even included something that looked like hot dogs and hamburgers.

The food was so good that they all ate ravenously. The owner walked over and queried everyone.

"Are you enjoying my cuisine? If so and there's not enough, just signal me. I'll send all you want."

Bret said, "There's already enough here for ten armies. We don't know how to thank you."

"Niz does me favors, I do him favors. It's my pleasure."

After the meal, they all felt like stuffed turkeys. Niz had another brainstorm.

"If nobody's too tired, I can get a cart and we can take a little tour of the island."

Their faces lit up. They were riding such a high. This was already the experience of a lifetime. Why not some more?

Niz stood up and waved to his friend in the restaurant. When he caught his eye, Niz made a motion like two hands on a steering wheel turning back and forth. The friend nodded and spoke to one of his staff while pointing to the cart lot.

It took just a few minutes for him to arrive at the table driving a four-seater. They piled in with Niz at the wheel, Bret in the passenger seat, and the women relaxing in the back.

Niz drove through the parts of town they hadn't seen, going up and down the side streets. Those were mainly filled with boutique type stores. He also drove to the far side of town where the park was. He showed the amenities and pointed out the road to the airport.

Niz retraced his route to pass the town and also went by the docks. He headed up the road disappearing into the forest. The road was paved, but the town was no longer in sight and all that could be seen on either side was a densely wooded area.

They drove around several curves. The last one presented them with a view of an enormous double steel gate. It rose about fifteen feet from the ground. There were concrete walls of the same height on both sides of the gates. They had razor wire up top and electrical wire attached. The walls disappeared into the thick forest.

A man on either side walked from the trees. They were wearing combat fatigues with green camouflage and both carried automatic rifles.

One of them stayed by the gate and the other started approaching the side where Niz was sitting. He wore a menacing look. While his weapon wasn't pointed at anyone, it wasn't pointed down either.

Essi dug her fingernails in Ani's forearm. She whispered because the look was enough to frighten anyone.

"I'm scared."

Patting her hand, Ani said, "Just relax and let Niz do the talking."

The gate guard stood by Niz silently. They stared eye to eye. The silence seemed like an eternity. Even Bret knew there was little he could do because of the danger to the women.

After some seconds, the guard started laughing.

"Mr. Niz, it's so good to see you again."

"How's the wife and children?"

"They're good. You know the expression about if mama isn't happy, nobody is."

He waved to the other guard to open the gate. Everyone sat back like a deflated tire. They started driving and the woods continued.

Essi said, "This is so secluded."

"Yes, but there are nice views on the other side of the island."

After coming around a bend, they saw huge mansions on either side. They weren't just mansions, they were closer to palaces. They extended as far as the eye could see.

Bret asked, "Only two guards to protect people like these?"

"They're just there to scare away any pain in the neck tourists. I assure you, there's no danger. I'll explain in a bit."

Niz started explaining these people weren't just wealthy. The owners were the most important people in the world. It's next to impossible to have a place here.

"Even heads of state are not necessarily welcome. There's no other place like this on the earth."

"What protects them?"

Niz pointed to a road they were approaching.

"That leads to the airfield and military base."

"You allow tourists to land there?"

"Only the homeowners and military can land. The other airport is the one you saw on the other side of the island."

"There still could be an attack."

"It won't happen for several reasons. Part of the requirements to live here is to donate one or more pieces of powerful equipment. There's artillery, attack helicopters, fighter jets, etc. There's even a small nuclear missile."

"What if a country attacks?"

"The protecting forces are made up of the most powerful nations, even those who are traditional enemies. A devastating force can be deployed in minutes."

"Did it ever happen?"

"Only once. I think they were mercenaries. They never reached the shore. Their craft was quickly destroyed."

They kept driving. Niz pointed to another road that led to a country club for this area. The club had everything from golf to tennis to card and billiard rooms. The restaurant was world-class.

They finally reached the end. In front of them were fields of flowers dividing the last two palaces. Niz pulled up to the one on the right. He said he could give them a bit more info and the girls would be welcome to walk the field.

"It's sort of a botanical garden."

Ani said, "Are you sure the boss of this place wouldn't get angry if strangers like us were walking around?"

"Don't worry. I know the boss would allow it."

"How can you be so sure?"

"Because I'm the boss. We're in front of my place."

All of their jaws dropped. The simultaneous questions spewed such as how and why. Niz explained many years ago he was in the area. He landed on this island and it was inhabited by only a few native people. They told him they were moving to a nearby island where the rest of their families lived. This island would be abandoned.

Since there were thousands of small islands in the area, many hadn't been claimed by nations. Niz offered them a fair price if they would deed it to him. They accepted. He registered it on the mainland.

Since it wasn't officially part of any sovereignty and in international waters, Niz formed his own country. He simply called it Nizland.

He made his own currency, stamps, flag, and national anthem. Since he fit within the Montevideo convention and declaratory theory, there could be no doubt of his right to do this under international law. Only a military overthrow could stop him.

He realized his dream to build something like this. All the rules of the island are passed by the majority of the residents in this area except Niz has the final word.

"I guess you can call me president or king or whatever."

They all laughed.

Bret said, "I was wondering what that flag I saw with an

N represented."

They could see a man in the doorway across the street, next to the garden. They waved and he did also. Niz told Ani and Essi they're welcome to explore the garden. Bret could do that or come with Niz. Niz had some business with the owner.

"You can come see him. He's a good man."

Bret opted to go with Niz. They walked to the door which the person they saw had vacated. Niz knocked and walked in. They indoor foyer was as big as a house.

The man was attending to some boxes on the floor. He stood up and turned around. It was the chief mate.

"You're awfully young to have a place like this."

"It's not mine. I'm just helping out."

"You know, we've spent hours together and I don't even know your name."

"My name's Steve. A lot of people just call me Little Niz."

"You mean you're—"

Steve reached out his hand to shake and said, "That's correct. My dad told me so much about you. It's an honor to meet you, sir."

Steve started bringing the boxes outside. Niz took Bret's arm.

"Come, I want you to meet the owner."

As they walked, they heard a dog barking behind a door.

"Don't tell me the owner's a dog."

"Not hardly. The owner's over there."

Niz pointed to the wall. There was a full-length mirror.

"What kind of joke is this?"

"It's no joke. The place is yours."

"That's insane. There has to be another person. It's not new."

"There was a couple but they passed away with no heirs."

"They died together? That's unusual."

"Bret, they died at the hands of those pirates. Their yacht was hijacked. The way they were tortured by those animals … nobody deserves to die like that. They were good people, moral people, tender people, caring people. Along with you and Steve, they were the best people I ever met."

"Now I understand your intensity during that battle."

"Bret, they're the ones who raised Steve."

"But why me? I didn't give any weapons to these people."

"You remember that nuclear missile you gave me? I gave it in your name. The vote was unanimous."

"This place is worth zillions."

"It cost me nothing."

By that time, Steve had returned. Niz told Steve to go ahead and let the dog out. He was barking like crazy. When Steve opened the door, the dog bolted out and flew past Niz and Steve. With a flying leap, it knocked Bret down and started washing his face.

The dog looked like his old dog Micah. It wasn't just a likeness, it was an exact match. The purebred German Shepherd, the ears not standing, the bald spot, the check mark on his head, everything.

Niz said that he'll wait outside, along with Steve. That way Bret could get acquainted with the dog. They closed the front door behind them.

Bret and the dog were staring at each other as he got down to eye level. He figured the likeness was so close, Niz had a clone made.

"I know you look like him. I'll love and take care of you. I just can't love you as much as my Micah."

The dog got up and walked over to Bret. He gave his cheek a soft lick and gave the brief whine that sheps are famous for. That noise put an image on Bret's brain almost like it was ESP. It was the dog saying, "I am Micah!"

Bret fell backwards on his butt while shaking his head and talking to himself.

Bret said, "Ok, Bret, it's been a rough time during your odyssey. I know you're cracking up. Stay together for the girls."

The dog stood there and repeated the same procedure … a lick followed by a whine and a voice in Bret's head, "I am Micah!"

"It can't be. It just can't be."

Bret moved a few feet away. They were still staring at each other.

"Ok, if you're Micah, prove it. It's still my imagination, I think."

The dog stood up on one leg and started hopping. He winked his eye. He said, "Wawa."

That was all Bret needed. He started bawling like a baby. He hugged and kissed the dog.

"It's you! It's really you!"

Bret went out front with Micah by his side. Niz and Steve were standing there.

"He's more than a clone. I know it. But how?"

"You remember the discovery for altering DNA? We sold it to that high-tech company."

"They did this?"

"I don't understand the scientific stuff, but here's what I know."

Essi gave Niz permission to take samples from the puppy and Micah. The tech company first discovered they were an exact match, which is almost impossible.

They knew for a long time the brain is a receiver of signals. Nobody knows how that works. Every time they altered the DNA of an animal, it wouldn't only remember things of the animal it matched, it mimicked the animal's behavior exactly.

When they cloned Micah, the brain waves matched their DNA alteration.

"Yes, Bret, that's Micah. Whatever you want to call it—a soul, a spirit, whatever makes a being special to itself—has been received and put into this dog's brain."

"How long will he live?"

"Nobody knows but they found a way to keep the telomeres long."

"What the heck is that?"

Niz said that's a string attached to the DNA that gets shorter as you age. It determines a normal lifespan.

"Their best guess is at least forty years for him, but who knows. You just might have the eternal dog."

As they were talking, a strange animal walked from the back of the house. It looked like a combination of a wolf, fox, and dog. It was about half the size of Micah.

"Ok, I'll bite. What is that?"

"It's called a warrah."

Micah walked over to it.

"Are they going to fight?"

"I doubt it. She's pregnant with Micah's pups."

They licked each other and both approached the humans.

"Is she friendly to people?"

"They were all friendly."

"Were?"

"They've been extinct for 150 years. That tech company gave her to me, but they wouldn't say how they did it. She prefers to sleep outside while Micah prefers to sleep indoors. Otherwise, they're inseparable."

She sniffed Bret and kissed his hand, then walked away.

"We'll have to take the ship to the mainland tomorrow to get your things and such."

Steve said, "Dad, don't you remember I need it? We have a business deal tomorrow."

"Oh, that's right. We can use Bret's ship."

Bret was once again stunned.

"I have a ship?"

"Remember the yacht we pulled next to? That's yours."

"Hey, back up. This is getting more ridiculous. You mean that floating hotel?"

"It's a graduation gift for you. Listen, Bret. Steve and I have more money than we can spend in three lifetimes. Besides, it was Steve's idea. Go argue with him."

Steve just smiled and walked away as he said he needed to get the yacht prepared for tomorrow.

Ani and Essi were back by the cart. The men walked over with the new companion.

"Doesn't that look like Micah?" Essi said.

Bret said, "I'll explain later."

Bret invited Ani to see the other house while Niz took Essi for a walk in the garden. There was a bench by the cliff facing the sea. They sat and watched.

"You know Bret has a place to live now."

"Oh, really?"

"That home. He and I will be neighbors. Essi, I was thinking …"

"Go ahead and say it."

"They need their privacy and I'm all alone."

"You want me to live with you? What about those young bikini girls on the beach?"

"Those pretty, young girls couldn't hold a candle to a real woman like you, Essi."

"I don't know about that."

"What about me? I look like an unmade bed. Could you live with an ugly, old guy like me?"

"To me, you and Bret are the two most beautiful men in the world."

Essi put her head on his shoulder. They held hands and looked at the sea.

When Bret broke the news to Ani, she had her usual cynical reaction.

"When does the real owner get home and kick us out?"

Bret explained the circumstances and the vote to give him this place. She was beside herself. It was getting late, so they decided to look at the whole house tomorrow. She looked tired like when she was sick.

They decided to go upstairs to the master bedroom. Before the room, Bret picked Ani up.

"I might as well carry you over the threshold."

They walked in and the size of the room was more like a football field. Bret stopped and put Ani down. She wondered what was wrong. He pointed to the bed.

Micah was sprawled across the bed, sleeping. There was still plenty of room for two people.

"I hope you don't kick me off the bed, now that my dog is trespassing."

"I wouldn't do that, baby. Besides, I'm in no condition to kick you anywhere."

Bret put his clasped hands on his head.

"I knew you weren't well. I could see it. We went through all this and now I'm going to lose you."

"Calm down with the melodrama. I'm just a little tired. It's not what I meant."

"So what's wrong?"

"Nothing wrong. I'm just going to have your baby."

Bret was just made the happiest man in the world.

ROBERT MIRANDA

Bob Miranda was born in Queens, NY. He started working after school hours at age twelve. It taught him discipline and respect for hardworking people, men and women, citizens and refugees, healthy and challenged individuals. He has three degrees: BS in Meteorology, MBA in Accounting, and PhD in Natural Health.

Bob worked with thousands of people from all walks of life. Bob's writing shares his life impressions of the way real people are and real human emotions of people in a fictional manner.